SHW

ST. ALBANS
FIRE

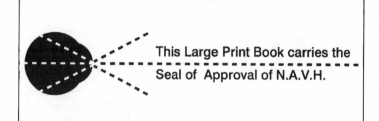

ST. ALBANS FIRE

ARCHER MAYOR

Published in 2006 by arrangement with Warner Books, Inc.

Wheeler Large Print Hardcover.

The text of this Large Print edition is unabridged.
Other aspects of the book may vary from the original edition.

Set in 16 pt. Plantin by Ramona Watson.

Printed in the United States on permanent paper.

Library of Congress Cataloging-in-Publication Data

Mayor, Archer.
    St. Albans fire / by Archer Mayor.
      p. cm.
    ISBN 1-59722-186-4 (lg. print : hc : alk. paper)
    1. Gunther, Joe (Fictitious character) — Fiction.
2. Police — Vermont — Fiction. 3. Saint Albans (Vt.) — Fiction. 4. Arson — Fiction. 5. Large type books.
I. Title: Saint Albans fire. II. Title.
PS3563.A965S73 2006
  813'.54—dc22   2005033296

To Paula Yandow, her family and friends, without whom this book would never have begun

As the Founder/CEO of NAVH, the only national health agency solely devoted to those who, although not totally blind, have an eye disease which could lead to serious visual impairment, I am pleased to recognize Thorndike Press* as one of the leading publishers in the large print field.

Founded in 1954 in San Francisco to prepare large print textbooks for partially seeing children, NAVH became the pioneer and standard setting agency in the preparation of large type.

Today, those publishers who meet our standards carry the prestigious "Seal of Approval" indicating high quality large print. We are delighted that Thorndike Press is one of the publishers whose titles meet these standards. We are also pleased to recognize the significant contribution Thorndike Press is making in this important and growing field.

Lorraine H. Marchi, L.H.D.
Founder/CEO
NAVH

* Thorndike Press encompasses the following imprints: Thorndike, Wheeler, Walker and Large Print Press.

ACKNOWLEDGMENTS

As always in this series of books, I owe a great deal of thanks to all the people who help me with research, editing, and fact-checking. For while the plots are all entirely fictional, the procedures and protocols, the geographical backgrounds, and the historical facts are all as accurate as I know how to make them.

That having been said, I cannot in good conscience let anyone else take the rap if errors are discovered in the tale that follows. So, my thanks to all those listed below — and to many others besides — but please blame me for any mistakes you may note.

John Martin
Paula Yandow
Kathryn Tolbert
Michael Morris
Michael Luker
Patrick Todd
Doug & Bobbi Flack
Gordon "Sonny" Boomhower, Jr.
Pete & Patty Stickney

Castle Freeman, Jr.
Paco Aumand
Brian Corliss
Marion & Marie Minor
Office of the Prosecutor, Essex Co. NJ
Jeff Cartwright
Jordan Carpenter
Victor Panico
David Kircher
John Nichols
Robert Larson
Dr. Steve Wadsworth
Julie Wolcott
Carolyn Boomhower
Julie Lavorgna
Damien Boomhower
Tom Minor
Luke Howrigan
Dick Marek

CHAPTER 1

Bobby Cutts lay on his bed, watching the bedroom ceiling, its shadowy surface painted by the downstairs porch light in a pattern he'd known forever. This room and the barn across the road had always been his sanctuaries — places of private celebration during high times, as when Beverly Cable allowed him a kiss in the eighth grade — and harbors to which he retired in pain, as now, when Marianne had once again suggested that they should try seeing other people.

He hated that euphemism, knowing too well what it meant. Marianne and he had been dating for a year, and it had happened twice already, counting this one. In fact, he'd been the one being "seen" when they first met, as she was dumping Barry Newhouse. He remembered the groping at the drive-in, the more serious stuff on her uncle's office couch one afternoon, and finally those hours in complete silence in her bedroom as her parents slept down the hall. Recalling that night — the smells of her, the taste of her kisses, her willingness at last to let him remove all her clothes — ran at odds with his frustration now, lust interfering with indignation.

He sat up and swung his legs over the side of the bed, staring moodily out the window, his anger back on track, ignoring the winter chill radiating off the glass before him. He wondered who she was with right now, since sneaking boys into her bedroom had become a moot point, she being eighteen and her parents no longer caring. He ran a catalog of possibilities through his mind — from high school friends to some of the young men who worked on her father's farm. No one fit. Everyone fit. His own mother had told him she'd seen Marianne kissing a boy in the front seat of a car in the supermarket parking lot. In broad daylight. He'd asked if his mom had recognized the guy. She claimed not to have, but he had his doubts.

He got up abruptly and reached for his jeans, the room suddenly too tight to breathe in. The barn beckoned to him with its panoply of distractions. He'd been on this farm for all his seventeen years, making the barn as natural an environment to him as a ship might be to a man raised at sea.

And right now he needed every distraction he could stand.

Bobby made his way along the short, dark hallway to the narrow stairs leading down, the wall of framed photographs beside him a celebration of the lives sleeping all around — his smiling parents, his sister, Linda, and her husband and two children. Also, himself as a child, and later posing for the yearbook in his football uniform, crouched down, knuckles on the turf, ball tightly tucked into the curve of his other arm. A life of rural Vermont, spent on a dairy farm, as snug as that ball in the crook of a culture dating back a hundred and fifty years. Bobby Cutts, for all his present anxieties, had that if nothing else: He was a young man as firmly ensconced in his society as farming was in the only world he knew.

He paused in the kitchen to add a log to the wood stove, losing himself for a moment in the red embers at the stove's heart, the eddies of hot air reaching up for him as from the heart of a chunk of lava.

In the cluttered mudroom beyond, he removed his insulated coveralls from the hook on the wall, paying no attention to their pungent odor, and stepped into his equally soiled barn boots, all of which were

11

banned from the rest of the house.

Encased in warm clothes, Bobby shoved the outer door open and stepped into the freezing night air, the shock of the cold a comfort to a boy who welcomed its biting familiarity.

By the porch light, he walked across the snowy yard, the soles of his boots creaking as he went, enjoying how his breath formed a cloud around his head with each exhalation.

Despite his dark mood, he paused halfway between the house and the hulking barn to take in his surroundings. His father had taught him this: Never just walk from one place to another. Take notice of what's around you. The beauty you find there is God's gift to the observant.

The full moon above him proved the old man right. Its colorless iridescence imbued the snow with an inner glow and touched the ridgepole of the barn ahead with a near electrical intensity. To the southeast, over the pale and featureless field next door and the trees barely visible beyond, the blackened smudge of a distant ski mountain was pinpricked by the tiny quivering of crisscrossing snow-grooming machines, crawling through the night like earthbound fireflies.

Try as he might to keep his anger stoked

against Marianne, Bobby felt it dying down. If she was that eager to do all that seeing of other people, did it make any sense for him to want her for himself?

But then the image of her in the arms of some anonymous other flared up in him again. He resumed walking toward the barn across the dirt road dividing the property.

The entrance they used most was down the far embankment and through a tiny door into the milk room, an oddity given the size of the overall structure. This was technically a bank barn, built against the lower edge of the road to allow direct access to the second floor. It towered forty feet at its apex, ran ninety feet in length, and included a hayloft so vaulting that Bobby's father, Calvin, had made room for a small, rough-floored basketball area to accommodate the occasional pickup game.

Bobby stamped his feet out of habit as he entered the sweet-smelling, warm milk room, although no fresh snow had fallen in over a week. Winter was on the wane, even in these upper reaches of Vermont's northwest corner, and tonight's cold notwithstanding, he knew from long experience that the year's first thaw was not far off, and with it the accompanying flurry of the

13

region's fast and furious maple sugar harvest — along with the gluey mess of mud season.

By the glow of one of the night-lights placed throughout the barn, Bobby glanced at the glimmering steel milk tank sitting like a rocket's spare part in the center of the room. This was nothing new — the use of milk cans and individual deliveries to the local creamery were long gone — but Bobby still found the holding tanks and their tangle of umbilical tubing disconcerting. In contrast to the rest of the barn, filled with livestock, hay, insects, and the smell of manure, the milk room was representative of a faintly menacing future — the tank looking more like an alien incubator than a simple repository.

Bobby quickly passed into the long, low stable where he spent most of his time, his nostrils instinctively flaring in the damp, cloying atmosphere. In the half-light, he could make out the rows of cows, tied in their stalls, many of them settled on their flanks, back sides overhanging the full and gleaming gutters running down each aisle. A cheap battered radio played softly on the far wall, soothing the cows with an endless cycle of innocuous love songs.

Bobby unconsciously let out a sigh at the

sight of the room, its floor permanently wet with urine, near-liquid manure, and the water used to routinely wash it all away. Everything was encrusted with manure and/or mud, administered from floor to ceiling by the flickings of cows' tails and the rebound splashings from their round-the-clock voidings. Had it not been for the almost seductive nature of its odor, this whole place by rights would have smelled like a sewer. Instead, to Bobby as to so many others, it ran from being almost unnoticeable to pleasantly familiar.

He glanced over his shoulder at the several portable milk suction units hanging beside him, designed to be moved from cow to cow with a minimum of fuss, and made sure they'd been properly stored. Bobby Cutts might not have been directly in line to inherit all this — his sister and brother-in-law, Jeff, were before him — but he still had a family member's proprietary interest in making sure things stayed ship-shape.

That was one of the things that had so disappointed him with Marianne. He'd envisioned her here, with him, working by his side in the barn, sharing a lifestyle that he'd been taught by his father and which he cherished as among the best in the

15

world. But that was before he'd woken up to her true nature. It was pretty clear now he'd been fantasizing from the start, fueled entirely by his hunger for her.

Unconsciously, he reached out and laid his hand on the smooth haunch of a nearby cow, taking comfort from its warmth. Now that he was here, surrounded by all that gave him sustenance, he recognized how foolish he'd been, and how, in fact, he might end up having to thank Marianne for dumping him.

Not that he was quite ready for that yet.

A sudden lowing from near the stable's far wall made him move quickly in that direction, both the sound and his experience preparing him for what he soon saw. A large cow was lying in a calving pen apart from the stalls, her benign expression at odds with the obvious tension rippling through her body. From her hind quarters, a glistening, milky white sack, the size of a duffel bag, was working its way into the half-lit world.

Gently, Bobby entered the stall. "Hey there, Annie," he said quietly, "you're rushing things. You were supposed to wait a few more days."

He positioned himself behind her and cradled the wet, slippery sack as it continued to emerge from the birth canal, the calf's front feet and nose visible through the thin membrane. Excited and fearful at his lucky timing, Bobby seized the feet as the sack ripped open, and half caught, half eased the bundle onto the hay-covered ground, straining against both the weight and the awkwardness of his package.

Now on his knees, covered with blood, viscous fluid, and the wet, powerful smell of afterbirth, he struggled against Annie's large, inquisitive nose as she tried to push him out of the way to conduct a maternal inspection.

"Easy, girl. Let me do this," he urged, struggling with the small, slimy creature in an attempt to lift its hind leg and check its sex. Successful at last, he smiled at what he found. "Nice, Annie — a future milker. Good girl."

Free to get to work, Annie's enormous tongue immediately began rasping against the calf's nose and eyes with surprising force, cleaning it off as it snorted and shook its head.

Bobby moved back and sat on his haunches, smiling broadly, all thoughts of Marianne banished, and admired the scene, pleased not only by the sight but also by the fact that he'd worked without direction or help. In the morning, he'd surprise his father with this tale of serendipity.

Which thought brought him back to reality. His job wasn't done yet, and what he had to do was way beyond Annie's capabilities. After cleaning up the mess and spreading more sawdust, he traveled back the length of the stable to the milk room and opened up the cabinet housing the drugs and medicines. After setting out two buckets to be filled with tepid water for Annie, he prepared one 2 cc syringe for injection into the calf's nostril and loaded a pill gun so he could deliver a bolus of medicine straight down its throat. He then returned to the pen and distracted the mother with the water, which she gulped down in a thirsty panic while he set out to medicate the newcomer.

Now he was done, he thought, stepping back at last and slipping the syringe into his breast pocket for later disposal. Almost.

Still smiling, he made for the nearest shortcut to the vast hayloft overhead: a broad wooden ladder punching through an open trapdoor in the ceiling. The least he could do was supply the happy twosome with some fresh hay.

Climbing with the ease of a seasoned sailor up a ratline, Bobby broke through to the hayloft floor in seconds, its suddenly enormous, domed, black vastness emphasized by its emptiness. So late in the season, there was but one towering pile of bales left, against the far south wall. The rest of the expansive floor space was bare, aside from a six-inch layer of chaff rustling underfoot.

He started walking toward the bales, feeling confident and restored, when he froze abruptly, suddenly concentrating. Like most people brought up in a world dependent on tools and machines, he had an ear for mechanisms in action and often monitored this ancient and gigantic barn as much by ear as by sight.

There didn't seem to be anything amiss. Bobby could feel more than hear the fans and pumps and motors throughout the building, as soft and delicate to him as the inner workings of a living entity. But he could swear that he'd heard a hissing of sorts — clear and distinct. And, more important, all his instincts were telling him that there was something distinctly wrong.

He stood absolutely still in the near total blackness, searching for some form of confirmation. Slowly, as lethal as the message it carried, the smell of smoke reached his nostrils.

A farmer's nightmares are full of fire, from a carelessly tossed match to a spark from a worn electrical wire to a fluke bolt of lightning. Even the hay itself, if put up too damp and packed too tightly, can spontaneously ignite and bring about disaster. More than one farmer in Bobby's experience, Calvin Cutts included, wrapped up every day by giving the barn a final fire check before bed. To say that such vigilance smacked of paranoia was to miss the larger point: Fire to a farmer was like a diagnosis of cancer — survivable perhaps, but only following a long and crippling struggle, and only if you were lucky.

Bobby had two choices: to investigate and perhaps stifle the fire before it got worse, or to run back to the house, raise the alarm, and get as many people and as much equipment coming as possible.

Typically, but unsurprisingly, he yielded to a young man's faith in his own abilities and set out to discover what was wrong.

Bobby's sense of smell led him away from the bales and toward the sealed-off so-called fuel room that Calvin had built as far from any flammable materials as possible. Here was kept the gas and oil and diesel for their machines, locked behind a heavy wooden door.

He could hear more clearly now, as he approached that door, the hissing sound that had drawn his attention. But as he unhooked the key from a nearby post and freed the fire extinguisher hanging beneath it, he remained convinced of his course of action. It was a closed room; whatever lay within it was contained and could thus be controlled.

Which is when he heard a second sudden hissing behind him, accompanied by a distinct snap — sharp, harsh, like the bite of a rat trap — far across the loft.

He swung around, startled — frightened. He'd been wrong. The noise beyond the door wasn't his only problem. And this second one, he realized with a sickening feeling, was accompanied by a flickering glow. A second fire had started near where he'd just been.

Bobby Cutts began to sweat.

Distracted now, not thinking clearly, he clung to his initial plan of action. First things first. Ignoring the heat radiating from the lock as he slipped in the key, he twisted back the dead bolt, readied the fire extinguisher, and threw open the door.

The resulting explosion lifted him off his feet and tossed him away like a discarded doll, landing him on the back of his head with a sickening thud. His mouth was bleeding copiously from where the extinguisher had broken several teeth as it flew from his hands.

Dazed and spitting blood, a huge, curling fireball lapping at his feet, Bobby tried scrambling backward, screaming in pain as he put weight on a shattered right hand. He rolled and crawled away as best he could, the smell of his own burned hair and skin strong in his nostrils. In the distance, at the loft's far end, he could see a second sheet of flame working its way up the face of the stacked hay bales.

He got to his knees, staggered to his feet, and began stumbling back toward the ladder, his remaining instincts telling him to return below and free as many cows as possible before escaping himself.

It wasn't easy. His eyes hurt and weren't focusing properly, he kept losing his balance, disoriented from a brain hemorrhage he knew nothing about, and as he reached the top of the ladder, the injury to his hand returned like a hot poker. The only saving grace was that he could see anything at all, the hayloft being high-ceilinged enough that the red, glowing smoke stayed above him.

He grabbed the ladder's upright with his

good hand, fumbled for the first rung, and began his descent, hearing the tethered animals starting to get restless.

Halfway down, just clear of the inferno overhead, he stopped for a moment to adjust to the stable's contrasting gloom. There, hanging by one hand, praying for salvation, he watched in stunned disbelief as all around him one bright rope of fire, then two, then three, magically appeared on the walls from the ceiling and dropped like fiery snakes to the floor, shooting off in different directions and leaving lines of fire in their wakes, stimulating a loud, startled chorus of bellows from the frightened creatures below him.

The fire spread as if shot from a wand, in defiance of logic or comprehension, racing from one hay pile to another. Bobby watched, transfixed. The cows had panicked in mere seconds and were now, all sixty of them, struggling and stamping and heaving against their restraints, lowing and roaring as the encircling fire, progressing with supernatural speed, changed from a series of separate flames into the sheer embodiment of heat.

One by one, the animals broke loose. Stampeding without direction, corralled by fire, they began generating a stench of burning flesh in the smoky, scream-filled vortex of swirling, lung-searing air. A broiling wind built up as it passed by the dying boy, the trapdoor directly above him now transformed into a chimney flue. Bobby Cutts clung to his ladder as to the mast of a sinking ship, weeping openly, the fire overhead filling the square opening with the blinding, bloodred heat of a falling sun.

His hair smoking, all feeling gone from his burning body, he gazed between his feet into the twisting shroud of noise and flames and fog of char, no longer aware of the contorting bodies of the dying beasts slamming into his ladder, splintering it apart, and uncaring as he finally toppled into their midst, vanishing beneath a flurry of hooves.

CHAPTER 2

Jonathon Michael stood under the open sky in the remains of the stable, dressed in heavy boots and coveralls, swathed in an acrid atmosphere of burned wood, insulation, and the sweet smell of cooked meat. The word "Police" was embroidered in block letters between his shoulder blades. He was empty-handed, his arms crossed, his expression pensive. After eighteen years as a state arson investigator, he'd learned that the first best rule in this work was to do nothing, or at least nothing physical. Time and again in the past, he'd seen others steamroll in, get distracted by the flashiest evidence, and reach the wrong conclusion — or at best waste a huge amount of time getting around to the right one. Truth be told, he had done just that more than once in the early days.

But not lately. He'd closed every case he'd handled over the last ten years, and while Vermont couldn't brag of the arson stats of New York or Boston, it still had its share of wackos, insurance defrauders, and just plain pissed-off people. And the state's

25

rural nature didn't necessarily mean a low average IQ among its crooks, either; some of the ones he'd arrested had done excellent, subtle work, making the end result look for all the world like a simple mishap.

So Michael took his time. He usually arrived without fanfare and out of uniform, walking around unnoticed and alone. Eventually, before he was done, he'd talk to the firefighters who battled the blaze, to the cops who controlled traffic and managed the crowd, to neighbors and friends, even sometimes to the press photographers and reporters, and finally to the family, all in the pursuit of telling details. Also — at some point in the midst of it all — he'd process the actual scene, occasionally taking days to do so. The pecking order for this complicated, often diplomatic procedure varied from case to case and usually, as now, was helped along by others, especially the Vermont Forensic Lab, which today was still on its way. Inevitably, however, sooner or later Michael found himself where he was right now: standing alone in the middle of a water-soaked, blackened, artificial swamp, trying to think through what might have led to its creation.

Traditionally, barn fires were among the worst. For the most part old, dry, wooden structures, barns were match heads to begin with, before they were stuffed with hay and chemicals and tractors and gas and oil and anything else highly flammable. By an overwhelming margin, when it came to investigating barn fires, Jonathon Michael found himself the tallest thing standing in a clotted field of tangled char.

This one was the rare exception. For reasons he hoped to discover — through his own reconstruction and from witness accounts — this barn had not been reduced to a cellar hole. It wasn't salvageable by any means — the entire hayloft overhead was missing, for one thing — but there were remnants of the building still standing, if only to an eye as practiced as his, which meant that he had a great deal more to work with than usual.

This was especially good news, since the primary reason he was standing here instead of running preliminary interviews was the strong possibility that a young man lay dead at his feet somewhere.

Joe Gunther carefully replaced the phone.

Gail Zigman glanced up at him. "Trouble?"

"Yeah," he answered tiredly. "A possible

arson way up northwest, St. Albans area."

She raised her eyebrows. "They called you?"

"Someone died," he answered.

Her face softened. "Ah," she murmured, once more struck by how often death played an intimate third to their relationship. She and Joe had been together for a long time now — decades, in fact — long enough to give her pause occasionally.

"You going?" she asked him, a coffee mug halfway to her lips.

He stretched and arched his back, causing the newspaper spread across his lap to slip onto the floor. "Yup. Not much choice. Sorry."

She took a sip and then shook her head. "No, no. I understand. I have work to do anyhow."

They were tucked into her small Montpelier condo, where she now spent most of her time. She'd recently been elected to the Vermont State Senate — a low-paying, part-time job in a citizen legislature that functioned only half of each year, although such a description didn't do justice to either the job's real demands or Gail's ability to transform potentially light labor into something all-consuming. Gail Zigman was nothing if not passionate, and did few things halfway. As a result, her large home in Brattleboro — which she'd briefly shared with Joe a few years back — had become little more than a place to touch base. Certainly, Joe, if he wanted time with her, had learned to drive here for it, usually rationalizing the trip by also checking in with his Vermont Bureau of Investigation headquarters in nearby Waterbury.

Joe got to his feet and went in search of his shoes by the front door. "This'll probably take a while — maybe a few days. I'll give you a call."

"Sure," she answered. "No problem." She added, suddenly concerned, "This is safe, right?"

He looked up at her, one shoe in his hand, and smiled. "Yeah. Probably an insurance thing gone wrong. Maybe a feud. We'll just be cleaning up the mess. Nobody shooting at us, at least not till the lawyers show up."

She nodded at the feigned humor and let him get back to his task, but the small smile she offered was entirely false. He'd almost died a couple of times on the job, once in a car accident and once when a knife thrust put him in a coma for weeks — not to mention too many lesser injuries and close calls to count.

Reacting to these thoughts, she, too, rose from her chair and crossed over to him, putting her arms around his waist and giving him a tight hug.

He chuckled tentatively and rubbed her back, burying his nose in her hair and breathing her in as he loved to do. "You okay?" he asked. "What's this about?"

She pulled back and looked into his eyes, her expression serious. "Nothing. I'll miss you. Do call."

Jonathon Michael watched as the medical examiner and the funeral home crew wrestled the gurney bearing Bobby Cutts along the narrow trench that Michael had, for safety's sake, allowed to be cut through the debris, despite it all being a probable crime scene. The volunteer EMT/ firefighters had been a huge help there — shoveling a pathway in barely twenty minutes. No surprise, of course; they were routinely reliable if you treated them right, hanging around long after their job was done, eager to assist, sometimes to a fault. Michael had pulled the leash on them more than once in the past to preserve potential evidence from being trampled or destroyed. Among cops, the inside joke was that EMT actually stood for "evidence mangling technician." Still, he remained grateful — they were cooperative, interested, and instinctively hard workers, especially when it came to the heavy lifting he so commonly required. In his experience, few of his own law enforcement colleagues were as useful — or, to be fair, as plentiful.

The gurney crew reached the edge of the barn's foundation and the trampled, soiled snowfield beyond, to be immediately enveloped by Bobby's family — assuming that what they'd found was Bobby. Luckily for the medical examiner, given what was left, dental records and DNA would confirm the identity of what had taken hours to locate. Michael's thermal imager had finally done the trick, just barely distinguishing Bobby's curled-up form from the smoking timbers and carcasses around it. In fact, when he'd turned the machine off to confirm his discovery, he couldn't tell the difference.

Michael shook his head gently and returned to work. He'd allowed for the removal as soon as he'd dared, but it still had taken hours for him and the forensics crew to measure, take pictures, and make sketches and notes, all while the family anxiously hovered. He'd met with them earlier, briefly — the mother catatonic, the father stoic and helpful, identifying his son from his partially burned boots, the sister and brother-in-law emulating their elders, although the sister had also given in to occasional bouts of pain so fierce that Michael had thought they might be stomach cramps.

No one had been able to tell him much. This was a bolt from the blue, without context or explanation. Michael hadn't pressed for more. It was early yet. He'd really only wanted first impressions, maybe an inkling of something amiss. He'd gotten only sorrow and grief.

The barn, by contrast, had bordered on the eloquent. From the moment he'd set eyes on it, he'd had his hopes, which is why he'd alerted his superiors. Arson investigation textbooks tell you to look for multiple sources of primary ignition — often those places that show the heaviest char, called alligatoring for obvious reasons. That's where this building's not having burned to the ground came in handy, the consensus being that if you burn anything long enough, it all becomes char.

Here there was enough left standing, or enough that could be re-erected with the firefighters' help, that Michael had been able to identify several sources of primary ignition. Not only that, but glancing about, especially in the remains of the stable, he'd discovered what looked like trailer lines — burned traces of a flammable substance used to carry fire from one spot to another. As a child, he'd seen his father light a brush pile using gasoline this way, dribbling a line of it along the ground from the soaking pile to a safe distance away. Jonathon had delighted in how the flame from a single match would tear off like a blazing ground ball to ignite the brush with explosive force. The overall effect had made a permanent impression. Never again had he treated fire with anything but respect.

Looking around, he had no idea what Bobby Cutts's last moments had been like in this scorched place, but if he'd been as surrounded by such images as Jonathon was conjuring up, a better picture of hell had never been imagined.

"Is it okay to approach?"

He looked up from his reverie at the sound of the familiar voice. A relaxed-looking older man, also in insulated coveralls, was standing just outside the encircling yellow crime tape.

Michael smiled and waved him in. "Hi, Joe. Sure. Watch where you step, though. It's a little tricky."

The younger man looked as his boss ducked under the tape and headed gingerly toward him, ignored by the other investigators, all dressed in white Tyvek, who dotted the blighted scene like slow-moving, stooped astronauts exploring a lunar landscape. Typically, Joe Gunther's coveralls were a little ragged and not marked in any way, not unlike the man wearing them. Gunther by now was a legend in Vermont, at least among fellow police officers. Once a Brattleboro cop and seemingly fated to stay forever as such, he had surprised everyone by abruptly transferring to the number two position in the Vermont Bureau of Investigation when the latter was born a few years earlier via a stroke of the governor's pen.

This turned out to have been a major event in Jonathon Michael's life, since Gunther's decision had done much to influence him to follow suit, in his case by leaving the state police. At the time, most cops had warily viewed the new VBI as a political stunt designed to gut the state police's own investigative arm and lure away the best detectives from all the municipal departments. But after Gunther was made field force commander and demonstrated that this exclusively major crimes unit would only enter local investigations by invitation, perceptions began to soften. Of course, the irony was that both the state police and the municipals did take huge hits, since the VBI package and its high-level mandate were so attractive, but, in the end, that only irritated a small number of management types — the working cops and the populations they served were delighted. The VBI turned out to be efficient, effective, well funded, and self-effacing, always ensuring that local politicians and law enforcement leaders were first in line when credit was doled out and reporters present.

Joe Gunther stuck his hand out as he drew near. "Jonathon, long time."

Michael shook hands warmly. They had worked together in the past, and he had always enjoyed the older man's style — a disarming and subtle combination of authority and diplomacy.

"Joe, how're you doing?"

"Pretty well. How's Diane?"

Michael chuckled. That was typical. His wife had undergone gallbladder surgery several weeks ago. Not an emergency, and although obviously of concern to the family, it was certainly nothing that had been made public. But Joe had known about it. By comparison, Jonathon wasn't even aware of Joe's marital status.

"She's doing fine. Took advantage of the recovery to go on a diet. Thanks for asking."

Gunther took in the devastation around them and sighed. "How 'bout you? I saw them loading the hearse. Was it bad?"

"Bad enough. I hope he went quick. I'm okay, though. The family may be something else."

"You talk to them?"

"A bit. Not in depth. Thought I'd leave that to you, if you're interested."

His boss shrugged. "I know Johnson's on vacation from your office. How's Ross doing with the Wilkens homicide?"

Michael knew Gunther was merely being polite. It was unlikely he hadn't been keeping tabs, but again, the man had his own style. "He's pretty busy. I doubt anyone's nose'll be put out of joint if you pitch in, and I'd appreciate the help. I'm more of a hardware man. Not too crazy about dealing with grieving families."

Gunther nodded as if he'd just been invited, instead of having driven all this way to participate. "Okay, if you're sure. Is it definitely arson?"

"Yup. I got multiple sources, trailer lines, what I think is glue spread on the walls to carry the fire down from upstairs."

"It started up there?" Gunther asked, surprised.

"Yeah, the hayloft. I found the remains of some sort of chemical squib near where all the bales were stacked — that and an odor of sulfuric acid. I collected samples for the lab, but right now I'm thinking a one-two ignition on opposite ends of the hayloft, involving chem timers, what looks like a potassium chlorate/sugar mix, and a series of trailer lines made of gas and/or glue, depending. They carried the fire down here and spread it to a series of secondary ignition sources — potato chips and piles of hay or whatever was lying around. Pretty organized work."

"Potato chips?"

Michael smiled grimly. "People don't realize it, but if they get the right brand, what they're munching on is a primo combustible — better than an oily rag and easier to get hold of."

"But why start upstairs?" Gunther asked. "Fire spreads up. Seems kind of complicated to fight Mother Nature."

Jonathon Michael looked vaguely uncomfortable. He preferred facts and evidence over speculation, which was one of the reasons he'd stuck with arson as a specialty. "More flammable materials?"

"Implying an inexperienced torch?"

Here Michael felt himself on firmer ground. "Not from what I've put together. This was no rookie."

Gunther was thoughtful for a few moments, while Michael quietly waited. Joe had an impressive record for closing complicated cases, after all — a man after Jonathon's own heart. He wasn't about to rush him.

"Anything familiar about his handiwork?" Joe finally asked. "You've done most of the big fires in the state."

Michael had already considered that. "Nope. I'll be running him through the computer, but I've never seen any of this before."

Another pause.

"How 'bout the family?"

"Could one of them have done it?" Michael asked rhetorically. "Anything's possible, I guess. Farmers can pretty much do what they put their minds to, at least mechanically, and I haven't had a chance to check out the insurance on this. But if you're looking for a gut reaction, I'd say no. They seem too shook up. And the word so far is they're super tight-knit."

Joe Gunther stared down at his soot-smeared boots for a moment before looking back up. "Guess we got an old-fashioned murder, then," he said sadly.

CHAPTER 3

Joe Gunther sat on the edge of his car's open trunk, slipping his coveralls off and storing them behind him. He was parked among a half dozen other official vehicles in the farm's dooryard, between the remains of the barn and the farmhouse across the road. The contrast was harsh and resonant — on the one side, the picturesque, if worn, well-loved shelter of a hardworking family, and on the other, the still-smoking heap of what had once been their livelihood. If ever there was a snapshot defining the financial tightrope such people walked, this was it.

He stood, slammed the trunk, and headed toward the house, on the front porch of which stood a very large sheriff's deputy, his shoulders slightly hunched against the cold. Gunther stepped carefully, mindful of the slippery hard-packed snow beneath his feet. He was wearing boots, as most everyone did in this country, which was still no guarantee against the odd slider.

"Deputy," he greeted the man at the door, displaying his badge.

The man nodded silently in acknowledgment, not really checking.

"The whole family inside?"

"Yes, sir."

"You want to take the chill off and get some coffee, they've got a thermos in the back of one of the pickup trucks near the forensics van. I'll take responsibility."

The deputy's face broke into a grateful smile. "Think I will. Thanks."

Joe entered the house quietly and stood in the foyer for a moment, listening. To his left was what appeared to be a small library or office, before him a bathroom and staircase leading up, and to his right were two doors, one to a living room, the other to the kitchen. Sounds of crying and muted consoling came from the former; the kitchen had someone rattling dishes and speaking softly. He headed there first.

Around the corner, he discovered two small children, a boy and a girl, sitting at a long wooden dinner table. The girl was drawing with crayons, the boy picking at a bowl of dry Cheerios.

Across the room, with his back turned toward them, a young man stood before the sink, running water over some plates and saying in a low voice, "Cindy, you sure you don't want something to eat?"

The boy saw Joe instantly.

"Are you a policeman?" he asked, causing both the girl and the man at the sink to look at him.

Gunther smiled slightly. "Yes. My name's Joe."

"You have a badge?"

The man stepped away from the sink, drying his palms on his jeans. "Quiet, Mike." He stuck out a damp hand as he approached. "Sorry. Jeff Padgett."

Joe shook Padgett's hand. "Joe Gunther. Vermont Bureau of Investigation." He pulled out his badge and laid it on the table before the boy. "Honest."

The two men watched the children peer at the gold shield as if it might suddenly move.

"I'm sorry for your loss," Joe murmured to Padgett, who he knew from Jonathon to be the deceased's brother-in-law.

The young man shook his head in disbelief. "It's like I'm dreaming, you know?"

"You going to find out why Bobby died?" the boy asked suddenly, looking up, his scrutiny over. His sister had already gone back to her drawing.

"That's why I'm here," Joe answered, pocketing the badge. He glanced at Padgett. "Is this an okay time to talk?"

Jeff Padgett hesitated a moment before asking his son, "Mike, you want to work on the model a little?"

Mike was clearly surprised. "Without you?"

"Sure. You can sort out the pieces. Make sure we got everything."

The boy's face lit up. "Sure, Dad. Thanks." He left the table at a run and disappeared out the door. They could hear his feet on the stairs.

Satisfied, Padgett nodded toward his daughter, the younger of the two. "She'll be happy forever doing that. We can talk over here." He pointed at a small gathering of worn armchairs near a far bow window overlooking the back field.

"You want coffee or anything?" the young man asked as he led the way.

"I'm fine, thanks."

They settled down opposite each other under the window, bathed in the sunlight coming off the pure white field.

"What do you want to know?" Padgett asked.

"I guess for starters, what was Bobby doing in the barn late at night? Was that normal for him?"

Padgett shrugged. "Depends. Would be if he heard something. You sleep with one

43

ear open in this business, you know?"

In fact, Gunther did know, having been brought up in a house just like this. "What might he have heard? You been having problems?"

"Not particularly, but you know how it goes. Shi— I mean, stuff happens all the time. Something goes wrong with one of the cows and she lets out a yell, that might've woken him up. Or something falling 'cause it gets knocked over. Maybe he just couldn't sleep. I go out there once in a while when Linda and I aren't gettin' along. Helps quiet me down."

"How did Bobby seem lately?" Joe asked.

Padgett tilted his large, round head to one side. "Fine, I guess. Having a hard time with his love life, but who doesn't, right?" He smiled suddenly, the flash of teeth startlingly out of context. Joe couldn't resist responding in kind.

"One girl, one too many, or none at all?" he asked.

Padgett laughed sadly. "Oh, it was one, all right. Poor guy couldn't see straight 'cause of her."

"How do you mean?"

He glanced over at his daughter, making sure she wasn't listening in. He continued

44

in a low voice. "Bobby wasn't a ladies' man. Kind of shy and retiring. Somehow or another he hooked up with Marianne Kotch, which nobody could believe, and it totally messed him up."

"Not a match made in heaven?"

"Not a match made anywhere. I told him to his face he was headin' for trouble with her, but he just got mad. She only picked him to piss off her ex-boyfriend. It wasn't serious for her. But old Bobby, I swear, he was making plans from the first night."

"So they were intimate?"

Jeff was lost enough in his story that the reason for telling it was temporarily over-shadowed. He chuckled. "Marianne Kotch makes it a point to get intimate with just about every man she meets. That's what I mean about her not being serious."

"But they continued being an item?"

"I think she felt sorry for him. She tried dumping him once. He went crying to her in the middle of the night. Made a big fuss. So she took him back. She wasn't happy about it, though. Everybody but him could see it."

"How were they lately?"

Padgett scratched his cheek. "Same, I guess — him the love puppy and her trying to find a way out. After he chewed me a new one, I generally avoided the subject."

Gunther glanced out the window at the glaring, snow-covered view, a portrait of Bobby Cutts emerging like a ghost at the bottom of a pool of water. He knew this process well, and knew also that at this stage, it was difficult to tell reality from whatever he might be hearing, making it both easy and dangerous to jump to conclusions.

"Would you say Bobby was depressed?" he asked quietly.

"Frustrated is more like it."

"What about Marianne? She must have been pretty frustrated, too. She ever complain that you know of?"

Jeff shook his head. "Nah. It was more how she acted around him, all pouty and resentful. But she and I don't talk. Linda wouldn't like it, not that Marianne's my age or my type. But you know women."

"I would never claim that."

Padgett laughed.

"How's the farming business been lately?" Gunther asked conversationally, hoping to coast on the genial mood between them.

His companion looked at him dubiously, his eyebrows arched, almost snide. "Lately? I'd have to say not too good."

Joe shook his head, irritated with himself, but also caught off guard by the sudden sarcasm in Padgett's voice. "I meant before. Any financial troubles?"

Padgett placed his hand on his forehead theatrically and gave Joe a quizzical look. "You know anything *about* farming?"

Gunther leaned forward in his seat, the edge in his voice designed to settle the man down a notch. "My father farmed his whole life. That's where I was born. I'm talking reality here, not the all-farmers-are-martyrs-for-feeding-America line. I know about that, and I don't argue the point. I'm asking about unusual financial problems, for you folks — personally."

Jeff Padgett didn't take offense. He actually laughed, albeit shortly. "I like that — martyrs. I never heard that one. Sad but true, though." He looked at the floor in contemplation for a moment, before adding, "God, it sure does get complicated, don't it? I mean, you're right. We do sort of walk around holier-than-thou sometimes. I used to get tired of teachers doing the same thing, complaining about how they were underpaid and unappreciated." He waved his hand in mock surrender at Gunther. "Okay, I get the point. The answer is no, we didn't have any more money headaches than the next guy, I guess. I can't say what this fire will do, though. Bobby's death could change everything."

"What was the insurance?"

Padgett made a face. "Less than it should have been, like everybody else I know."

"Little enough to shut you down?"

The young man looked wistful. "You met Cal?" he asked.

Joe knew Calvin Cutts to be Jeff's father-in-law. "Not yet. Thought I'd talk to you first."

"He took me in as a teenager. Believed in me when most people figured they'd be visiting me in prison next. He put me to work, set me straight, treated me like a son, even took it in stride when Linda and I got together. And after I proved myself and she and I got married, he told me this place would be ours — the same place he got from his father before him."

He pointed in the direction of the barn. "When something like this happens, it's one of a farmer's biggest fears. I suppose you know that, coming from where you do. But you deal with it. Hanging by a thread is who we are. And Cal is among the best I know at making it work."

He paused, as if worried this might be

taken as bravado, and returned to the shadow haunting them all. "I don't know about Bobby, though. That's gonna be rough."

"Could you handle the load alone if Cal called it quits?" Joe asked.

Padgett sighed. "Depends on the money, like always. I'd do everything I could, I'll tell you that. I say the same thing to the developers who come by, trying to buy us out. I do this because Cal used it to save my life. I owe it to him, to Linda and the kids, and because it's all I want to do anyhow."

This wasn't said with any fervor. Instead, in contrast to moments earlier, the words came out almost mournfully, as if Jeff Padgett weren't so much proud as resigned to what fate had decreed. But there was more, which Joe recognized from his own experience. He'd watched his father carry the same sense of destiny, as if farming, with all its insecurities and dangers and hardships, simply boiled down to the reason he'd been put on earth.

"Did Bobby get along with his parents?" Joe asked, mindful of all the odd feelings that feed a survivor's grief, sometimes including an emotion that has little to do with love and harmony.

"Yeah," Jeff said, immediately and un-equivocally. "He really did. I mean, they'd have their disagreements, Marianne being a whopper, but it never ran to much. This whole family just seems to keep on going, you know what I mean? Like a tribe or something." He paused and added thoughtfully, "I suppose that's why I feel the way I do being taken in. It's pretty special. You'll see why when you meet Cal."

Joe nodded. "I'll do that next. I'm al-most done, by the way. Just a couple more questions. When did you last see Bobby?"

"Gosh, let me think. We pretty much hang around the TV set at night, but some of us come and go."

"You live here, too?" Joe asked, sur-prised.

Padgett gave a slightly crooked smile. "Yeah. I know it's weird, but this is a whole lot nicer than anything I could afford if we were on our own."

Gunther made a dismissive gesture. "No, no. Of course. Makes perfect sense. I just didn't realize, is all."

"Yeah," the young man agreed. "A lot of families have almost done the same thing, though, building houses right next to each other and spending nearly every night together." He hesitated and then added, "It is a little embarrassing sometimes, not to mention crowded."

Joe moved him along. "You were telling me when you last saw Bobby."

"Right," Padgett exclaimed, clearly relieved. "I think it was on the early side, to be honest. I remember him saying he had something to do in his room."

"How did he seem?"

"Normal, considering. I mean, I told you he was bummed out generally, but that was it."

Joe followed that up. "You mentioned that Marianne probably took up with Bobby to get even with her last boyfriend. Did the boyfriend hold Bobby responsible?"

"Barry?" Padgett asked. "Oh, I doubt that. I mean, he is a jerk, and a bad drunk, but he'd probably just take it out on his animals. You should see his farm. There's the flip side to Cal. Barry's father is what gives farmers a bad name, and the apple didn't fall far from the tree. Whole family's a waste of time. But I doubt any of them would go that far." He waved toward the barn.

"What's the last name?" Joe asked, not as ready to dismiss the possibility that

Barry might have gone hunting for his rival, especially given his own family dynamics. It was clear by now that despite an apparently rocky youth, Jeff Padgett had become a genuinely nice guy and less inclined to think ill of his fellows.

"Newhouse. The old man's Wayne. They're three farms down, to the right. You can smell it before you see it."

"Given their different styles and how close-knit this community is," Joe continued, "how would you describe the relationship between Newhouse and Cal?"

"I wouldn't. They barely talk to each other. That's not a big deal, though, 'cause close-knit ain't it. Lots of folks don't particularly like each other around here. That's one of the nice things about being surrounded by land — helps you keep your distance. The close-knit thing is mostly inside each family. The fact that Newhouse is a slob and a thief and out to screw everybody for a buck is more his problem than ours. And I'd still bet my bottom dollar he had nothing to do with that fire."

"Why not?" Joe asked.

"What's to be gained? It's not like the properties abut, and Newhouse is sure as shit not in a position to buy anyone out, even if it was a distress sale."

They both turned as young Mike ran into the room, his eyes bright. "Dad, I counted the pieces. There're a hundred and forty-three. Can we put some of them together?"

Joe Gunther rose to his feet, making sure his last question of Michael's father wasn't misconstrued — and thus passed along the grapevine. "I'll let you go. I wasn't saying Newhouse had anything to gain, by the way. I just have to ask everything I can think of."

Padgett stood also, stroking his son's head as the boy wrapped his arms around his father's leg. "I know, and I'm not saying him or Barry *didn't* do it. I just don't know why they would."

Joe shook his hand in parting. "If there's one thing I've discovered in this job, it's never to be surprised by the whys."

CHAPTER 4

Gunther stepped back into the Cuttses' front hall and paused before the open living room door, again listening for telling sounds. Unlike the first time, there was no crying or murmured consoling. Only silence.

He approached the threshold and peered inside. A worn-looking couple, no older than he but certainly more battered, sat beside one another on a sagging couch facing a blank TV. It was a rough-and-tumble room, clearly decorated to absorb whatever human tornado might pass through it, from riotous small children to a Super Bowl party. The floor was bare wood aside from two old, thick rugs; the furniture sturdy and functional, and the walls covered with photographs and crayon drawings. Here and there, in an ornate lamp or a dark oil painting, were signs of family heirlooms; but otherwise, the room's history reflected only the present — a point in time now as potentially stalled as the silent grandfather clock in the corner.

Calvin and Marie Cutts sat hand in hand, quiet and dry-eyed, pale and drawn, like two weary travelers awaiting transport at a bus station.

Gunther stepped inside the room. "Mr. and Mrs. Cutts? My name's Joe Gunther. I'm with the police."

Calvin Cutts rose quickly to his feet, a strained smile on his face, extending his hand in greeting. "Call me Cal. I'm not big on formalities."

"Same here," Gunther replied. "I'm Joe."

Cutts indicated his wife, who stayed resolutely staring at the darkened TV set. "This is Marie."

Joe nodded toward her, delivering the sad, appropriate, but curiously tinny phrase "I'm sorry for your loss."

"Would you like to have a seat?" Calvin asked, touching the edge of an armchair off to one side of the couch. "Or maybe a cup of coffee?"

Gunther accepted the seat, saying, "No, thanks. Your son-in-law already offered. Nice guy."

Cutts resumed his seat next to his wife, who still didn't seem to have noticed Joe's arrival. "We're very proud of Jeff. We and Linda both got lucky when he joined the family."

Joe smiled broadly. "Yeah. He told me the story. That must've been a little surprising when he and Linda got together."

But Cal shook his head pleasantly. "Most natural thing in the world. Didn't surprise me in the least."

"Did me," Marie said shortly, not moving her eyes.

Both men hesitated, then Cal laughed carefully. "Well, I wasn't bothered at all. You could tell they had eyes for each other from the moment he found us. Part of me wonders why it took as long as it did to surface. Guess they had to work out the 'are we brother/sister or not?' part first."

His wife snorted.

Calvin looked a little tense. "After that, it didn't take long. Anyhow, what can we do to help?"

Joe was still thinking how best to approach them. For his purposes, this was hardly ideal — both of them together, tangled in grief and something older and more complicated that he knew nothing about. He wished he could find a way to split them up, preferably remaining with the man.

"To begin with, I just wanted to repeat how sorry I am to be meeting under these circumstances. I and everyone involved in this case will do everything we can to move things along quickly." He pulled a business card from his pocket and gave it to Calvin Cutts. "If anything comes up you'd like to talk about along the way, no matter how small, don't hesitate to call."

The farmer slipped the card into his breast pocket after studying it politely for a moment. "Thank you. Don't worry about us, though. You just do your job."

Joe nodded. "We will, and please tell your daughter the same thing — anything at all. Where is she, by the way? I sort of thought she'd be here with you, or with her husband."

"She went upstairs," Cutts said without further explanation.

"She all right?"

Marie Cutts, finally looked straight at him, her eyes narrow with anger. "Her brother was just burned to death. No, she's not all right. Are you the idiot who's supposed to catch who did this? God help us."

"Marie," her husband cautioned.

"I understand how you feel, Mrs. Cutts," Joe began.

"Oh, spare me," she cut him off sharply. "And can the sympathy. You don't know us from Adam's off ox. This is your job, and if we're lucky, your ambition will give us what we want, which is the son of a bitch who burned my son alive."

"Maybe you should check on Linda," Cal suggested gently.

"Check on her yourself," came the quick reply. "This man wants answers. I'm going to give them to him."

Cutts looked at a loss, suddenly on the hooks of his own suggestion.

"Go on," she ordered him. "You're wasting time."

Hesitantly, he rose to his feet, smiling awkwardly at Joe. "Maybe a good idea. She's taken this pretty hard. I won't be long."

His heart sinking, Joe conceded. "Take however long you need."

They both waited until Calvin had left the room.

"What do you want to know?" Marie Cutts demanded.

Joe took the direct route, hoping it might earn him some small amount of credit. "For one thing, I'd like to reconstruct the last hours of Bobby's life — maybe find out why he was out there in the middle of the night."

"He went up to his room early, mooning about that tramp he was stuck on, and that's the last we know."

"What made you aware the barn was on fire?"

She made a sour face. "You think sixty cows and the barn they're in burn without a sound? Mister, you haven't lived till you've heard that." She tapped her temple. "That'll stick in my head till I die, 'cause somewhere in the middle of it, I'll always think my son was calling for help, with no one to hear him. You don't think that's a mother's nightmare, you're stupider than I thought."

Gunther sat forward, resting his elbows on his knees, his placid demeanor hiding the anger he now showed in his voice. "Mrs. Cutts, if you want me to stuff the sympathy and act like someone who's just punching the clock, fine. But do me a favor. You stuff the attitude. I don't need a lesson in heartbreak from you, 'cause you know absolutely nothing about me."

Marie Cutts's mouth opened in shock. For a long, measured moment, she said nothing. Joe waited, wondering how this version of a splash of cold water would work.

Finally, she pursed her lips, frowned, looked down at her hands for a slow count of five, and then glanced up — serious, honest, and for the first time, vulnerable.

"I'm sorry. You're right. It was the noise that woke us up. I called 911 as Jeff and my husband ran out, but it was already too late. We couldn't even free the animals. It seemed like the fire was everywhere. And that sound . . ."

Joe spoke softly. "Do you know of anyone, for any reason, who might have wished this on you?"

Her hands clenched tighter in her lap, but her eyes remained on his. "So it was set?"

He hedged. "We're making that presumption so as not to miss anything."

She shook her head. "People are so crazy nowadays. What's it take to push them over the edge? Not getting a parking place or not wanting to wait in line any longer? I don't know. We do our work, we mind our own business. It's not like in the city, where people get on each other's nerves." She suddenly waved at the view out the window, similar to the one he and Jeff had shared earlier. "Look. We can't even see our neighbors. We might as well be living on the moon."

Joe let her calm down a few seconds before suggesting, "But you don't live on the moon. You have neighbors, you belong to the dairy co-op, you interact with people in town. What's the farm's financial situation?"

She sighed. "Like everybody else's. You borrow money against the year's production, and then you keep your fingers crossed you'll have something to produce. We have good years and bad. I heard the average farmer's income in the U.S. is like twenty thousand a year, net. That fits us, if nothing falls on our head. This last year wasn't too bad. But we have debts, if that's what you're asking. Cal and Jeff work all summer baling other people's hay, to tilt the balance a little, 'cause Cal's got the equipment for it when most others don't."

"And Jeff's still set to take over when you and Cal retire?"

She looked surprised. "Where did you . . . ?" Her voice then flattened, catching him off guard, and she turned away. "Oh, you were talking to him. Yes, that's right."

He studied her staring at the blank TV again. Her tone had turned hostile, as when the topic of Jeff Padgett marrying Linda had come up.

"You don't seem very happy about it," he said quietly.

Her eyes didn't move. "It's not my farm."

Ouch, he thought, and pursued this new

vein, taking an only slightly educated guess. "And it wasn't going to be Bobby's, either?"

She cut him an angry look. "What's your name again?"

"Joe Gunther."

"Well, Mr. Joe Gunther, if you want me to clean up my attitude, then you can stay the hell out of our private business. Bobby's death has nothing to do with who gets what in this family. You do not get a free pass to poke around, leastwise not from me."

Joe nodded. "Fair enough. You made it pretty clear you weren't super fond of the girl Bobby was dating."

"Marianne Kotch is a slut; that's why."

"How rocky could things get between them? I gather they had their ups and downs."

Marie Cutts looked scornful. "Jeff tell you that? He's just jealous. Probably wishes Linda wore tight clothes and no bra, too."

"Is it true, though?"

"They weren't happy," she conceded. "Marianne tried to dump him once. I don't know how they were doing lately, but my guess is, she was putting him through hell. I warned him about her, but that's all he needed to make a big deal out of it. I even caught her in the supermarket parking lot, not long ago, making out with some long-haired greasy guy in a car. She was all over him. I told Bobby, like it would make any difference. I swear that half his interest in that girl was just to spite me."

"You know who the greasy guy was?"

"No. I mean, I've seen him around. He's a St. Albans kid. No good."

"You have a name?"

Her eyes narrowed again. "What is it with you? We're talking about a teenage whore making out in the parking lot. Who cares? You think either one of them killed Bobby? They know how to do one thing, and it isn't striking matches, unless it's to light a joint."

Joe just watched her in silence.

Losing the staring contest, she looked away again. "It was John Frantz's boy. I don't know his name. Frantz runs a feedstore in town. You can find out that way."

"How did Bobby react when you told him?"

"I didn't actually tell him who it was. He pretended like he knew anyhow. Said he and Marianne had already talked about it, but I could tell he was lying. I saw the hurt in his eyes."

"Would he have confronted this boy, do you think, had he known who he was?"

"I wish he had," she said hotly. "Bobby would have kicked his skinny ass."

"But he didn't, as far as you know?"

"No," she admitted mournfully. "Bobby was too much like his father that way. Not much of a fighter."

As if on cue, Calvin Cutts appeared at the doorway, his expression telling Joe that he'd overheard — and that he was used to it. "Linda's asleep, finally," he said quietly, regaining his seat beside his wife. He reached out to take her hand again, but she moved it away.

Gunther kept focused on Marie. "What about Barry Newhouse? Jeff told me Marianne dumped him and used Bobby to rub it in. Barry lives nearby, doesn't he?"

Marie turned on her husband, rather than answering. "Would you tell your fair-haired boy to mind his own business? He's been shooting his mouth off with all sorts of crap about Bobby's love life, none of which will have anything to do with the price of eggs in the end, assuming there is an end."

She stood up abruptly, her husband's return clearly triggering the fury she'd been barely controlling so far. "My son was just killed," she addressed Cal, "along with your entire herd. Everything we worked for, saved for, everything we sacrificed for, is a pile of ashes. And what are we doing? We're letting a cop give us the third degree based on a bunch of gossip from Jeff Precious Padgett."

She'd been pacing the floor during this diatribe, and now came to a dead stop in the middle of the room, finally rendered motionless by her outrage. Her arms stiff by her sides, her fists clenched, she tilted her head back and yelled at the ceiling, "Goddamn you all," before storming out the door, slamming it behind her.

The two men stared at the door in silence before Calvin Cutts said in a soft voice, "This is hard on her."

Joe shifted his glance to him, aware that he was speaking of far more than their son's death.

"And maybe a bit on you, too?"

"Yeah," Cal said softly. "A bit."

CHAPTER 5

"Bobby didn't have what it takes to own a farm," Calvin Cutts said sadly. "Marie could never accept that. And when I gave it to Jeff and Linda instead — or at least made it clear that they would inherit it — she saw it as my betraying her family tree." He shook his head. "She's never been able to get past that."

Gunther was confused by the reference to her family tree, also remembering that moments ago Marie had referred to Bobby as her son and the destroyed cows as Cal's herd. "How were you betraying her family tree? Wasn't Bobby both of yours?"

"Oh, yes. But Jeff isn't. That's the rub. Marie's father lost the farm she grew up on. She's a woman of some pride and saw his failure as a stain on her family honor. That farm had been theirs for a lot longer than this place has been in my family. To this day, she claims the bank did the old man in, but he fell apart and hit the bottle. From the time Bobby was born, she always saw him taking over here as a kind of redemption: a son of hers setting the legacy right."

They were still in the Cuttses' living room, the door closed since Marie's violent departure.

"And instead you gave it to a troubled kid off the street," Joe mused.

"Kind of, yeah," Cutts admitted. "Actually, Jeff wasn't such a stranger. I knew his folks before they split up and disappeared and left him behind. I always knew he was good at heart. He just needed a break."

"How did Bobby see his joining the family?" Joe asked.

"He was okay with it," Cal answered carefully. "I suppose there might've been some rivalry early on. But Jeff's nine years older. It didn't take them long to sort it out, and after that, they were like brothers. The way I see it, Bobby was actually kind of grateful. He was always better as a number two man — wasn't comfortable running things. That's what I meant before."

"Your wife must have been upset, seeing an outsider doing so well at her son's expense."

Calvin hesitated before repeating, "My wife has a lot of pride."

Gunther wasn't going to argue with what had obviously become a mantra of sorts.

He changed directions slightly. "Sounds like Barry Newhouse has good reason to be pretty angry at Bobby. What do you think he's capable of?"

Cal echoed his son-in-law. "Not much besides drinking and wasting time."

"He wouldn't want to get even?"

Cutts paused, clearly rethinking his response, given Joe's implication. "Ah," he said. "He might. He's had run-ins with the law before." He dropped his gaze to the floor and let out a deep sigh. "My God," he added softly, "what have we come to?"

Gunther kept going, hoping to keep the man functional. "What can you tell me about John Frantz's son?"

Cal looked up, his eyebrows arched. "Rick? Good Lord. I don't know. He'll probably put his father into an early grave, but that may be as much John's fault as Rick's. John's a little straightlaced. Why do you ask?"

Joe kept his reply vague. "I heard he might be seeing Marianne, too. Would you call Rick a violent kid?"

Cal pushed his lips out and reflected. "I honestly don't know. All the black leather clothes and body piercing. The violent message is there, but I don't know if he's ever carried it out. He could certainly hold his own if it came to a fight, I guess." He gave Joe a hapless look. "Sorry."

Joe rose to his feet and crossed to the window. Leaning against the cold glass, he asked, "I'm sorry to get more personal, but I need to know a couple of private things."

Still sitting on the couch, Cutts looked up at him open-faced. "Sure. Whatever you need."

"How were your finances before the fire?"

Cal smiled wryly as he answered, "Blame the patient for the illness?"

But Joe shook his head. "If by that you mean that I'm thinking insurance fraud, I don't believe you're a man who would sacrifice his animals, much less risk killing someone. I do have to ask, though. Not to mention that you may not be the only one to benefit from the loss of this farm."

Cutts sighed. "Finances were fine; at least normal. I own the farm free and clear, I have an equipment loan from the farm service agency with about thirteen thousand left on it, and I was about to take out ten thousand more to plant this coming season, as usual." He paused before adding, "Now, though . . ."

In the silence, Joe repeated the question

he'd asked of Calvin's wife: "Insurance?"

"Some," he answered wearily. "Not enough." He stopped again, this time clearly arrested by some pressing thought, and then he placed both palms against his forehead. "God."

"What?" Joe asked.

"Sugaring time's almost here," Cutts said, not looking up. "Bobby, Jeff, and I were going to set the taps next week."

Gunther knew what this meant from having helped his own father years ago. Maple sugaring — far from the quaint hobby that many vacationers assume it to be — is a serious moneymaker for many farmers. Having been told of the farm's physical assets by Jonathon, Joe calculated that Calvin could probably place about two thousand tree taps, generate some five hundred gallons of syrup, and maybe gross $10,000 a year selling wholesale — hard cash. No small change to someone netting only twice that much every twelve months. What Calvin Cutts had just heard was the metaphorical final coffin nail being driven home, assuming he hadn't already reached that point. Part of the rationale behind sugaring was that you could do it with available resources: free scrap wood to run the evaporator, free sap, and free manpower, since it tended to be a family business. With his son dead and his spirit broken, however, Cutts was unlikely to have the heart to manage a sugar run, no matter how much money it might generate.

Joe wouldn't pursue how this news struck him here and now; callous as it seemed, he had his own immediate needs to address. But he made a mental note to see what could be done about gathering this man's sap for him, at the very least.

"Cal," he said quietly, "I hate to keep at this, but I need to know something else. Assuming Bobby had nothing to do with the fire — that he was just an innocent victim — can you think of any reason why someone might want to put you out of business?"

Cutts looked up at him. Gunther wasn't sure he didn't have tears in his eyes. "Enough to destroy a man's family? No."

"Let me put it another way, then," Joe persisted. "Have you done anything at all in the last several years that might've pissed somebody off?"

Calvin ran his hand through his hair. "Jesus, who hasn't? For one thing, I'm a registered Democrat. That pisses my wife off right there."

"Something you did," Joe suggested. "Maybe involving a family member or a neighbor. A business deal."

Cutts sat back in his seat, suddenly staring at Gunther in wonder. "My God, you think it could've been?"

"Anything's possible," Joe answered, not knowing where this was headed.

"Christ," the other man murmured. "Last year, Billy St. Cyr and I had another run-in, but it couldn't have anything to do with all this. That's just too crazy."

"Tell me about it anyway."

Cutts still looked incredulous. "It was stupid. He drained a small wetland into my cornfield, and I called him on it. Instead of damming the ditch he'd just dug, like I suggested, he called the local ag agent on something he thought I'd done. He claimed I'd planted illegally close to a streambed, which I hadn't — he got the regulation wrong. Anyhow, he was fined for his violation almost as soon as the agent showed up. It was totally crazy. He should have kept his mouth shut. Instead, he ended up losing a bundle and blaming me."

"That was it?" Joe asked. "How big was the fine?"

"Not huge, and Billy's got the money.

He's doing well. He takes advantage of every subsidy, every handout, and every financial incentive that comes down the pike, plus he sells off overpriced parcels of land to flatlanders looking for a piece of God's country. He's not a bad farmer, truth be told, but he's a little shy on scruples."

"He ever make an offer for your place?"

"No. If anything, he wants to get out."

Gunther pulled on an earlobe, reviewing what he'd just heard. "You said this was *another* run-in. There were others?"

Cutts waved his hand tiredly. "All the time. Something like twenty years ago I sold Billy a truck that seized two months after he bought it, probably because he didn't change the oil. He said I knew it was a lemon and that I should buy it back. I refused, and that was the start of it. He's hated me ever since."

"Has it escalated over time?" Joe asked.

Calvin shook his head. "Nope. It's always piddly stuff, and it always comes up when he's got nothing better to do."

There was a knock on the door, and Jeff Padgett poked his head in. "Dad? The minister's here. He was wondering if you'd like to see him."

Calvin Cutts looked inquiringly at Joe, who immediately nodded. "Fine with me,

Cal. I was pretty much done anyhow. You go ahead."

Joe followed them both back into the front hall, and from there, saw a somber-suited man standing with Marie in the kitchen, speaking quietly. She looked thin and insubstantial next to him, her bony arms crossed tightly, her eyes glued to the floor. Joe couldn't tell from this distance whether she was benefiting from the man's words or simply waiting till he was done before tearing his head off. Her body language looked suitable for either option. For both their sakes, Joe wished for the former.

Without further ceremony, he let himself out, pausing on the front porch alongside the deputy sheriff standing guard — the same one he'd encouraged earlier to get a cup of coffee against the cold.

"Everything okay in there?" the man asked.

Surreptitiously, Joe noticed his name tag said "Davis." "As okay as can be. Pretty hard knock to take. You find that coffee?"

The man smiled and nodded. "You bet. Felt good all the way down. 'Preciate it."

"No problem." Joe figured him to be in his mid-fifties, probably a lifelong cop like himself, but content to stay local and work the same patch he'd been born on. The way he was built conjured up a duffel bag wrapped in a coat.

"Guess you know the folks around here pretty well," Joe suggested.

Davis chuckled. "If I don't, I never will. The old-timers, that is. Lot of people coming in from away. Don't know them so well."

"Anything you can tell me about the Cuttses?"

The deputy made a face. "Not much to tell. They keep to themselves, like most farmers. None of them has any time to do much else."

"No run-ins with you guys?"

Davis smiled. "Had a few with Jeff before he straightened out. That boy could drive like nobody I know. Old Calvin here saved his butt, sure as hell. But that's ancient history — maybe fifteen years back, now."

"What about Bobby?"

He shook his head. "Nope. Straight arrow. The girlfriend's bad news, but I figured that was just a short walk on the wild side. Marie would've seen to that soon enough."

Joe tilted his chin in the direction of the barn's blackened skeleton. "Could she or her playmates have had anything to do with this?"

Davis mulled that over. "Anything's possible, I guess, but nothing rings a bell. I'm talking sex, drugs, and booze with them. Nothing more violent than a domestic now and then — maybe disturbing the peace on a Friday night. The kind of stuff Jeff was getting into before Cal got hold of him. But Bobby wasn't doin' any of that. He just had the hots for Marianne. He didn't hang with her crowd." He gave a frown. "I can't say I see this being connected to them. You could prove me a liar, though. Wouldn't be the first time."

Joe patted his shoulder once before stepping off the porch onto the hard-packed snow. "Well, let's hope we get lucky. I hate for this to drag on for too long."

"Yeah," Davis agreed. "Especially when they begin to pile up. People start getting antsy."

Joe fixed him with a stare. "Pile up? What do you mean?"

The deputy looked surprised. "Barn fires. This is the third one in three weeks. You didn't know?"

CHAPTER 6

Joe found Jonathon Michael in the back of the crime lab van, labeling one of the shiny paint cans he used to collect evidence.

"How's progress?" he asked, propping one foot up on the tailstep.

Michael looked over his shoulder. "Hey, Joe. Slow, but we're gainin'. How 'bout you? You talk to the family?"

"Most of them. The daughter's asleep. I also got a little local background from the deputy guarding the front door."

The other man laughed. "Yeah — I saw him. Big as a bear."

"Right," Joe agreed affably, adding, "He told me this is the third barn fire in as many weeks."

Michael paused to reflect, but wasn't as surprised as Joe was expecting. "I know of two, counting this one, but that's it."

Joe worked to hide his irritation. "You knew about another one? Why didn't you mention it?"

Jonathon straightened to work out a kink in his back. "It was an accidental electrical fire. Took out the milk room and half the stable. The farmer admitted to repairing an extension cord with duct tape. It overheated, and *poof*." He snapped his fingers.

"You were the investigator?"

"Yeah," he said. "It was pretty straightforward."

"How come you don't know about the third one?"

Jonathon smiled. "This is my first day back on the job. What with Diane's surgery and all, I decided to take two weeks' accrued time. One of the other guys must've handled it. I didn't know about it because I haven't even been to the office yet. I got paged for this at home at the crack of dawn."

"Who should we talk to?" Joe asked, mollified. "Seems like we ought to compare notes at least."

"Oh, yeah," he readily agreed. "For sure. Tim Shafer's the one you want. He was covering for me out of St. Johnsbury."

St. Johnsbury was in the opposite corner of the state, in what was referred to as Vermont's Northeast Kingdom. Shafer being based there and yet having covered a fire near St. Albans was a perfect demonstration of both the state's small size and how a handful of people had to cover vast portions of it.

"I can bring Muhammad to the mountain and ask him to meet us over here with whatever he has on file," Michael continued. "He loves getting out of the office."

Tim Shafer was not a big fan of the Vermont Bureau of Investigation. An ex-trooper like so many of his new colleagues, he'd made the switch for purely practical reasons. As he saw it, the Vermont State Police's own investigative unit, the BCI, had been robbed of its eminence, the VSP brass had sold the agency out politically, and the troopers' union had been either asleep at the wheel or in cahoots with someone.

His line of reasoning differed depending on who was listening, but the final leap remained the same: Shafer had joined the VBI because no one listed above had protected him from it.

He still had all his benefits, the same pay, and seniority, and was now lined up for a better pension. He also had the same statewide jurisdictional reach as before, if not slightly better, and from within a leaner, less bureaucratic, more autonomous organization. Nevertheless, his heart remained with the Green and the Gold of the state police, even as — it was hard to deny — he'd clearly thrown them over.

Such contradictions aside, Shafer remained a generally personable sort, if a little overbearing when it came to debating certain topics. This was a good thing right now, as his upbeat nature had been tested by the apprehension of being summoned from afar by the VBI's second-highest-ranking officer — and told to bring just one particular case file.

Not surprisingly, Joe Gunther knew all this, and thus greeted a suspicious Tim Shafer with the friendliness of a doting uncle as the latter entered the St. Albans restaurant specifically chosen for this meeting.

"Tim," Joe exclaimed, getting to his feet and waving the younger man over to join them at a quiet booth far removed from both the front door and the kitchen. "Hope you don't mind the setting — we were getting sick of the office. Meal's on me if you're hungry."

Shafer was hungry, which, along with his opinions, was also a well-known given. He wasn't a fat man, although he was solidly built, but he ate enough for a wrestling team. Gunther had selected an environment at once disarming and seductive.

Jonathon Michael smiled wryly as he

greeted his fellow arson investigator, the reason for Joe's earlier suggestion of a restaurant now becoming clear. At the moment, Tim Shafer was a reluctant ally, which made this neutral and flattering way station part of a careful pitch, indicative of a meeting of equals. As Shafer slid his bulk along the smooth surface of the fake-leather bench, Jonathon could see him visibly relaxing.

"You want to see a menu?" Joe asked, summoning the waitress.

Shafer accepted the glossy card, studied its contents before ordering a Coke and a burger, and sat back to see what would happen.

Joe pointed to the thick accordion file Shafer had walked in with. "That the file?"

Shafer pushed it farther into the middle of the table. "As requested," he said neutrally.

"Definitely an arson?" Joe asked.

"Oh, yeah."

"You have anyone for it?"

"Not yet." Shafer was watching both of them carefully.

Joe smiled and nodded to Jonathon. "We just picked up a case of our own. Thought we should compare notes, since they're both barn fires."

Shafer looked surprised, as much by the coincidence as by the implied confirmation that he was not in trouble. "Sure," he said. "What've you got?"

Jonathon filled him in, pulling notes, sketches, and photographs from the briefcase by his side. Taking Joe's diplomatic cue, he detailed everything without asking Shafer to divulge his own investigation, until the other man's growing enthusiasm made the point moot. Shafer began regularly interrupting with "Just like mine" and "Same as me."

By the time Jonathon was wrapping things up, the burger plate had been pushed aside uneaten and half the contents of Shafer's file lay spread across the table.

"It's gotta be the same guy," he was saying. "The chemical timers look the same, the trace evidence of potato chips and glue trailers, the weird detail about setting it in the hayloft first."

"What do you make of that last part?" Joe asked.

Shafer looked baffled. "I couldn't figure it out. It's like the guy just went for the biggest source of fuel, regardless that it was up top. Not that it mattered, since the barn was a total loss. I mean, it worked, whatever we think about it." He picked up one of Michael's pictures of the devastated stable. "And he cooked the whole herd, huh? Least I didn't have that to go through, not to mention the kid."

Joe had been drinking coffee quietly through most of this, making comments only rarely. Now he sat back and eyed his investigators thoughtfully. "Okay, so we're pretty sure the same torch did both barns. What do you make of your farmer, Tim?"

"Not much. Kind of pathetic, really, named Farley Noon, if you can believe it. I kept trying to get him to take a guess on who might've done him in, but he didn't care. He just kept saying he was too old and too tired to give a damn anymore."

"Another case of being underinsured?" Joe asked.

"A little. He could have built something pretty close to the original. But I guess he'd finally run out of gas. He'd been having a string of bad luck — contaminated milk."

"How so?" Joe asked.

"Antibiotics. Any whiff of that stuff in the milk and the co-op puts you on notice."

"But he must have had insurance for that, too," Jonathon protested.

Shafer smiled wryly. "He did the first

time. But he got stuck twice, one right after the other — that's two truckloads of his milk and everybody else's on the pickup route. Cost him six thousand dollars, not to mention that the state took him apart, going over all his books and procedures. He had to take out an additional loan to cover the loss, the co-op shut him off till he tested clean a few times in a row . . . You get the idea. The barn going up in smoke turned out to be the last straw."

"What was the story behind the antibiotics?" Joe asked.

Shafer shrugged. "Nobody knows. Noon swears he wasn't treating any animals, which is usually how it gets into the milk — through the bloodstream. The presumption was that he was sabotaged. But that's almost impossible to prove. One cow gets shot up with a single load of penicillin, her milk'll screw up everything in the holding tank for three days running, while everybody runs around trying to find out which animal is dirty. It's a near-perfect-crime type of scenario."

Jonathon absorbed all that and then asked, "The fire broke out midafternoon?"

"Right. Two-thirty."

Joe got the point. "When all the cows

were outside," he mused. "Interesting difference between the two."

Both men looked at him.

"What're you thinking?" Shafer asked.

"What did Farley end up doing?" Joe asked instead.

"Sold out."

"I'm thinking that somebody knew all too well how the business works, assuming the contamination was connected. Who was the buyer?"

"His neighbor."

"Did he also get the cows?" Jonathon asked.

Shafer was looking a little uncomfortable, as if he hadn't given this fairly obvious point the attention it deserved. Joe had been expecting such an awkward moment, sooner or later. It usually cropped up when several investigators compared notes — one of them began to feel he was unfairly being put under scrutiny.

"Yeah," Shafer admitted.

"Probably neither here nor there," Joe said placidly, and moved the conversation along. "Was there bad blood between the two?"

"No," Shafer answered with just a bit more force than necessary. "That was the whole point. They got along fine. The neighbor wanted the acreage, sure, but it was always up-front — had been for years — and he seemed more upset by the burning than Noon. Plus, with the barn gone, he had to blow a bunch of extra bucks to build one of those oversize plastic Quonset hut–type things to house the extra cows. I gave both of them a real going-over — bank accounts, neighbor interviews, the local cops, you name it — they always came up real straight. And the neighbor's supply of penicillin was all accounted for."

Joe stared at the two piles of documents thoughtfully for a couple of moments, deciding how best to move on. "Where was the third fire geographically in relation to Farley Noon's and Calvin Cutts's?"

They both looked at him inquiringly.

"The so-called accidental electric fire that started in the milk room?" he prompted.

"Oh, yeah," Michael said. "It was over near Lake Champlain." He pawed through some of Shafer's paperwork until he located a map. He slid it before his boss and tapped on a spot with his fingertip. "Somewhere around there. I may be off a hair, but that's about right."

Joe studied the map. "A mile from

Farley's. Do you remember what happened to that farmer afterward?"

Jonathon's silence was telling. Shafer smiled to himself, feeling safely free of the spotlight.

"He sold out," Michael finally admitted.

"A neighbor again?"

"That's what I'm trying to remember. No. It was a developer, someone out of St. Albans. Clark Wolff — that was it. Wolff Properties. They handle a bit of everything: rentals, home sales, development projects."

"You know what they have planned?" Joe asked.

Michael shook his head. "Nope. It just happened, so it may still be under wraps." He glanced at the map again. "Given its proximity to both the town and the lake, though, it's probably housing. That's what's hot right now."

Joe pushed the map away and sat back to cross his legs. "Tough question, Jonathon, but without one iota of criticism intended, okay?"

Michael was already ahead of him. "How sure am I it was accidental?"

Gunther raised an eyebrow. "Three barn fires, two almost within sight of each other, all in short order. And with the end result that two out of the three unloaded their farms, and the third's barely hanging on. You gotta wonder."

"I *was* sure," the other responded, emphasizing the past tense. "But there's no way I'm not rechecking it now."

"I know it's a lot, given what's on your plate already . . ."

Again, Michael headed him off. "No, I can do it, and I don't need any help. I know the players, who to call. I can do it faster alone."

Both men paid him the respect of accepting this small face-saving fiction. Mirroring Joe's overall courtesy, Tim Shafer even shifted the emphasis somewhat. "If the torch did two barns the same way, without hiding that they were arsons, why would he disguise the third?"

"Too early to tell," Joe answered. "We don't even know it was set. But it wasn't the third chronologically; it was the first. Could he have entered the barn through the milk room, like everyone does, immediately saw the cob-job wiring running to the tank, and figured what the hell? He took it as a gimme."

"It ties to the other two being set from the top down, too," Jonathon suggested.

"How's that?" Shafer asked.

His colleague backed up slightly. "I didn't mean directly. I meant that he may be a guy who works with whatever opportunity is staring him in the face." He tapped the map again. "At my guy's — Loomis is his name — he sees the bad wiring and uses that; at Noon's, according to your sketches here, he sees access to a full hayloft right outside the door connecting the milk room to the stable; and at Cutts's — given his success at Noon's — he just repeats himself. I mean, think of it, we've all been in cow stables before, right?"

The other men nodded.

"What's the reaction going to be from the cows when a stranger walks in, possibly carrying gas and/or glue as accelerants? Tim," he added suddenly, warming to his hypothesis, "what style stable was Noon's — tied or free stalls?"

"Free."

Jonathon smiled. "There you have it." He then answered his own earlier question: "They start moving. The skittish ones first, then the others. If this torch isn't used to being in a barn, a free-stall stable with a bunch of huge cows moving around is not going to be the place to start setting up squibs and laying out trailers — not if you're scared of being stepped on or crushed."

Joe couldn't resist smiling. "Nice — for a total piece of fiction."

Shafer laughed, finally completely at ease. "Yeah, well, that's how a lot of cases come together, right? You tell stories until you like one enough to chase it down."

Joe conceded the point. "I do like it, I'll admit that, but it only takes us so far. Assuming the Loomis fire is arson, which is a stretch, then what's the connection between all three?"

"The farmers sold out, like you said," Jonathon said quickly.

"Two of them did," Shafer corrected.

Joe made a face. "Right — as far as we know. But if the point was to make each one sell out, then why? The properties aren't contiguous, and one is miles away. Also, the two buyers we do have so far couldn't be more disconnected."

"Age?" Jonathon suggested, clearly thinking in overdrive, both stimulated by the challenge and embarrassed by his possible mistake with the Loomis investigation. "All three farmers were long in the tooth."

Shafer and Gunther stayed silent for a while, until Joe suggested, "Okay. I don't know what to do with that yet, but let's keep it in mind. What else?"

No one answered. "How about a smoke screen?" he continued. "The old theory that you hide a needle best among other needles. Could be only one of the arsons really counts."

"Then which one is the needle we want?" Shafer asked.

Gunther smiled. "That's easier than it sounds. It may not matter. Again assuming that Loomis is an arson, we have three felonies to investigate anyhow. If you want to get technical, we don't want to rule out two to find the one left over; we need to solve them all. If we're successful, we'll find out at the end."

Now it was Michael's turn to sit back. "But that was true from the start."

Shafer couldn't resist the dig. "Except that until now, we didn't know to give Loomis a second look."

Gunther gave Jonathon high marks — he merely pressed his lips together briefly before admitting, "Point taken."

Joe tried to clear the air. "Okay, there are three of us and three roads to go down. Tim, you stick with Farley Noon; Jonathon, I know you have some of the Cutts case to organize, but while you recheck Loomis, let me carry the investigative load there. I suggest we get in touch every couple of days, face-to-face or by e-mail or phone, just to share updates. Also, I'm going to have someone at headquarters make a few calls, find out how many other farms in the area have gone on the block — when, where, why, and who bought them."

He slid off the booth bench and stood up, looking down at them both. "You wanted something to chase, Tim. Guess we all got lucky — in spades."

CHAPTER 7

Deputy Sheriff Leon Ledoux rolled his cruiser slowly to a stop at the edge of the shopping mall parking lot, far away from the nearest light source. In general, his assignment here was simply to patrol the lot, giving comfort to merchants and instilling caution in those planning mischief. But he'd done that earlier, as he'd been doing for more years than he could count, and it had been as effective — or not — as usual. The trouble with such gestures, he'd discovered — the reason they were so void of satisfaction — was that success was measured by the absence of activity.

His immediate boss, the chief deputy, always asked him the same question when he checked in every night: "See anything at the mall?" And to Leon's perpetual "Not a thing," he always responded, "Good. That'll teach 'em."

Leon had a good idea who the "them" were. He was less convinced about the value of his supposed teaching.

Not that it mattered in the long run, since that conversation only applied to when the stores were open and people milling about. Later, there was no doubt about either Leon's lesson plan or the people he hungered to instruct. All ambivalence or frustration was replaced by the thrill of the hunt.

For right now, long after hours, the chief deputy was asleep in his bed and Leon Ledoux was out to catch bad guys.

He'd been doing this for ten years, ever since he left the Marines and joined the department. By day, he served papers, stood around court, drove prisoners from one spot to another, and chased taillights — and made those "demonstrations of force" so dear to his boss's heart. But by night, with the setting of the sun, as the glow from his car's dashboard slowly replaced daylight, Leon felt his nondescript, bulky, uniformed persona metamorphose into something predatory and lithe, like a watchful panther.

Leon Ledoux lived for the night.

His cruiser dark, its engine running, he reached for the binoculars he kept under his seat, and trained them on a tight circle of figures clustered around a car before the abandoned Ames department store across the parking lot. The store's black and featureless windows supplied a suggestively apocalyptic backdrop to what was clearly a drug deal under way.

"I got you, you bastard," he murmured, still staring through the binoculars.

Leon lowered the glasses and surveyed the snow-dusted ground between him and his target, as if he were planning an attack on an enemy pillbox. In fact, his approach would be simplicity itself: His only real choice was to emerge from the shadows and cross the lot as quickly as possible, blue strobes flashing, hoping against reason that his prey would stay put.

He sighed slightly, as if in recognition of reality not quite matching fantasy. In truth, the people he busted were mostly teenagers or assorted losers that he'd dealt with from virtually his first day on duty. Barring the few exceptions who appeared periodically from out of town — usually from nearby Canada — they were as familiar as the horses on a carousel and just as prone to coming around with monotonous regularity, circling out of sight into jail before returning for each repeat performance.

There were an elite few, however, who fit the truly rare category of the bad news local who had never been arrested — so far. They were a source of special irritation to Leon Ledoux, and he had one of them right now, literally in his sights: Rick Frantz.

He unhooked his radio mike and keyed the transmit button to update dispatch. Not in detail, of course — he didn't want company messing up a drug bust. He merely mentioned he was investigating some suspicious activity.

After that, he studied the scene before him one last time — memorizing the players — before gunning his engine, hitting his lights, and peeling out of hiding like the avenging angel he felt himself to be. Partway across the parking lot, he switched on his public address loudspeaker and barked out, "This is the police. You are under arrest. Do not move."

Of the five people he'd cataloged, three froze and two bolted. Frantz took off on foot, while the driver of the car hit the gas so hard, his back end began fishtailing on the slippery snow.

Ledoux had eyes only for Frantz, as the latter ran the length of the abandoned department store and headed for a dark alleyway between it and its neighbor.

This undivided attention, however, carried a cost. In exchange for only tracking Frantz, Leon took his eyes off the other car, whose rear wheels now suddenly found purchase on the asphalt under the snow and launched the vehicle straight at the cruiser.

Ledoux watched in horror as the young driver, caught like a ghost in the cop's headlights, abandoned his steering wheel and covered his face with his hands. Ledoux swerved, lost control, and met the other car in a perfect T-bone configuration.

Shouting a string of curses, ignoring the pain in his neck, he leaped from his vehicle and ran to the other driver's open side window.

"You son of a bitch," Ledoux yelled, ignoring the blood that was pouring from the driver's nose and lip. "You're under arrest. Put your hands on the wheel. One above and one through the middle. Now."

Dumbly, the boy complied. Ledoux slapped his cuffs on his wrists, locking him to the steering wheel. He then reached past him and pulled the key from the ignition.

"Where is Frantz headed?" he demanded, peering into the gloom.

But the boy was now crying.

The deputy stepped back, quickly surveying the damage to his own vehicle. "God *damn* it," he swore, and kicked the door before him, making the driver jump in surprise.

Ledoux pulled his radio from his belt. "Dispatch, this is oh-eight. I've been in a ten-fifty at the mall. Am in pursuit of a subject heading behind the Ames store along the north wall. Need assistance."

Paying no attention to the dispatcher calmly repeating his message, Leon replaced the radio and began running. Coming abreast of the three young men still standing rooted in place, he only slowed enough to yell at one of them, "I got all your names, Carl. You move one foot from where you are, and you are screwed for life. You got that?"

All three merely nodded as he passed.

Despite the extent of this turmoil, Rick Frantz had been gone for only a little over a minute.

Ledoux arrived at the entrance to the alleyway, sweating and out of breath. Already, in the distance, he could hear sirens approaching. He didn't have much time.

He poked his head around the corner. The alleyway ran straight and narrow to a streetlight at the far end, allowing him to see that there was no one in sight. Still, crouched low, he entered the narrow space warily, watching and listening.

About halfway down, he found something. A side door into the empty building was slightly ajar. Using his flashlight, Ledoux saw a set of melting footprints leading inside.

"You dumb bastard," he said in a low voice, killing his light and silently stepping through the doorway.

It was cold in the building, almost as cold as it was outside, and very dark. The only light came from the parking lot fixtures, far away and filtered through the long row of dusty front windows. The room was huge, as befitted a space that once housed a department store and was now only home to a scattered jumble of counters, broken shelving units, forgotten furniture, and dozens of boxes.

It was otherworldly in its stillness and oddly disconcerting, since above a certain height, all obstacles ceased to exist, the abandoned rubble not reaching above five or six feet. It was like being in an enormous movie soundstage, designed for cameras and lights to fly overhead for hundreds of feet, totally unimpeded.

Except that Leon had no access to airborne lights or cameras. He was stuck on the ground, and that ground was increasingly resembling a maze of potential ambushes.

He hesitated, considering his options.

He knew he was in trouble. The car crash had reduced his derring-do to the swagger of a reckless cowboy. His choices, as he saw them, were to retreat and face some serious disciplining, despite having taken in all but one of the suspects, or to finish the job, make a clean sweep, and hope that his success might offset his transgressions.

It wasn't even a contest. Walking on the balls of his feet, Ledoux advanced into the cavernous room, keenly aware of his shoes crunching on the debris underfoot.

Even with the tumult before him, he could pick out the ordered pattern of erstwhile aisles, and began calculating what route Rick Frantz might have taken. He then moved toward the long back wall, instinctively bent over, and got the dim light coming through the far windows to reflect off whatever wet footprints were still visible.

Feeling surer now, and further stimulated by the appearance of blue strobe lights in the parking lot, he killed his radio and pager so they wouldn't give him away, removed his heavy shoes, and silently began traveling parallel to Frantz's glistening tracks.

He moved fast. Even buried inside the building, he could hear car doors slamming outside, along with a few muffled shouted commands. It wouldn't be long before his colleagues followed his example, informed by the kids he'd left behind, and found the same door he had in the alleyway. He needed to get his hands on Frantz before that happened.

He was nearing a collection of tall shelf units, lined up like dominos, row on row, when at last the footprints inevitably faded to nothing. Undeterred, Ledoux remained against the far wall so that as he worked the row of shelves, he only had to look in one direction. He hadn't seen a weapon during his earlier surveillance, but by now, he was beginning to fantasize that one reason Frantz alone had taken off was that he was probably armed. Instinctively, Ledoux slipped his gun from its holster.

He glanced down the first alley-like aisle and stopped dead in his tracks. The shelves were too tightly packed to allow the light from the front windows much access. Disappointed, he pulled his flashlight free, aimed it down the shadowy corridor, and hit the switch for just an instant. In a burst of light barely longer than a camera's flash, Ledoux saw only empty floor space. He slipped along the wall to the next aisle.

He'd worked his way up five rows in this

fashion, his tension increasing with each flash of his light, when he suddenly heard the loud crash of a door opening far behind him, making him jump.

"This is the police," came a shouted, nervous voice. "If anyone's in here, come out with your hands up."

Ledoux swore under his breath. Things were not improving. Hedging his bets between remaining silent and letting out a shout, he turned his radio back on and murmured into the mike, "It's Leon. I'm in the Ames store. I got him cornered. Block the door so he can't get out."

Instead of the answer he was hoping for, he heard, "Unit calling. I can't copy."

He was about to respond, bluntly and loudly, when a small sound drew his attention. He looked up the aisle beside him, just in time to see a shadow flit past its far opening.

He gave up the radio and bolted down the aisle. At its far end, he turned toward where the shadow had been heading, assumed a shooter's stance — one hand holding the gun, the other the flashlight — and shouted, "Police. Don't move." He then switched on the light and captured Rick Frantz out in the middle of the room, one hand holding a small canvas bag.

Damn, he thought, I got you.

But it wasn't to be. A split second later, bank by bank, in rapid succession, the ceiling's rows of fluorescent lighting stuttered awake, causing both Ledoux and Frantz to instinctively freeze, their eyes cast heavenward.

With the light came a burst of shouted voices, causing them both to whirl and face the side entrance.

"Don't move."

"Police. Freeze."

"He's got a gun."

To his horror, Ledoux saw not one but four of his colleagues on either side of the door, all of them with drawn weapons, half of which were pointed directly at him.

"It's me," he shouted, and waved his hands.

It was the wrong thing to do. One shot rang out, the bullet thudding into the shelf unit by his head, followed by another, which only elicited a small grunt from Rick Frantz.

Ledoux spun back in time to see the boy crumple to the floor, dropping his small bag.

"You stupid bastards," Leon screamed, fighting the impulse to return fire. "It's me."

He ran over to Frantz's side, seeing a pool of blood already seeping out from under the body.

He came to a stop in his stocking feet, holstered his gun in an embarrassed quick gesture, and stared at the end result of his evening's work.

"Shit."

CHAPTER 8

Generally speaking, bodies aren't buried during the winter in Vermont. The ground's hard, covered in snow, and the expense of dealing with both is too great. Most people attend a service away from the cemetery, comfort the grieving family, and bid farewell to the casket, not considering that the body will spend the rest of the season in cold storage before being quietly interred a few months later.

Most people were not Marie Cutts, however. Despite the family's financial misfortune, she was sparing no expense. Her son was to be buried properly and promptly, with no practical discussions being broached.

The morning following Leon Ledoux's series of poor decisions, Joe Gunther parked behind a long line of vehicles — mostly pickups — that was tucked against the embankment of a narrow dirt road at the top of a hill. He got out, turned up the collar of his coat against the chill morning air, and made for a small metal gate in the wrought-iron fence ringing the cemetery.

It wasn't large, as burial grounds go, but it was perfectly perched on the hill's very cap, so that as he climbed the path toward the backs of the assembled crowd, Joe felt the sky opening up all around him. And as he reached the crest, this faintly biblical impression was only enhanced by the view suddenly yawning at his feet. Instead of seeing more hills, which was the norm in a state as geologically lumpy as Vermont, he was faced with a vast and dizzying emptiness, sweeping away into the Lake Champlain valley, across the flats cradling a miniaturized St. Albans, over the frozen slab of the lake itself, and only then coming to a halt against the distant and forbidding wall of New York State's Adirondack Mountains. It was a view to impress even the dullest onlooker, made all the more stark by being clad entirely in snow and ice. To the horizon's hard edge, under a blinding sun and a sky as blue as the base of a torch's flame, the whole world looked as cold as when glaciers had scoured the trough in which the lake's waters were now frozen.

It was at once beautiful and repellent — a fanciful glimpse of the Paleolithic past and a future conjured up by science fiction writers too depressed to imagine anything less bleak.

A perfect setting, Joe thought, for this particular funeral.

He found Jonathon Michael standing apart from the crowd, dark-suited like Joe and wearing a thick topcoat. He'd found a small knoll to stand on, presumably chosen to give him a vague sense of distance and objectivity, and which, Joe found as he joined him there, also served well as an observation post.

"You hear the latest?" Joe murmured to Jonathon after exchanging nodded greetings.

Michael merely raised his eyebrows questioningly.

"Rick Frantz is in a coma, shot by some nervous deputy last night during a drug deal."

"We can't talk to him?"

"Not if we want him to talk back."

They were silent for a few moments, watching the somber group slowly reorganizing around both casket and minister, a few settling into the folding chairs reserved for the immediate family.

"It would be a drag if Frantz is our guy," Jonathan said in a low voice, "and we never got to find out."

The same thought had occurred to Joe. "It's early yet. I wouldn't worry too much.

You know who that is? Looks like a basket-ball player with a weight problem."

Jonathan nodded. "Billy St. Cyr. Neighboring farmer to the south."

"No kidding?" Joe remembered the name. "He's the one Cal said he's been arguing with for twenty years."

They inventoried the assembled faces, exchanging information on the few they knew so far. Joe figured that before this was resolved, they'd probably have a conversation with almost everyone here.

"How 'bout the blonde?" he asked eventually.

Michael cast him a look. "You didn't meet her? That's Linda, Jeff's wife."

Joe grunted softly. "She was asleep when I met the others. She's very pretty."

Jonathon didn't respond, leaving Joe to his own reflections. In fact, Linda Cutts Padgett was a beauty. Even tired to near haggardness, she was endowed with the same soft and vulnerable radiance that had made the young Julie Christie such a hit in *Doctor Zhivago*. On her looks alone, Jeff had to count himself a lucky man.

Joe shifted his focus to the rest of the family, noticing that the grief he'd witnessed the day of the fire had changed into a different, more volatile, complicated kind of tension.

The minister became its first victim, attempting to arrange the seating. His hopes had clearly been to line them up patriarchally with Cal first, then Marie, followed by Jeff, Linda, and the two kids. But Marie would have none of it. She brusquely pulled Cal down the line, placed him between her and Jeff — casting a loathing glare at the latter — and fired a quick snarling comment at the minister that brought him up short.

Jeff showed no notice. He was tending to his children, getting them to settle down, while his wife merely stood there, staring blankly at the ground, a thousand miles away. When it came time for them all to sit, Jeff gently lowered her to her chair, as if tending to an ancient Alzheimer's victim.

By then, Joe's eyes were on Calvin. When they'd first met, he'd taken the farmer to be an appeaser by instinct, naturally resolving all conflicts within range. But he wasn't that way here. Despite the minister looking at him imploringly, there was no deflecting of Marie's both barrels from Cal. In a rough approximation of his daughter's apparent catatonia, he seemed to be functioning on automatic pilot.

The service had barely begun when, from their elevated knoll, the two police officers saw another car pull up by the side of the road. From it, a young woman began making her way up the path toward the group.

Joe took in the short skirt, streaked hair, and a glint of silver from an eyebrow post, before turning back to the family, his attention drawn by a sudden sharp sound.

Marie Cutts was standing, her arms rigid, her chair toppled backward. Seen this way, thin and tensioned, her profile highlighted by the sun, she was pure gargoyle of old, perched in muted mimicry of some demonic spirit.

Until she let out a scream.

"No. Not her. Not here. Get her away."

The minister stalled in midsentence, Calvin looked up at her quizzically, as if she'd shattered a profound daydream. Jeff was the first to act, reaching across his father-in-law to offer comfort. But, of course, that was precisely wrong. Marie recoiled from his touch as if he'd been on fire, violently jarring the minister, who had to lurch not to drop his Bible.

Jonathon Michael was dispassion personified, whispering, "Let me guess: Marianne Kotch? Should we do something?"

Joe said, barely moving his lips, "Not yet."

His book safe, the minister rallied, grabbing Marie by the shoulders, his body language supportive but disciplining, as if warning her to behave or else. He steered her back to her chair, which Jeff had righted, and almost pushed her back into it. He then nodded to the young newcomer, directed her to a spot as far from Marie as possible, reopened his Bible, and asked of his audience, "Shall we resume?"

They did, including Marie, who sat beside her husband in furious, silent, impotent defeat, as glowering as Cal appeared lost.

"Wow," muttered Jonathon, "I wonder why she showed up."

Joe was still watching Marianne Kotch, her head held high but her stance suggestive of a deer's about to bolt.

"I think I'll ask her," he said.

He had the opportunity after the service. Because of where the minister had placed her, and her own reluctance to mingle, Marianne stayed far back of the crowd, among the other headstones, biding her time until she got a clear run to her car.

Gunther stepped off his small mound and approached her casually.

"Marianne?" he asked as he drew near.

She eyed him suspiciously. "So?"

"Nothing much," he responded affably. "Nice of you to pay your respects."

"Not according to the mom from hell." Her voice had a sulky false confidence he was all too used to hearing.

"She's suffered, too."

"It's not my fault he's dead," Marianne said petulantly.

"Seeing the world through her kind of pain hardly makes you clear-sighted."

She frowned and stared at him. "You a preacher?"

He laughed softly. "Cop. I'm looking into his death."

She took a half step back, bumping into a headstone. "I should've known," she said angrily.

Gunther kept his voice quiet and comforting. "Should've known what? That we'd investigate? Don't you want to know who killed him?"

She looked troubled. "He was killed, then? It wasn't an accident?"

"Until we hear otherwise, we're assuming it wasn't. That's why we're finding out as much about Bobby as possible."

Marianne's expression soured. "Bet you got an earful about me."

Joe nodded. "That must be hard, knowing that."

She flared up again. "They can all get fucked. What I do is my business. I don't care what they say."

He smiled. "I can see that."

Her face flushed. "Up yours," she spat, and tried to walk away.

He took a risk and caught her arm, hoping it wouldn't cause an uproar. He got lucky. As soon as he stopped her, she seemed to deflate and just stood there, staring at the ground, breathing fast.

"I'm sorry, Marianne. I'm sorry that he died, and I'm sorry that Marie can't see what he meant to you."

She looked up at him, her eyes glistening. "You don't get it. I dumped him. I thought he was a pain in the ass — a moony-eyed, shit-on-his-shoes, lovesick pain in the ass."

Joe thought back to Rick Frantz, who, days before being shot in mid–drug deal, had been seen kissing this girl in a parked car. "And who may have been the most decent boyfriend you ever had," he suggested.

Her eyes wandered to about halfway down the buttons of his coat. "Yeah . . . Well, maybe. Turned out decent and boring were kind of the same."

"Still, he didn't deserve this."

She wiped her eyes with the heels of her hands, smearing her makeup and making herself look even younger than she was. "He wasn't my type, but he had his moments."

"Can you tell me a bit about him?" Joe asked.

She gave him a questioning look. "Tell you about him? That's what I meant. There wasn't anything *to* tell. All he wanted was to hold hands."

Gunther didn't respond, choosing instead to wait her out. As if reacting to a question, she added, "Okay, maybe more than that, but it was still like a big frigging deal. I mean, Jesus, he asked me to marry him. How stupid is that?"

"What were his plans after you got married? He must've said."

She laughed sadly. "Shit, yeah. Did he ever. Can you believe it? We were supposed to settle down and live with his folks. 'Just like Jeff and Linda,' was what he said." She spread her arms wide. "Look at me, for Christ's sake. Do I look like I belong on a farm, much less playing house with the Dragon Lady? Jesus, that would've been World War III right there."

He couldn't repress a smile. "It does seem like a tight fit."

She shook her head. "Tight like a straitjacket. You got that right."

"I heard you took up with him in the first place to get back at Barry Newhouse."

She was caught by surprise. "You been getting around." She let out a sigh. "Well, I wish they were wrong, but I guess that's true. Barry was being an asshole. Bobby seemed the perfect way to stick it up his butt."

Again, Joe remained still.

And again, she reacted as if accused. "Well, Bobby was perfect. Like a choirboy. And it's not like I stayed with him just because of Barry."

"You fell in love with him, after all?"

She tossed her head, the tough girl regaining her dignity. "Yeah, right. Not likely. Talk about a match made in hell. No, I didn't fall in love. But you couldn't not like the guy. He was so . . . you know . . . earnest. It was so dopey, it was cute. For a while."

"You dumped him once earlier."

She looked uncomfortable. "Shit, what *don't* you know?" she said. "I tried, yeah. But he took it so hard, I felt sorry for him. The second time, though, I wasn't backing down."

"That was just before the fire?" Joe asked.

Her eyes widened. "That's what I was telling you. It was the same day. When I first heard about it, I thought maybe he'd killed himself."

"You don't still think so?"

Her mouth dropped open. "Holy shit. I didn't know that's what happened."

Joe held up both hands to stop her in her tracks. "No, no. It didn't. But I need to ask you: Was he that depressed that night?"

"He wasn't happy. Pulled the same routine he did the first time — crying and everything. But it didn't get to me as much. I thought maybe even he knew we weren't too good for each other by then."

"Did he say what he'd be doing that night?"

She looked rueful. "What? Like killing himself? No. He was wicked bummed out, and he left. That was it."

Joe returned to an earlier topic. "What about Barry? He must've been angry after you and he split up."

"He wasn't happy," she admitted.

"Did he say he might go after Bobby?"

Her tone was dismissive. "He said he'd break him in two, but it didn't mean anything. Barry's all talk. That's one of the reasons I dumped him. Plus, if it ever got down to it, Bobby probably could've kicked his butt. Barry's not in great shape, and Bobby was pretty strong." She paused before adding, "That would've been fun to see."

"So Barry didn't say anything specific?"

"No."

"What about Rick Frantz?" he asked.

She stiffened. "What about him?"

"You were seen kissing him in the supermarket parking lot. Rick must've wanted you to himself."

"You don't know Rick. Even *with* all your snooping around."

"So it's not serious between you two?"

"Nothing's serious with Rick. I was with him because I was sick of Bobby and needed a break. Who told you about that anyhow? I can't believe this place. You can't take a shit around here without everybody knowing."

Joe ignored her. "You went to school with Bobby, didn't you?"

"Till I blew out of there, yeah. I was a year ahead of him." She added with unintentional irony, "I'm older."

"How was he treated there? Any troubles?"

Her expression darkened. "His troubles

weren't at school. They were at home, with that mother."

Joe rested against a large granite stone behind him, hiking one leg up for comfort. Most of the mourners were gone by now, and a small crew of workers had appeared to tidy up the burial site. Jonathon Michael was chatting with someone by the distant road. In the opposite direction, there was, just discernible, the tiny streak of a boat's wake far out in the middle of the lake, where the water was no longer frozen.

"Did he and his mom have a bad relationship?" Joe asked.

"You saw how she is," Marianne burst out, pointing down the road.

"That doesn't tell me how they were with each other."

She made a face. "Weird, if you ask me. She's got a mouth on her like nobody's business — always tearing people down, including her own family. But Bobby seemed clueless."

"Did she spoil him?"

"No. She gave him shit, too. But it wasn't as bad, and he didn't seem to mind, so they kind of canceled each other out."

"Like a mutual understanding?"

"Yeah," she agreed. "Not that you could really tell. It was just something I noticed."

Joe reflected a moment on what he'd learned so far. "Was Bobby a happy guy?" he finally asked.

She crouched down and gathered a little snow in her hand. The presence of snow seemed at odds with the pleasant temperature. It was a good sign for maple sugarers, who needed warm days and cold nights.

"Yeah," she said simply. "He was looking forward to a good life."

"No conflict with the way his sister and Jeff got the farm instead of him?"

Marianne looked up, surprised. "Oh, no. That worked out perfect. He thought Jeff was a great farmer."

She straightened and tossed her tiny snowball underhanded so that it landed without a sound on top of another grave. "Maybe that's what I noticed about him and his mom. It really drove me crazy. Nothing bothered him — working for his brother-in-law like a hired hand, the Dragon Lady's bitchiness, being trapped in that house with all those whacked-out people. He totally didn't get it when I said I'd sooner be dead than move in there."

A combination of compassion and curiosity about part of her story made Joe bring up a subject he'd avoided until now.

"I was sorry to hear about Rick Frantz."

She shook her head like a mother dismissing a mischievous pet. "Yeah. What a jerk, huh?"

It wasn't the reaction he'd expected, and confirmed the lack of seriousness she'd claimed concerning the kiss Marie had witnessed.

"You're not surprised?" he asked.

She turned and tilted her chin toward the fresh hole now filled with Bobby Cutts's body. "*That* surprised me. Rick getting shot is right up there with water being wet. Bobby was supposed to find some girl who liked cows as much as he did and make babies with her."

She looked over her shoulder at him, her face suddenly much older. "Guess that shows you, huh? You done with me?"

He nodded. "Yeah. Thanks for your help."

"No sweat."

Joe watched Marianne walk unsteadily across the frozen ground in her high-heeled black boots, her hands out to both sides to keep her balance, her bright green fingernails flickering in the sunlight.

"Guess that shows you," he echoed softly.

CHAPTER 9

Gunther waited to return to the Cutts house until long after the funeral, close to nightfall. He didn't want to appear as people were still milling about as usual following a service, but he also didn't want too much time to elapse before asking the family more questions.

He used another approach to the house than he had on the day of the fire. Then he'd come from the south, where the road curved around and delivered him abruptly to the dooryard. The northern reach, however, was entirely different. Cresting a hill not a half mile away, it afforded a view that would have been picture-perfect before the black hole of the burned barn ruined everything. From the rolling fields and clumped trees in the foreground, to the pristine white farmhouse and scattered outbuildings, and finally to the far-distant ski mountain crowning the horizon, it was all so emblematic of Vermont's touted virtues as to moisten an adman's eye.

But the cremated remnants of the barn were just as symbolic, as Joe was discovering — not just of the tragedy now crushing its owners but of the broader plights of family dysfunction and grinding economic struggle. If tourists driving by such sylvan centerpieces only knew, he thought, they wouldn't see the rural life with such dewy-eyed romanticism.

He rode down the hill, pulled off the road, and got out of his car. Marie Cutts appeared at the farmhouse's front door as if on cue.

"What do you want?" she called out to him, her voice sharp and unpleasant.

"Hi, Mrs. Cutts. Sorry to bother you. I just wanted to ask a few more questions."

"We've done talking to you. You know what to do. Go out and do it."

He approached the building, walking slowly. "That's what we're doing. We have quite a few people working on this, each one of us making sure every detail is covered."

She glared at him suspiciously. "What're you saying?"

He smiled slightly. "That *my* job is making sure I've asked all the right questions here."

She wasn't buying it. "The right questions? The ones you like the answers to, you mean. My son was slaughtered the same as all those cows, but I'm starting to hear that the police think one of us had something to do with it. What the hell were you thinking, coming to my son's funeral?"

"I wanted to pay my respects . . ."

"That's bullshit. I saw you talking to that whore afterward."

Jeff Padgett appeared in the doorway behind her and placed his hands on her skinny shoulders. "It's okay, Mom. Let him come in."

She shrugged him off violently and pushed by him to leave, saying, "Don't you tell me what to do. It's not your place yet."

Padgett looked at the ground briefly before he slowly straightened and forced a smile. "It's been very tough on her."

"I'm sure it's been tough on you, too," Gunther said, stepping onto the porch and remembering a similar exchange with Calvin.

"I loved him, but he wasn't my son."

"Good point."

"Who would you like to talk to?" Jeff asked.

"Your wife, actually, if she's up to it."

Padgett nodded carefully. "I guess so. She seems a lot better. Got the wind back in her sails — better'n the rest of us."

"You don't sound convinced."

"Yeah," he admitted wryly. "I've seen her do this before when times were tough. First she crashes, then she rallies like a trouper, charging around putting everything right."

"And then she crashes again?" Joe surmised.

"Not always. I never know. Makes me nervous; we've never had anything hit us this bad before." He paused. "She's in the kitchen, you want to see her."

"I do," Joe said, "but first I was wondering, since you brought it up, what *are* you and Cal going to do now?"

"I don't know," he answered simply. "We're meeting with the insurance people, then the bank. Guess we'll know what we're facing after that."

Joe slipped by him across the threshold and patted his arm. "Well, good luck."

"Thanks."

Gunther walked through to the kitchen door, hoping Marie wouldn't also be in attendance. He breathed a quiet sigh of relief as he saw only Linda, the two kids, and Calvin, who was sitting at the dining table reading the funnies to the little girl. Linda was showing her son how to load the dishwasher.

His quiet arrival allowed him to survey the scene unobserved, which, despite its domestic appearance, did strike him as Jeff had implied — a thing of infinite fragility. Cal reminded him of the haunting pictures of Lincoln shortly before his death. His appearance was ravaged by grief and sleeplessness, his eyes dark-rimmed and sunken, surrounded by careworn creases. His voice was soothing and quiet.

Linda, by contrast, was the epitome of brittle cheer, like a lightbulb whose filament was burning dangerously bright. She fussed about, instructing and teasing her son, her voice high-pitched and nervous, her hands fluttering like cornered birds, grasping plates and glasses, then lighting on the boy's narrow back as she directed him.

As at the service, however, Joe was again struck by her beauty. Even now, dressed in an old flannel shirt and jeans, she was distractingly attractive — slim-hipped, athletic, and graceful, with shoulder-length, thick blond hair that always fell perfectly in place as she moved.

He cleared his throat, causing the four of them to look his way.

"Sorry," he said. "I was just wondering if I could ask Mrs. Padgett a few questions, since we missed each other the first time."

There was an awkward silence as father and daughter exchanged glances, using body language to determine how to handle the kids.

Cal finally rose and waved young Mike over to join him. "Why don't we go up to the sugar house and see how Billy's doing?"

It was the right suggestion. Both children grasped their grandfather's hands and escorted him from the room, barraging him with eager questions.

With a sad cast to her face, Linda watched them leave. Afterward, she smiled weakly at Joe and pointed to a chair at the dining table. "Would you like some coffee? It's fresh."

He nodded as he sat. "That would be great. Thanks. I haven't had the chance until now, I'm afraid, but I wanted to extend my condolences."

She poured him a cup and brought it over to the table, sitting down opposite him. Facing her this close, he could see the exhaustion around her eyes and the slight pallor to her cheeks. This was a woman working hard to maintain her composure.

"Thank you," she said. "I keep waiting for it to sink in. Right now it's more like he's just running late or something."

"That's pretty common."

"I suppose you see this kind of thing a lot."

"Often enough," he admitted, before asking, "I heard Cal say that someone named Billy was at the sugar house. You going to do some sugaring, after all?"

"No. Billy St. Cyr volunteered to collect our sap and boil it down for us. He only wanted a percentage of the yield, so Dad said it was okay."

"St. Cyr?" Joe questioned, recalling the big man at the funeral. "I thought they didn't get along."

She smiled faintly. "Guess that's what tragedy will do. He came over this morning and offered to help. I've never seen him so sweet."

Joe took a sip from his mug before commenting, "That's what I hear about your brother — that he was a very sweet guy."

She cupped her cheek in her hand, her elbow resting on the tabletop, and stared into middle space. "Yeah," she said softly. "He was that."

He matched her tone of voice. "What do you think happened?"

Slowly, she refocused on his face. "It was an accident."

He waited for more, but she stayed silent, looking at him.

"How do you mean?"

"He wasn't supposed to be in the barn. I mean, it's not like he shouldn't have been. Annie was going to calve, although not for a few days. But there was no reason for him to be there." She scratched her forehead. "I guess I'm not making much sense."

"No, you're doing fine," Joe reassured her. "Did he often visit the barn at night?"

"We all do now and then. It's a peaceful place at night — not peaceful-quiet, mind — it's actually pretty noisy. But peaceful in that you feel all alone on the face of the earth, just you and the cows. I used to think it felt like what Noah's ark must've been. I'd stand at the window sometimes and imagine there was only water out there. I swear to God I could almost feel the floor rock under me a little, just like a ship." She sighed. "Maybe that's what he was feeling."

Joe doubted it. He'd been caught in a fire, years ago, and it had been nothing like being on board a boat.

"Did he have reason to seek out a little thinking space?" he asked instead.

She looked at him more directly.

"There'd been some trouble in his love life."

"Marianne Kotch?"

She smiled slightly. "I heard you'd been asking around. Yeah. Mom wasn't too keen on her. But then, that's kind of her way."

"Like when you and Jeff got together?"

"She wasn't too thrilled then, either."

"How did she react?"

Linda straightened and crossed her arms. "Angrily. She's never liked Jeff."

"Why?"

She glanced at the door, as if checking to see who might be listening. Her voice was barely audible when she spoke. "I think because he got in the way of Bobby."

"As a sort of surrogate son?"

"Yeah — that's a good way of putting it. The sad thing is that Bobby loved Jeff and was really happy when Dad said he'd give us the farm."

"Bobby didn't resent not getting it himself?"

She shook her head. "He was very happy being number two. Told us that straight-out when it happened, and I know he wasn't lying."

"Didn't he like farming?"

"He loved it. It was his whole life, which is a good way to look at it if you're going to do this. He just knew he had a lot to learn and that Jeff would be the perfect teacher, that's all."

"How 'bout you?" Joe asked suddenly, noticing how her phrasing became almost clinical at times.

She raised her eyebrows. "It's all I've ever known."

"But do you like it?"

"What's not to like? It's a good life."

"The hours are brutal, the work's tough and nonstop. I was born on a farm."

She gave a laugh. "Well, then you know. I kept milking and haying the fields and stacking bales even after the kids arrived, just so I could see my husband other than late at night, when he'd come in smelling of cow manure and engine oil and fall asleep with a beer in his hand."

Joe stared meditatively at his coffee, thinking back to his own father and how he, too, would come in exhausted every night, barely able to talk to his wife and two sons.

"I always wonder how women put up with it," he mused.

"They don't always," she commented. "Even though more and more women are becoming farmers themselves."

He looked up at her, studying her serious

blue eyes. "Your mom seemed to be having a hard time even before Bobby died."

Linda pursed her lips. "That goes way back," she admitted. "Her father's to blame."

"How so?" he asked, remembering the story Calvin had told to him.

"You heard he was a drinker?"

He nodded.

"Well, that's it in a nutshell. 'He drank the farm and five generations' worth of hard work.' That's how Mom puts it. She hated him for it, and maybe she hated the farm for pushing him too hard, 'cause she loved him, too."

"And then she married a farmer?" Joe asked. "Risky move."

"She didn't feel she had a choice. For some of us, it's all we know, till we wake up too late."

"Does that include you?" he asked.

She smiled. "No. I married Jeff, and my dad's nothing like my grandfather. My mother's disappointments aren't my own."

"But you are in a pickle now," he said. "What happens if this farm can't recover?"

She held his gaze. "The farm may not, but we'll recover. We'll just do something else. Dad can retire. Jeff can get another job. IBM's hiring all the time in

Burlington. Or he can do something else. There's no telling what the bank and the insurance company will say. Maybe something will work out." She leaned forward again for emphasis. "The point is, it's not what you're doing so much as who you're doing it with. As long as our family's okay, we'll be okay."

He took one last sip of his coffee and stood up. "Well, it's getting late. I ought to get out of your hair. I do thank you for talking with me. It helps to get as much background as possible."

She stood up with him, in the process brushing against a corkboard hanging on the wall. He noticed, among the snapshots, children's drawings, and assorted business cards, one from a Realtor named John Samuel Gregory, out of St. Albans.

He pointed at it, something tugging at his memory. "Quite the name."

She glanced over her shoulder. "People like him come by all the time, especially these last few years. Flatlanders pay top dollar for farmland. I've heard some of them say it's like getting back in touch with the land. They have no clue."

"He offer to list the place?"

"We didn't let him get that far. Do you

think you'll catch who did it?" she asked, circling the table.

"We'll do everything we can," he promised.

Linda escorted Joe out of the kitchen to the front door. "That's not the same thing, is it?"

He reflected on that for a moment, wondering what to say. He preferred to be honest, although official training on the subject suggested a little bravado never hurt, especially when people were feeling vulnerable.

"We'll catch him," he finally said, for that split second believing it himself.

Perhaps not surprisingly, she didn't break into applause. Instead, she studied him for a couple of seconds, reached out to touch his forearm lightly, and said, "I think you will do everything you can."

CHAPTER 10

Gail Zigman was daydreaming about Joe. Hardly a novelty. She did that a fair amount, when her mind was drifting. They had been a couple for so long that thinking about him was pretty much second nature.

Although lately, sadly, that hadn't been as comforting as it used to be. Gail was undergoing a change — a fundamental life change, she realized — and her relationship to Joe was looming large within it.

She blinked a couple of times and checked into what was happening around her. She was sitting in Senate committee room 7, the so-called Ag Committee, along with her five colleagues, listening to some ideologue ramble on about the perils of the United States falling behind the rest of the world in food production. Nothing to be learned or believed there, she thought, allowing herself to drift once more.

Gail had come to believe that her life was losing purpose. Born to wealthy New York parents, one of two daughters well trained, well traveled, and well educated, she'd hit the social tidal wave of the 1960s at just the right time and age to be swept completely off her expected course. She'd ended up in Vermont several overstimulated years later, in a commune outside Brattleboro, wearing cotton tie-dyes and pulling garden weeds, her brain foggy, her body worn, and her ideals a jumble of rehashed political and social rhetoric. That period had started a rebirthing process that had led her to running a successful realty business, to local and now statewide politics, and to completing an interrupted law degree and pursuing a short and tumultuous career as a deputy state's attorney.

In the midst of it all, she had met and fallen in love with Joe, whose steady, stalwart presence had often served as a crucial anchor in turbulent times, despite his being — on the surface, at least — her exact opposite: a farmer's son, a lifelong cop, and someone whose travels had been almost exclusively paid for by his employer, including the military, who'd seen fit to put him into combat at a tender age. To all her friends, he could not have been less suitable for any A-list of potential suitors.

Except that in her mind, she, like Joe,

had made a life of being purposeful, successful, and of use to others, especially after she'd left the commune.

But something else had happened during these years just past, something so overwhelmingly pervasive that it had truly changed her life. She'd been raped. She'd survived, of course, had suffered no physical handicap, and had seemingly resumed a healthy, normal life, whatever that meant. But she'd never been the same. It was following the rape that she returned to law school, became a prosecutor and later — by contrast — an environmental lobbyist, and then accepted the urgings of friends to run for state office. The rape started her on what had first appeared as a random progression but which, looking back, now seemed like a blueprint for political ambition, including high-profile stints on both ends of the polemical spectrum.

And one of the reasons that this evolution hadn't appeared contrived or cynical was that she'd devoted herself completely to each step, with no thought about the next until she'd found herself taking it with a true believer's zeal. It was only now, in hindsight, that she recognized that a series of haphazard choices born of trauma and emotion had turned out looking like a coherent plan. Even so, Gail was slowly realizing — long after most of her friends, including Joe — that, as a result, she might be poised on the threshold of her most exciting stage yet.

She cleared her head enough to once more check in on what was unfolding before her. The witness had broken out hard-backed charts that he was holding up to buttress his argument in favor of genetically modified plant seeds — charts already included in the folders he'd handed out earlier. Eyes open and expression intent, she retreated back into her thoughts.

So why was she constantly returning to Joe during these ruminations? It wasn't like things were amiss in their relationship. If anything, his switch from the Brattleboro Police Department, where he'd worked from the start, to the VBI had done them both some good, exposing him to new challenges and making their own conversations more interesting — to her, at least.

One of her colleagues, a liberal Democrat from Chittenden County, interrupted the witness to challenge him on a point he'd just made. Gail sat forward in her chair, using her own mental autopilot to retrieve from her subconscious what had just been said. It was a long-standing and handy talent, being able to do two completely separate things at once, even if one of them was daydreaming.

The topic being discussed — if not the speaker — was actually of great interest to her: the exponential use of so-called GMO seeds versus the concerns about their potential long-term effects. Vermont, frequently a hotbed of political controversy, was, as usual, garnering national headlines with the debate, and the statehouse was buzzing with a pending showdown between the two camps, of which this small piece of boring testimony was just a preliminary twitch. E-mails and phone calls were already escalating as interested parties began waking up. It was looking as though Vermont might be made a litmus test on the subject.

But not right now, Gail thought, watching the bland face of the man addressing them. This one was a bench-warmer she doubted would be around for the final showdown. And that, she had to admit, was a battle she was looking forward to.

The mere thought of it brought her back to the here and now, and Joe was allowed to slip from her mind as she asked a pointed question of her own.

★ ★ ★

The setting this time wasn't a restaurant. For one thing, no restaurant had a big enough table for what these three men required. For another, Tim Shafer was now safely on board and no longer in need of a nurturing environment. As a result, he found himself lugging his two boxes of files down a narrow hallway and into the conference room in the Vermont State Police barracks building in St. Albans. There Joe Gunther and Jonathon Michael were already setting up their own paperwork piles along the length of a large wooden table. A thermos of fresh coffee was parked in the middle like a surveyor's cairn.

"Hey, Tim," Michael greeted him as Shafer bumped the door open with his hip. "You need help?"

"Nah," Shafer grunted, dumping the stacked boxes on the table's one clear area. He began opening them up and distributing their contents, mimicking his two colleagues. "You wouldn't think traffic in Vermont would be anything to bitch about, but Burlington is going straight to the dogs, if you ask me. Be faster to use the back roads."

Burlington, also along the shore of Lake Champlain, and the state's largest town,

139

was about twenty-five miles to the south. Gunther checked the clock on the wall. "It's after five. You must've hit rush hour."

That did little to calm Shafer down. "Story of my life."

Michael was oblivious, still shuffling his paperwork. "I heard Chittenden County's population is growing every week."

"Well," Shafer countered, "you can have it. I'm happy living in St. J. with two wood-chucks and a cow next door."

Joe, the first to have arrived, chose a seat and propped one foot on the edge of the table, waiting for the others to catch up. "Not to get the cart ahead of the horse, Jonathon, but did you ever find out why that developer bought out Loomis?" Loomis was the farmer who'd lost his farm to a presumed electrical fire.

Michael didn't bother looking up. "Nope. I talked to the buyer again — Clark Wolff — and he told me it was a pure investment. That the same urban sprawl that just gave Tim fits in Burlington is heading this way. According to him, it was money well spent. In the meantime, he's leasing out the fields to neighboring farmers."

Joe tapped the side of his head. "Wolff — that's why it rang a bell. When I was interviewing Linda Padgett, I saw a business card on the bulletin board in her kitchen. Belonged to someone called John Samuel Gregory — sounded a little over-the-top, so I commented on it. But now I remember the card said he was with the Wolff firm."

"He put a price on the farm?" Jonathon asked.

"Wasn't that kind of conversation. He may have wanted it to be, but I think all he got to do was leave behind that card."

"I met him," Jonathon admitted. "He was in the office when I was talking to Wolff. Slick — snappy dresser, smooth talker. Just the type that gives me the willies. Stuck out like a sore thumb. I assumed the Porsche parked out front was his."

"You happen to ask Wolff what other properties he's bought recently?" Joe asked.

Jonathon tapped his last little pile straight and immediately swooped down on a file he'd placed earlier, opening it up. "Yeah. I kept it to farms only, since he's a jack-of-all-trades, selling, leasing, and renting damn near anything he can list. He couldn't tell me what deals might still be in the works with the other people who work out of his office, like Gregory, but" — he extracted a single sheet of paper and slid it across the table to Joe — "here's his list."

He continued speaking as Joe glanced at the document. "Not much to it, like you can see. There's the Loomis place and two others. I included the names, dates, prices, phone numbers, and everything else he gave me. I also double-checked the land records at the various town offices, to make sure he wasn't bullshitting me, but I guess he was telling me the truth. He seems like a pretty straight guy."

Joe put the report aside as Jonathon also found a seat and settled down.

"And what about a cause for the Loomis fire?" he asked. "Your last e-mail said you were still digging."

Michael looked disappointed. "That hasn't changed. When we were at the restaurant and arson first came up, I was scared I'd dropped the ball somehow." He held up his hand quickly, adding, "I'm not saying I didn't, but I went back over everything, down to the last detail, and the only thing I'd change now is to leave the cause as undetermined, instead of electrical mishap. I jumped the gun a little there."

Tim looked up from his housekeeping. "Too much damage?"

Jonathon nodded. "The place was

trashed. I could trace it to the milk room and the bulk tank wiring, no problem, but that's about it. Loomis admitted right off he'd fooled with the wires and that it might not have been the best job in the world. I went from there. But to be honest, I never could find anything you'd call a positive source of ignition. If it was arson, it was well done, and designed to look like faulty wiring."

"Things just get too hot for any evidence to survive," Tim chimed in supportively. "It happens a lot."

"Yeah, I've seen that," Joe agreed appeasingly. "So there's nothing to go on at all?"

Jonathon smiled and extracted another document. "Maybe. I reinterviewed everyone as well, and this time I asked if anything unusual or suspicious was noticed before the fire. I did that the first time, of course," he added quickly, "but now I was a little more persistent." Again, he handed over what he was holding to his boss. "That's a statement from Butch Yeaw, Loomis's hired hand. He claims to have noticed a dark sedan with out-of-state plates drive by a couple of times the same week as the fire. He didn't get where it was from, just that the plates were light-colored. It stuck in his mind because it seemed like a city car to him — four-door sedan, American-made. But that was pretty much it."

"He couldn't describe the driver?" Joe asked.

"Only that he was alone and wearing a brimmed hat. Yeaw also said the car was going slowly, as if the guy was a tourist, except that the feeling was all wrong."

"We talking reality here, or too many cop shows?" Joe wondered out loud, staring at the cover of the statement.

Jonathon didn't take offense. "Butch Yeaw doesn't seem overequipped in the imagination department. I think he tells things pretty much like they are."

Joe paused to think a moment — a mason considering what stone to use next. "Rick Frantz is still in a coma. It might be interesting to find out if he had access to an out-of-state car."

"And the hat could've been a disguise," Jonathon suggested. "Local boy throwing suspicion on some mysterious flatlander."

By now Tim Shafer had sat down, his unpacking finished. "I have a sighting of a man in a brimmed hat," he said, holding up a statement. "Right here: 'Looked like somebody from the city — short leather coat and a hat like one of those gangster

144

shows from the seventies — a fedora.' That's according to Farley Noon himself, who saw the guy a couple of days before his barn went up."

"No car?" Joe asked.

"Nope."

"Still," Joe mused, "that's a connection, if only a small one, between Loomis and one of the other two. It gives a little more credibility to Loomis's being an arson." He then asked no one in particular, "I wonder if Loomis knows Rick Frantz." He turned to Tim. "You get any further into your case?"

Shafer looked equivocal. "I went back over it all and conducted a few more interviews, but to be honest, I don't have much more than before. It doesn't seem like there was a reason to burn down Noon's barn. Nobody benefited except the neighbor, who bought the place, like I said, and he looks squeaky-clean."

"I might have something," Joe finally admitted, unfolding a map and spreading it open on the table. The other two left their chairs to gather beside him.

"I had somebody at headquarters call around for all the local farm sales over the last half year. This is what they came up with. I've circled the acreages in red."

The map showed Lake Champlain on the left, speckled with various-size islands looking like stepping-stones, and the Vermont shore to the right, with St. Albans at the top and the outer reaches of Burlington lining the bottom.

"Huh," Shafer grunted softly. "That's interesting."

From a distance, the small cluster of eight red circles looked like a shotgun blast, the brunt of which covered a patch of land between the water and Interstate 91, which in turn pointed like a blue ruler line straight at the Canadian border.

"God," Jonathon commented. "If I ever saw a blueprint for a development project, this is it."

"Big, too," Shafer agreed. "Huge, in fact."

"Maybe," Joe cautioned. "Some of these properties are three hundred acres or more. If these clustered sales are related — which is a major if, since no one buyer stands out — then it's possible the actual point of interest is something like this." He placed his fingertip on a remote crossroads bordered by three of the circled properties. "Right there you have a prime, commercial, two-acre spot owned by three different people. For all we know, the plan is to build a gas station and make a killing on the side by selling off the excess acreage."

Both arson experts looked at him dubiously.

Gunther laughed and shook his head. "I'm talking theoretically, guys. The point is that something unusual is going on, we have no clue what it is, and it isn't on the up-and-up. 'Cause here" — he stabbed the map among the red circles — "is the Loomis place, and here" — he stabbed again nearby — "is Noon's."

"But Cutts is nowhere near there," Jonathon said.

Joe looked up from the map, his eyes bright. "Exactly." He pointed to the outermost property, far inland and distant from the rest of the cluster. It was outlined in blue, distinguishing it from the land sales. "It's way out in left field. Interesting, huh? For some reason, the same guy who burned Noon's and may have burned Loomis's — assuming he's the man in the brimmed hat — traveled way over here to torch the Cutts place, too. The question is why?"

The others remained silent.

"And to add to the mystery," Joe added, "I heard this morning that Billy St. Cyr, the same neighbor who's been ragging at Cutts for two decades but all of a sudden showed up at the funeral and is doing Cal's sugaring for him, has just offered to buy his place, lock, stock, and barrel."

"They going to accept?" Jonathon asked.

Joe shrugged. "Don't know. I just got it through the grapevine. The catch there is that when I interviewed Cal, he said that St. Cyr is looking to get out of the farming business, not wade in deeper. Makes you wonder about the sudden change of heart."

Shafer was doubtful. "You're not saying it's all connected, are you?"

Gunther moved away from the table and began pacing. "God, no." He waved vaguely at the spread-out map. "It would be totally paranoid to tie everything together. But by the same token, it could be that the torch is a local guy, or was in town on a separate contract, and that St. Cyr hired him coincidentally, just to do the one job."

Joe took a breath and added, "There's something else: I also had the circumstances of every one of these sales looked into, to see if the profile of the seller fit an older farmer who might be less inclined to rebuild after a disaster, like Loomis, or one who got an extra push, like Noon did with his tainted milk. Turns out one of them was killed in a tractor accident, leaving the widow to sell out. And another sold after almost dying from exposure to silage gas."

"Come again?" Shafer asked.

"He was checking on the contents of his silo by sticking his head through one of the side portals. Silage produces gas — I guess it's methane or something; I don't know — but it put him in a coma for two weeks. Damned near killed him. I've heard of that before. Even a half-minute exposure can knock you out if you're not careful. Anyhow, he was in his late sixties and his family insisted he get out of the business after that."

"Did anyone check on the tractor accident?" Jonathon asked.

"No," Joe told him. "It was written off as an accident and ascribed to 'owner error,' pretty much like Noon and his milk. Also, to add insult to injury, according to the widow, the tractor was declared totaled by the insurance company and disposed of." He smiled, seeing his colleagues' expressions, and admitted, "The same thought crossed my mind — I could buy the silage gas as accidental. The guy survived, after all, but the tractor? Sounded too much like a barn burning. Suspicious."

"Speaking of the torch," Jonathon said,

perhaps seeking firmer ground, "Tim and I put together a profile of his signature — the potassium chlorate squibs, the use of glue trailers, the chips, and the rest — and ran it by the Alcohol, Tobacco, and Firearms databank, just to see if we got lucky."

"And?" Joe asked.

"Still waiting. But I'd like to use my laptop to check if they've kicked anything back."

"Go for it," his boss urged.

Michael opened his computer, connected it to the high-speed line in the wall, and began typing. As he progressed toward the site he was after, Joe reflected at the ease of it all. The year he started out as a patrol officer in Brattleboro, long before even simple radios were common, much less computers, one of his colleagues had been reduced to summoning help by firing a shot into the air, Old West style. Times had changed fast.

"Got it," Michael said.

"Who is it?" Shafer asked, peering over his shoulder.

"It's not a who. It's a where. According to ATF, a similar unascribed signature was filed with them by the Essex County arson task force, in New Jersey, to be kept on record for future reference."

"Essex County?"

Joe stopped his pacing and faced them both from across the room. "That's Newark."

There was a long silence between the three men before Jonathon finally asked, "What do you want to do with that?"

Joe stared at the floor for a moment before answering, "We're not making much progress here. A field trip might help."

Shafer smiled, the very phrase an enticement. "I can take that, if you want."

But he was disappointed by Gunther's response. "No. You and Jonathon have enough on your plates already. Plus, I'm adding a couple of things: Order a check of all the surrounding gas stations and motels. We're looking for a man in a fedora driving an out-of-state, dark four-door sedan — possibly from New Jersey — who was in the area around the three dates of the Loomis, Noon, and Cutts fires. And if there are any surveillance tapes on file, all the better. Also, that loose thread with Rick Frantz is still bugging me. Look into him more — his background, his whereabouts when the arsons took place, how and where he might've picked up that kind of knowledge. Find out if he or his father knows Loomis. I don't want to get so distracted by a guy in a hat that I miss

151

who might be right under our noses."

He thought a little more, rerunning their conversation in his head. "And Billy St. Cyr. What's going on there? First he's a jerk, then he's Mr. Sweetness and Light; he doesn't want to keep farming, then he wants to buy more acreage. Interview him, see if we can get a look at his finances. Also, remember Barry Newhouse? The guy Marianne Kotch dumped for Bobby Cutts? She said he was all talk, but he did threaten to break Bobby in two. I'm not saying she's wrong, but he's worth sweating a little, just to make sure."

He walked back to his pile of documents and began gathering them up. "I'll go to Newark. And I know exactly who I want riding shotgun."

CHAPTER 11

"Newark?" Willy Kunkle reacted. "I'd sooner eat shit."

Gunther laughed, unperturbed. Willy Kunkle was one of his own squad members, out of Brattleboro, in the opposite corner of the state from where the arsons had occurred. Joe had driven all the way here to ask Kunkle to join him on his trip to New Jersey.

"Have you ever been there?" Willy asked incredulously.

"I've driven by."

"What? The airport, at eighty miles an hour? Hardly the same thing. You do know what their town symbol is, like New York has the Empire State Building and St. Louis has the arch? They have a thirty-foot rusty metal bottle perched on top of an abandoned brewery. People in Newark tell each other to 'Meet me west of the bottle,' like other people say, 'Meet me at the Central Park Zoo,' except that there's an outside chance you won't get shot at the zoo. Newark is a pit."

Kunkle had been brought up in northern

Manhattan and had first cut his teeth as a New York City cop. Joe didn't doubt that he knew what he was talking about, even while he was sure that his viewpoint was as badly skewed as it was about most everything.

"Do you know anyone who works there?" Joe asked mildly.

They were in the VBI office on the top floor of Brattleboro's Municipal Building, a single room as spare, unadorned, and poorly equipped as all the other Bureau offices scattered across Vermont. The VBI hadn't been around long enough to accumulate much junk or, for that matter, much respect from other agencies, despite its lofty major crimes unit status.

"I know a few," Kunkle conceded, adding, "Or I used to."

"How 'bout on the arson task force?"

"The county prosecutor's office?" Kunkle asked, demonstrating the precise insider's knowledge Joe was after. In New Jersey, county prosecutors had police working directly for them in special units, unlike in Vermont, where the state's attorneys no longer even had in-house investigators.

"Yeah," Joe said.

Willy shook his head. "No. The guys I hung out with were city cops, mostly crooked, and I haven't talked to any of them since. Probably dead or busted by now. Urban renewal."

"But you know the town?" Joe persisted.

"Like the inside of a toilet, and that's how much I want to go back. What's this all about anyhow?"

"An arson case up north," Joe explained. "It's in the dailies, if you'd read them. For that matter, it was front-page news. Teenage kid died along with sixty cows."

Willy was sitting behind his desk, his feet up and his chair tilted back against the wall. He'd placed the desk at a diagonal across a windowless corner so he could survey the room as from a machine-gun nest. It said much about the man.

"I heard about it," he said dismissively.

"Well, that arson looks like it was one of two, maybe three, around St. Albans, so Jonathon Michael ran the torch's signature by ATF and was told that the arson task force in Essex County had filed the same signature less than a year ago."

"But with no name attached," Willy suggested.

"Right — just to have it on record."

Willy rolled his eyes and pulled on his ear with his powerful right hand. That, of course, was his own signature: He was a cop with only one functional arm. The left one, still attached but atrophied, useless, and generally pinned in place by its hand being shoved into Willy's pants pocket, had been ruined by a sniper round some fifteen years earlier. He was still on the job thanks to the Disabilities Act, his own pugnacious ability to pass the agility tests, and Joe Gunther, who'd gone to bat for him despite unanimous suggestions that the crippling of Willy Kunkle was a clear sign from God that such men shouldn't be allowed inside law enforcement.

What Joe continued to see in Willy had so thoroughly eluded everyone else that even Joe was no longer sure what it was, except that somewhere in the center of this irascible, infuriating, corrosively sarcastic person lay the heart of a man Joe could trust with his life.

"So," Willy reflected, "based on that kind of airtight evidence, you figured you'd wander down to Newark and bring this torch to justice?"

Joe chose to play along. "Something like that."

"Even though the guy might have burned a couple of buildings in Newark just like he did in Vermont, and maybe like he's done in half a dozen other places, before returning home to Ames, Iowa, or Christ knows where?"

Gunther remained silent. In fact, with the myopia that often affects an investigator when he tumbles to an attractive notion, it hadn't crossed his mind that his quarry might have no more attachment to Newark than he did to St. Albans, or even — to play devil's advocate — that he could be a Vermonter who'd visited the city with evil intent, instead of the other way around.

Willy laughed at his boss's expression. "Gotcha, didn't I?" He then added with uncharacteristic generosity, "Been there, done that. It's a bitch getting caught stupid."

Not overly diplomatic, Joe mused painfully, but fair enough. "That mean I'm on my own?"

Still smiling, Willy considered him sadly. "Nah. You'd be a babe in the woods. I better go just so you don't get killed."

At approximately the same time, in Montpelier, Gail Zigman stepped out of the capitol building to get some lunch, using the huge front doors instead of the more convenient side entrance only because she loved the view off the columned portico, overlooking downtown. Instead, she was confronted with a large crowd of winter-clad protesters, many carrying signs in opposition to the very GMOs she'd been hearing about in committee. At her appearance, even though there was no indication that she wasn't merely a tourist or a clerk, a surge of chants and shouted slogans rose to greet her.

If not downright irony, there was a certain poetry to the moment that Gail, the newly minted legislator, could appreciate. Not only had she been a protester herself throughout her adult life, holding various signs for various causes, but she'd even been a lobbyist for VermontGreen, the state's most outspoken environmental group, an organizer of such protests, and a staunch critic of GMOs.

Without hesitation, she descended the broad marble steps, approached the front row of protesters, and introduced herself to a young woman who appeared to be a leader. Within five minutes, lunch long forgotten, Gail had organized a sidewalk symposium on the topic of genetically modified products and ended up taking down names and contact information of people she wanted her committee chairman to consider as witnesses for the hearings.

An hour later, checking her watch, she bade farewell and retreated back up the capitol steps, feeling faintly as though she'd just played a part in some romantic black-and-white movie about the benefits of democracy. She crossed the threshold absentmindedly, sorting through the wad of notes and business cards she'd had thrust upon her, some from people she hadn't even noticed. Which is when she found a small folded note on an otherwise blank piece of paper.

Opening it, she read, "Be careful you're not playing with fire."

Newark, New Jersey, is one of the nation's oldest cities. In what must now be classified as an irony of near cosmic proportions, it was founded in 1666 by Puritan zealots hoping to establish a theocracy of equally close-minded people dedicated to, among other things, repelling civil governance and banishing corruption. It goes without saying that these two particular ambitions failed to thrive. Indeed, in the heyday of its notoriety — now blessedly past — Newark could arguably have posed as the national poster child for municipal graft.

Joe and Willy approached the city as

most everyone did, via crowded high-speed freeway, as unremarkable in their car as a single platelet coursing through an artery and, in Joe's case, feeling about as irrelevant.

"We meeting with anybody specific down here?" Willy asked as Newark's curiously old-fashioned skyline rose up like a postcard from World War II. "Or are we just showing up?"

"Special Deputy Attorney General Benjamin Silva," Joe intoned. "Director of the arson task force." He added the address he'd been given, on Glenwood.

Willy snorted. "Good location — in Orange. They don't have to commute far to work that way. Orange is close to most of the old Mob hangouts. I love the guy's title — sounds like something the Soviets would've come up with back when. He going to be of any use?"

Joe kept his eyes on the ever-changing traffic, cutting back and forth before him like a school of hyperactive fish. "He said he'd assign us a babysitter and make his resources available."

"Babysitter?" Willy sounded incredulous.

"My word," Joe corrected himself, "not his. I think he said liaison or something. Whatever he is, I'm hoping he'll open a few doors for us."

"Close 'em is more likely, from what I remember about the locals."

"Not very welcoming?"

"Hardly," Willy responded. He stared moodily out the window at the passing scenery, which by now had become a startling number of decrepit and/or abandoned buildings and vacant, weed-choked lots.

"Well, I'm not going to worry about it now," Joe told him cheerfully. "Between you and the babysitter, maybe we'll get lucky."

Willy turned to look at him sourly. "I wouldn't count on it." He pointed ahead. "You better take this exit if you don't want to explore the rest of Jersey."

Joe followed his subsequent directions, until Willy said twenty minutes later, "Glenwood's right up ahead."

Joe moved to the right lane. "How do you know this town so well?"

Kunkle's answer was typically terse. "Like I said, I used to visit."

The street Joe pulled into fit the overall neighborhood of nondescript one- and two-story buildings, until he came abreast of a glass and steel monstrosity — square, blockish, four floors tall — made of a mosaic of metal-framed rectangles, where every panel, if it wasn't a window, was made of an equally shiny, bright green plastic. It was the worst of historical salutes to 1970s architecture.

"This is it," he said, craning to see the number over the front door.

"Jesus," Willy commented. "That's some kind of ugly."

They drove alongside the building and found a space in the parking lot to the rear. As Joe got out of the car, he noticed that each three-window cluster looming overhead was sealed with the exception of a tiny, centrally located drop-open enclosure, reminiscent of the tray doors mounted on prison cells in the movies, and presumably designed for access to fresh air. Here they also looked vaguely like naval gunports, row on row.

"Kind of makes you homesick for the Municipal Building," he said softly, removing a briefcase from the back seat.

"Nah," Willy countered. "I bet this has plumbing."

They entered the front lobby, announced themselves to the guard at the desk, and were joined, minutes later, by a young man wearing a crew cut, jeans, a gun, and a T-shirt labeled "Arson Task Force" across the back. After the appropriate introductions, their escort led them into the elevator and up to the third floor.

"Pretty far from home, aren't you?" he asked, holding open the doors.

"We're not from Utah," Willy growled.

"Yeah," Joe said quickly, in response to their host's startled expression. "Can't get used to all the people. I like a little more elbow room."

Giving Willy a covert second glance, the cop proceeded down a hallway to what looked like an apartment door, punched in a code on the combination lock, and ushered them into a suite of offices.

"The director's office is right down here," he told them, leading the way. "He's expecting you."

Benjamin Silva was short, compact, bald on top, and equipped with a thick black mustache that matched his bushy eyebrows. He came at them from behind his desk like a tiny linebacker and shook both their hands vigorously, waving them toward two chairs opposite the desk.

"Welcome to Newark. Have a seat. Want some coffee? How was the trip? I never been to Vermont. Hear it's great." Without pausing to await any response, he glanced at their guide and ordered, "Get Lil in here, would you, Phil? Thanks."

Willy took him up on his offer. "Coffee would be good. Black."

Silva crossed to a side table and poured a mug from a thermos. "You, Agent Gunther?"

" 'Joe' is fine, and I'll pass. Thanks."

Silva handed the mug to Willy. "Great. I'm Ben. We're far from the flagpole over here, so we run things a little looser, too."

"I noticed the jeans," Willy said.

Silva nodded. "For example. At the head office, they're all bib-and-tuckered, but nobody likes it."

"Why're you in this building?" Joe asked.

"Dumb luck." Silva smiled, adding, "Plus a little string-pulling. The Essex County prosecutor's office actually has some five hundred people in it, including about a hundred and eighty investigators and a hundred and fifty lawyers. We have task forces like this one for homicide, child abuse, narcotics, rape, gangs, and internal affairs. That makes us the third largest law enforcement outfit in the county, behind the Newark PD and the sheriff, but by statute we're on top of the heap. Which is why, the farther away from headquarters I can get, the better."

"Politics?" Joe asked.

Silva laughed. "And how. Saying politics in Essex County is like saying snow in Vermont, I guess. It's everywhere, and it gets

164

into everything. One reason I wanted my squad out here in the boonies was to keep my people as free of it as I could."

"How many do you have?" Joe asked.

Silva had by now returned behind his desk. He tilted his chair and linked his fingers behind his neck. "There are two attorneys, one lieutenant, and five investigators."

"That's all?" Willy blurted out. "Newark's like the arson capital of the Northeast or something."

Ben Silva smiled. "True. At its peak, just a few years ago, we had up to four hundred car arsons a year. There was one location off the McCarter Highway, where one off-ramp led to a short street named Riverside Avenue, which then hooked right back up to the highway. Arsons were so common there, cars were sometimes backed up waiting for service. The state finally closed the off-ramp. And that," he added, "is just cars. We also have a ton of structure fires, since old-fashioned urban renewal is making a comeback. Either people who want to sell property torch the old factories and warehouses and abandoned buildings that sit on them, or they burn them to save money on demolition."

"How do you handle it all?" Joe asked.

"We don't," Silva said almost cheerily. "We cherry-pick the worst ones and, if we have time, deal with some of the others. Otherwise, we train as many cops and firefighters as we can to keep their eyes open and apply the skills we teach them. That having been said, we don't do too badly — the nation's arson solve rate is fifteen percent at best. Ours is anywhere from twenty-five to forty, depending."

Silva suddenly leaped to his feet again. "Lil. Glad you could join us. This is Willy Kunkle and Joe Gunther of the Vermont Bureau of Investigation. Lieutenant Lillian Farber, my second-in-command and the operational head of the squad."

Silva dragged another chair over from the corner and offered it to the newcomer, a slim, middle-aged woman with a no-nonsense set to her face.

Silva resumed speaking as he sat back down. "I was just giving them an overview of the operation."

"You want jobs?" she asked, smiling slightly. "I'll swap you. I'd take Vermont any day."

"That mean you're not going to say we're far from home?" Willy asked.

Lil Farber laughed outright. "Phil told me

166

what you said. He thinks you're a shit bird."

Willy joined her laughing — much to Silva's visible relief, Joe noted. He was a little surprised himself, if for another reason. Willy wasn't usually the bantering sort, especially on first meeting.

"I suppose now I have to watch out for payback," Willy said.

"In spades." Farber pointed at his useless left arm, now squashed between his body and the arm of the chair he was occupying. "What's the story there?"

Silva looked appalled at the bluntness, but Willy merely smiled. "Proof positive that anyone can be a cop in Vermont."

"Rifle round," Joe said briefly.

She nodded. "Tough break." She then looked at her boss. "So what's up?"

Silva in turn glanced at Gunther. "To be honest, I'm not sure. You two are after a torch you think has a Newark address?"

"Right," Joe answered, extracting a sheet of paper from his inner pocket. "We don't have a name, but after we ran his MO through the ATF database, they said you folks had filed a similar profile not long ago. This is what we have — what he used, how he used it."

Farber took it from him. As she read, Silva commented, "Must be a big case to send two of you all this way, especially on something this thin."

Joe heard Willy grunt his own skepticism softly as he answered, "It's a homicide. A seventeen-year-old kid."

"Sixty cows?" Lil Farber exclaimed, still reading. "That must've smelled good."

"We're looking at everything we can," Joe continued, "checking motives and backgrounds, but it was clear from the start that we had a pro on our hands, along with the strong likelihood that he was hired. When this Newark connection came up, I thought an alternate way to get to whoever's pulling the strings might be through the man he paid."

Silva nodded agreeably. "Sounds reasonable enough."

Farber handed the report back to Gunther. "The potassium chlorate and the potato chips sound like our guy. Also the way he pulled the fire downstairs from the hayloft with glue lines."

"We figure he did that because he didn't want overexposure to the cows," Joe told her.

"Could be," she admitted. "I wouldn't know. I'm Newark-born-and-bred. I just eat cows. With our fire — a warehouse — it was convenience. He had more combustibles available on an upper floor."

"Same with us," Willy said, again surprising Joe.

"Well, there you have it, then," she answered, "another similarity."

"But you don't have a name, either?" Joe asked.

She shook her head. "Nope. That's one reason we posted the MO. You don't have a description, maybe, or a car sighting?"

"We have sightings of a fedora," Willy said, "and a dark sedan that looks like it came from the city."

Both Farber and Silva stared at him.

"I know, I know," he said. "Lame."

"But not that lame," Gunther added. "I got an e-mail as I was leaving the office with a little more. I had all the area motels and gas stations checked for the time periods of each of our three arsons. One of the motels reported a guy in the hat checking in under the name S. Corleone."

Ben Silva laughed. "Sonny Corleone? A comedian."

"The rest of the registration," Joe continued, "was equally bogus, but the clerk picked up on the *Godfather* reference, too, and after Mr. Corleone had tucked himself in, the clerk went out to copy down the car license." Joe extracted a slip of paper from his pocket and handed it to Lil Farber. "We traced it to a rental place at the Newark airport."

Willy was clearly irritated at hearing this only now. "Fat lot of good that'll be. Busiest rental desk in the Northeast, probably. Which was exactly the point."

Joe was genuinely embarrassed by his oversight. This information had been so last second, he'd truly just shoved it into his pocket and forgotten about it. "I don't doubt it," he agreed soothingly.

But Farber wasn't playing. "I wouldn't say that," she said. "Not necessarily. We have pretty good relations with these outfits, since a lot of the car arsons involve rentals as getaway vehicles. We can give it a try, at least."

Ben Silva stood up again, making Joe wonder if perpetual motion was the man's primary form of exercise. "Great," he said, rubbing his hands like a pleased host. "Lil will be your official liaison during your stay. Anything you want, ask her. It goes without saying that we'd appreciate your doing all police work in her presence or with her knowledge, since you're out of your jurisdiction." He looked a little embarrassed by his own words. "Don't want you boys to get into any jams in the big city."

Willy gave him a predictably baleful look. "Right — goes without saying."

Joe grabbed his elbow and steered him toward the door, saying cheerfully, "Got it, Ben. Appreciate the help. We'll mind our manners. You want updates as we go?"

Silva seemed grateful for the fast exit. "Lil will keep me up to date, but come by anytime."

CHAPTER 12

Lil Farber was driving, with Joe up front and Willy in the center of the back seat, sitting slightly hunched forward. They were in Farber's unmarked SUV, heading toward downtown Newark.

"How long you been a cop?" Joe asked conversationally, looking out the window at what he believed was one of the most unremarkable urban centers he'd ever visited. It didn't always look bad or blighted, necessarily, barring the occasional weed-choked, empty city block. Mostly, it seemed like a jumble of spare parts borrowed from other communities — a little suburbia here, a little small-town America there, some anonymous big-city bits elsewhere. There was no particular rhyme or reason to it, and no overriding sense of identity. The only common thread Joe could see — in this section of town, at least — was the occasional glimpse of the New York skyline down several of the eastern-pointing streets — hovering enormously on the horizon like a supertanker bearing down, albeit far enough off to be only startling.

"Twenty-two years," she answered. "I came into the prosecutor's office straight out of college." She laughed and glanced at him to raise her eyebrows. "Did it for the money, if you can believe that. It was the best job offer I had going."

"Jesus," Willy commented. "What else were you looking at? Panhandler?"

"I can't complain," she said, ignoring him. "It's interesting work, and I have a business on the side. A lot of us do. I'm part owner of a restaurant."

"There it is," Willy exclaimed suddenly, his pointing finger appearing between the two of them. "I told you."

Joe looked ahead and saw looming into view an enormous rusty metal bottle perched on stilts atop an abandoned building.

"Hoffman bottling plant originally," Farber explained. "Then the Pabst brewery, before it went out of business. People never paid much attention that the beer bottle started out as a soda bottle."

"Close as Newark comes to a landmark," Willy repeated. "Like the Eiffel Tower."

Farber glanced over her shoulder quickly. "You're quite the asshole, aren't you?"

"One of our best," Joe agreed.

"I'm taking you on a small side trip," Farber explained, driving between two cemeteries, one Jewish, the other Catholic. "The Newark most people know is actually several municipalities, of which Newark's just one. They all fit together like puzzle pieces. There's Irvington, Orange — where we just came from — Belleville, Bloomfield, Glen Ridge, Nutley, and a few others. They all have their own governments, police and fire departments. New Jersey is one of the most heavily bureaucratic states around, and it's bloated with patronage and corruption. One reason that bottle stands out like it does is because everybody's too busy lining their own pockets to care much about civic pride.

"We have a beautiful old courthouse that looks like a palace," she continued, "built in 1907 for two million bucks. Not a hundred years later, it's been under renovation for six years, and supposedly the scaffolding cost more to put up than the original building. Tell me someone isn't making a profit on that one."

She indicated one of the empty lots that Joe had noticed earlier, and which had been increasing in number as they headed south. "You'll see those all over Newark. The really big ones were once either factories or public housing buildings, the smaller ones were usually properties that burned down during the '67 riots, back in the days of 'Burn, baby, burn.' "

"Forty years ago?" Joe asked, surprised.

"That's when the city started dying big-time," Willy added.

"Actually," their host continued, "it was dying way before then. The riots were just the last spasms. Whatever a town could do wrong, this one did, decade after decade, including taking all its poor and stuffing them like black powder into the biggest collection of public housing projects in the country. Talk about a time bomb. After the riots, of course, they tore them all down. No halfway measures here."

The neighborhood they were in now had disintegrated into a variation of what Joe had seen in New York's poorer sections a couple of years earlier. The streets were dirty, cars were abandoned everywhere, building after building was gutted and empty, windows gaping.

Farber waved her hand as if introducing a stage act. "So here's the latest version: Welcome to Irvington — our current time bomb. With the projects gone, Newark decided the next best move was to throw out its poor. Irvington became the trash barrel.

We had a surveillance we were running in Irvington Park a while back. It was broad daylight, middle of the week, but we couldn't get the job done because we were constantly distracted by all the crime going on around us, some of which was too bad to ignore."

With theatrical timing, they saw a man bolt from a doorway and run down the sidewalk, pursued by another brandishing a knife. Farber barely gave them a look. The duo vanished into a side alley. Joe glanced back at Willy, who silently shook his head.

"In 1975," she went on without a pause, "some magazine rated fifty cities in twenty-four categories. Three guesses on who came in dead last by a mile." She suddenly held up her hand. "Hear that?"

They heard two faint, very distant pops.

"Gunshots. There're about two killings a week in Irvington."

She turned a corner and began driving east. "We'll go check out those car rental records now."

Willy sat back in his seat and smiled. "Happy you got that out of your system?"

She looked into the rearview mirror at him. "What?"

"City mouse, country mouse?"

She laughed. "All right, so what city do you come from, as if I couldn't guess?"

"I used to drop by here when I was with the NYPD. It was like visiting a zoo."

"No argument from me," she said, still amused at being found out. "So how did you end up in cow country?"

The smile faded from his face, as Joe suspected it might. "Long story," was all he said.

To her credit, Farber merely quipped, "Then here's to a happy ending," before dropping the matter.

The central office of the car rental company was near the intersection of Broad and Market Streets, which Farber told them was Newark's original settlement site in 1666 and remained the heart of the city to this day.

Joe, however, was once more struck by the whole place's time-warped aura. To his eye, almost all that was necessary to make this a living snapshot of the 1940s was to replace every vehicle with its sixty-year-old equivalent.

Lil Farber took them into a large sandstone office building, still in tour director mode. "This is the flip side of places like Irvington. Old on the outside, jammed with modern electronics on the inside. And talk about ironies: Newark is second only to Hartford in its number of insurance companies. Very high-tech." She smiled broadly at that, adding, "Not a bad idea, given the number of local claims."

On the building's fifth floor, Farber delivered the court-signed paperwork she'd secured before setting out, earning in exchange the attentions of a young woman named Melanie, who studied the subpoena as if it were written in Latin and finally gave all three of them a hapless expression, along with the question "What do you want?"

Joe reached across the counter and tapped the form with his fingertip. "The registration listed there belongs to one of your cars. We want to know who was renting it on the date marked."

Melanie looked nonplussed. "That's it?"

"Too much?" Willy said caustically.

Thankfully, she didn't get it, her eyes on his arm and her smile doing its best. "Oh, no. This shouldn't be a big deal. I will have to get my supervisor, though."

The supervisor, a steely-haired man named Philpot, with too little power and too few opportunities to exercise it, wasted half an hour asking questions he wasn't entitled to have answers to, before finally delivering a copy of the rental contract. As with the motel registration in Vermont, it was signed "S. Corleone."

Joe showed it to Farber. "That home address do anything for you?" he asked her.

She studied it for a moment. "Yeah. Makes me think of the Hudson River. The street numbers there don't run that high."

Joe turned back to the supervisor. "We'll need the name and address of the employee who handled this contract."

Philpot rose to his full splendor. "I don't believe that falls into the purview of your subpoena. We have to protect our people from unwarranted harassment."

Having reached his limit, Willy shot his hand out, aiming for the man's throat. Joe saw it coming. He seized Willy's thick wrist in midair and brought it down with a thump onto the counter.

"What was that?" Philpot stuttered, his eyes wide. "What did he just do?"

Joe leaned forward, making the supervisor tuck in his chin nervously, as if expecting a punch. "Do you have any idea why three cops would come into your office with a court order looking for this information?"

Philpot looked stumped. "A crime?"

"A big one. Do you really want to hinder a murder investigation?"

Without further delay, a printout of the clerk's name and address was produced.

"Do you have a business card, Mr. Philpot?" Joe asked, handing the printout to Lil.

"Yes. Why?"

"So I can get my boss to write your boss a letter of thanks for your cooperation."

Looking suspicious, Philpot slowly produced a card from under the counter. Joe took it, smiled, and slipped it into his pocket. "Thank you."

On the ride down in the elevator, Willy said, "You should've let me kill him. Would've been faster."

Back in the car, Lil looked at the employee card and shook her head. "You don't actually think this person is going to remember renting a car to a guy in a hat weeks ago at the airport, do you? And even if he does, what's he going to tell us?"

"That had crossed my mind," Joe admitted.

"Let me try something else," she offered. "I don't want to step on any toes, but maybe a quick meeting with the rest of my guys might kick something loose. I keep thinking the hat'll help. It could be more than just something to keep the cold off, like a trademark. Fedoras aren't that common anymore."

Two hours later, Joe and Willy were sitting in a windowless conference room back on the third floor of the task force's garish building. Around the table were Lil Farber and all five of her investigators, something Joe took as an extraordinary show of professional courtesy, given — as he knew now — the overwhelming size of their workload.

Introductions completed, Joe addressed them: "I want to thank you first off for meeting with us . . ."

"We just wanted to see what you looked like," cracked a voice to general laughter.

". . . and to thank you also for putting up with my colleague," Joe continued.

Responding to the general mood, Willy shot them all the bird.

"As you have no doubt discovered by now," Joe went on, "he's our token New Yorker. We've had him Christ knows how long, and it hasn't done any good whatsoever."

"We could've told you that," said another voice.

181

"The reason we're here," Joe kept talking, "other than to give Willy a breath of polluted air, is because we've had a few fires in our neck of the woods which may have been started by one of your locals — certainly somebody whose MO is like the one you filed with ATF."

He began passing out stapled packets of all the relevant information, which he'd generated from a borrowed copier just prior to the meeting. "I'll give you a few minutes to familiarize yourselves with what we've got."

The room filled with the soft sound of pages being turned over and restless men shifting in uncomfortable seats. They were a seasoned group, with only one still in his twenties, casually dressed in khakis or jeans and clearly at ease with one another. Lil had told him earlier that her most recent member had five years with the unit, and the rest a lot more than that. This was a crucial detail, she'd said, because in a highly computerized world of databases and instant communications, the arson task force was just now getting its case information digitized. As a result, until that process was completed — God knew when — the archival intelligence of the unit would be only as good as the memories of the men around this table. It was a curiously quaint reminder that much of the high-tech razzle-dazzle portrayed on TV and assumed by the public was either downright fiction or only true for certain elite state and federal outfits. Not county cop shops like this one.

Joe waited for the last man to finish before he resumed. "It goes without saying that the evidence linking our torch to yours is pretty skimpy, but we're hoping against hope that maybe something in what you've just read will ring a bell."

"A man in a hat?" one of them asked.

"A fedora," Lil responded, coming to Joe's aid. "I suggested this meeting, thinking one of you might remember something like that. It's a Humphrey Bogart hat. Real distinctive. Might be a trademark."

A tall, heavyset man in a T-shirt spoke up. "We're not trying to bust your chops. And the thing with the chemical squibs and the chips and chasing the fire downstairs does fit our profile, but we don't have a name, either." He gave Joe a hapless look. "Maybe the hat *is* a trademark. We can add it to what we got, but . . ." He shrugged to show his conclusion.

"Give us more," another suggested. "He

rented a car at the airport, drove up north, rented a room, then what?"

"Looks like he scoped out his targets," Joe answered him. "Not bothering to dress locally or fit in. Either that, or he thought the hat would act as a disguise, which I guess it did, since that's all anyone remembers. At one place, he was just seen driving by; at the other, he was on foot."

"What was he wearing?"

"A short leather coat — another thing that stood out. We tend more toward wool or ski parkas or barn coats. Not a lot of leather."

There was silence in the room as everyone pondered the unlikeliness of success here. On pure impulse, Joe added, "He registered, both for the car and the motel room, under the name S. Corleone."

"Sonny Corleone?" asked the heavyset man.

"Presumably."

The man looked across the table at one of his colleagues. "*The Godfather.* Who's the *Godfather* freak? Talks about that fucking movie all the time."

"Gino?" was the response.

"That's it." The big man smiled and addressed Joe. "Gino Famolare. Used to be an electrician, till he moved up. Now he drives a truck out of the port — a long-haul man. Mob associate. A real Nicky Newark. I never pegged him for a torch, though."

"Nicky Newark?" Joe asked.

Lil smiled as she explained. "That's what we call the typical lowbrow Italian hood around here. They're not made men or Mafia bigwigs. Just small-time players — working-class Mob, if you like. They have real jobs, live regular lives, but when a favor needs doing, they can be found. We call the female counterpart Connie Cavone — it's kind of our version of Ken and Barbie."

Joe's optimism was guarded. "But there's no connection linking Famolare to arson?"

The big man didn't seem concerned. "Not yet. Not directly. But it may not be a big reach. Rog," he asked another squad member down the table, "remember Vinnie Stazio?"

"What's not to remember? You're right. They were real close."

"Who's Vinnie Stazio?" Joe asked.

"Big-time local torch," Rog answered. "A legend. I thought of him when this signature first surfaced. Vinnie used to like glue and a potassium chlorate/sugar mix, too, and he was a real mechanic. Did clever work. For fast timers, he would inject sulfuric acid into Ping-Pong balls and plant 'em in the potassium. Depending on the acid's concentration and makeup, it would take longer or shorter to melt through and ignite the mix. Amazing work."

"What happened to him?"

Lil answered that. "Dead. Maybe fifteen years ago, he was shot by a night watchman — an off-duty Newark cop. Shouldn't have happened. He wasn't armed. But I guess he ran. Supposedly, he threw something at the cop, who claimed he feared for his life as a result."

"Yeah, that was a whitewash," the man named Rog said. "I mean, I don't want to bust the guy's balls who shot him. I wasn't there. But I thought it was bogus he got off without even a loss of pay. Vinnie was at least a pro — always made sure nobody got hurt. I'm not standing up for him, but he was super careful that way."

"Could Gino have been an apprentice?" Joe asked, his hopes slowly rising.

"It's possible. The solve rate for arson being so low, if you know what you're doing, it wouldn't be surprising we never heard of you. Sure as hell Gino kept the right company if he wanted to learn the trade."

Lil rose from the table and crossed over to where a computer was perched on a counter along the wall. "Let's see what central records has on him, just for kicks."

Instinctively, most of the others got up also and gathered around behind her as she typed in her request. In a couple of minutes, the screen lit up with a photograph and a history. Lil intoned what she read for those behind her and for Willy, who typically hadn't stirred from his seat.

"Giorgino Ernesto Famolare, born Newark, 1963, middle of five kids. Father was a longshoreman, also connected. Gino was brought up in Silver Lake, attended the local schools, initially trained as an electrician . . ." She tapped the screen with her finger. "He still lives in the 'hood. Probably brings flowers to his mother, good boy. Two daughters, one teen, one just beyond and in college. Okay . . . here we go: some teenage stuff — vandalism, petty theft, trespassing. He gets older; here's a bookmaking rap, transportation of stolen goods. Sounds like he was a runner for the big boys. Then . . ." She scrolled down the screen. "Nothing. Clean as a whistle."

She pushed away from the computer, and the group around her returned to their seats. "Just another urban story," she concluded, sitting down.

"Suggestion," said Rog. "If you want to find out about somebody, you check out his friends. If we collect every name he was ever busted with and run their records, could be we find him lurking dirty in the background. It would give us a better picture of what he's been up to, even if he wasn't the one in cuffs."

Joe nodded in appreciation. In some police jurisdictions — and clearly this was one — note was made of everyone present at an individual's arrest, whether those extras were charged with anything or not. It was a useful intelligence tool for exactly this kind of situation. But this was the kind of homework one did on a personal case — not on behalf of some cop from out of town.

"Good idea," Lil said. "It'll fall to one of us to do it, though, since these guys don't know our computers."

"I can handle it," Rog said immediately. "Maybe it'll be worth a free ski pass someday."

The big man burst out laughing. "You? On skis? I would pay to see that."

"I would make you," Rog came back.

"Well," said Joe, "if not a ski pass, whatever you'd like. Our treat."

"Yeah," Willy added. "We'll show you mud season, ice fishing, and fifteen ways to slide off a road."

"Willy moonlights for the tourist industry," Joe explained amid the startled laughter that greeted Kunkle's comment.

"Okay," Lil said during the short lull following. "It's getting late. You two probably want to get settled. You have a place to stay?"

Joe answered that they were all set and gave her the name and number of the motel he'd booked from Brattleboro before setting out, to which one of the men responded, "Too bad. We could've put you up in Irvington for a whole lot less."

Outside Montpelier, Vermont, in a condo overlooking the valley and the town, Gail Zigman sat in her living room admiring how the setting sun slowly abandoned each roof to the coming night, leaving the sparkling gold dome of the capitol building until last.

"How was your trip?" she asked Joe on the phone.

"Strange," he admitted. "I still have a hard time figuring out what all these millions of people do."

She laughed. "Don't feel bad. A lot of

them were up here today. The GMO debate is heating up, and the troops are on the march. Everybody under the dome is running around looking for the best political cover they can find. How're the police down there?"

"Great," he answered. "They work directly for the prosecutor's office, which is a little weird, but they're good people. Incredibly helpful. They pulled our chains a little, doing the city cop, country cop routine, but that was par for the course."

"Us?" she asked. "Who'd you take with you?"

"Willy. He knows Newark from the old days."

Gail didn't respond immediately. Having a thorough dislike of Kunkle, she was hard-pressed to say anything positive.

Joe took advantage of the pause to ask, "What's the big debate about GMOs anyway? I wouldn't have thought there'd be much question."

"Not for me, there's not," she agreed. "But the Monsanto, Archer-Daniels-Midland types have done a good job brainwashing my conservative counterparts. They've got some powerful allies quoting the corporate scripture chapter and verse and making the organics and traditionalists look like a bunch of Chicken Littles.

"The problem," she continued, "is that the small operators are right. We can't compete with Iowa and Kansas, so we better concentrate on turning out specialty products. Ye olde Vermont farmer and the rest. Slap a premium price on everything from milk to sauerkraut and sell it like Ben & Jerry's. It's about our only trump card and we're about to give it up. The purchase of GMO seeds in this state has quadrupled in the last three or four years, to a half million pounds."

Now it was Joe's turn to remain silent. Politics was of no great interest to him, and not an advisable pursuit in his line of work. Plus, he often felt uncomfortable when Gail climbed onto one of her soapboxes. Her enthusiasm could feel like a steamroller.

As if on cue, she kept going. "I hate it that this entire nation's agriculture policy caters only to the megafarmers far from New England *and* is being driven by people who have no thought beyond the bottom line. I mean, everywhere you look, the biotechnology industry lords over both scientific research and regulation, including in Vermont. Our entire food chain is being controlled by a handful of global corporations located as far away from us as they can get.

"Sorry," she muttered after taking a breath, the vehemence of her outburst echoing in his silence. "Didn't mean to lecture. I know you hate that."

"No, no," he said quickly, embarrassed. "It does sound like things are heating up. Are you getting a lot of flak?"

Gail hesitated. The threatening note she'd received about playing with fire lay on the table by her side, unacted upon but certainly not forgotten. Given her personal history, she didn't take such gestures lightly. Still, she knew how political debates pushed people to where their passions got the better of them. She hadn't done anything about the note.

Nor did she mention it to Joe now.

"No more than usual," she said, and changed the subject.

CHAPTER 13

"Dug up some interesting stuff," Lil Farber told Willy and Joe when they walked into her office the next morning. She gestured to them to sit opposite her desk and handed them each a computer printout.

"Rog burned a little midnight oil last night. Guess he got all excited by Willy's description of Vermont. Anyway, since we found nothing when we ran Gino Famolare through the system all by himself, and nothing mentioning Gino when we ran the late Vinnie Stazio, Rog decided to step back from the main players. He compiled one list of Gino's known associates, and another of Stazio's, seeing if anyone overlapped." She paused to smile. "I think we may have gotten something. See where it mentions Antonio Lamano, linked to Stazio in May of '82? They were in a car together when Vinnie was pulled over for questioning, which is why Lamano's name pops up. He was an interesting guy — nicknamed Tony Hands. The Organized Crime unit has a small phone book on him, which Rog checked out.

"Lamano was a made guy. Old-time Mob soldier. He's presently doing forever time someplace like Rahway, and I remember hearing a while back that he wasn't faring too well, so maybe he's dead. But a lot of years ago, close to when that car was stopped" — she pointed at the printout in Joe's hand — "Lamano was being wiretapped around the clock by the feds. One of the deals mentioned on those tapes was a warehouse fire we're pretty sure was set by Stazio — had his signature all over it. That's one reason people were happy to find them both riding around together, 'cause generally, Stazio was pretty canny about who he was seen with and who he talked to.

"But here's the neat part," she continued. "On the tapes, Tony Hands actually talks about Stazio. Says how the guy's the best and blah, blah, blah, and then he mentions how Vinnie's got a fair-haired boy coming up. That's when he says, 'Gino's doin' good — a real live wire. Nice to see the traditions kept up.'"

Farber looked at them expectantly, her eyes bright, forcing Joe to comment politely, "Wow. That's great."

Willy, of course, wasn't buying it. "That's supposed to mean Famolare is

Stazio's prince-in-waiting? 'Gino's doin' good'? No wonder you're having such a hard time gettin' the Mob out of town."

Lil was not amused. "TV shows and know-nothing country cops notwithstanding," she said darkly, "we've done a damn good job putting them in jail. That's why Lamano's there now. The Mob in Newark is a fraction of what it was, and tapes like this helped do that." She sat back in her chair and propped a shoe up against the edge of her desk, her irritation smoldering.

"This kind of intel takes interpretation," she went on. "You don't actually expect these mopes to speak right up for the microphone, do you? To be honest, this is almost that straightforward, given some of the roundabout, oh-so-cute, coded bullshit I've heard when they think they're being bugged. This is worth pursuing, unless you're just down here to see the sights and blow off work."

Willy opened his mouth to respond, but Joe cut him off, saying forcefully, "Of course, we want to check it out, and we appreciate the effort Rog and whoever else must've put into getting us this. Did the Organized Crime unit pitch in, too?"

Lil nodded, somewhat appeased by Joe's

understanding. "Yeah. He got hold of them after he tumbled to the Lamano connection."

"I don't know the protocol," Joe said, "but if you could make sure Rog and they know how much we appreciate their help, that would be great."

Spontaneously, and much to Joe's surprise, Willy added, "I'm sorry. Didn't mean any disrespect."

Joe stared at him, causing Willy to bristle instantly. "What?" he asked sharply. "I screwed up, okay?"

"No, no," Joe responded, laughing now. "That's fine." He turned back to Lil. "What do you recommend we do now? Drop by and have a chat with Gino?"

She frowned at that. "You could if you want, but I doubt it would last longer than it would take him to call his lawyer. These guys do not talk to us, not unless we've got 'em by the balls."

"How 'bout checking out his time sheets and delivery records against the dates of our arsons? Or his vacation time and sick leave schedule?" Willy suggested, sounding to Joe as if he was trying to make amends — another first. "That might get us probable cause."

"We don't have enough for that kind of

court order yet," Lil said. "And, believe me, his particular trucking company is going to be very big on seeing one of those."

"Ask around the neighborhood maybe?" Joe offered. "Somebody might have overheard him saying he was heading up to Vermont."

Farber laughed, totally recovered from her earlier irritation. "That neighborhood, I think it's safe to say you *might* be able to get the time of day. Otherwise, you'd get more conversation out of a brick. Joe, not to be condescending — I promise — but I think you'll find that people down here react a lot differently to cops than what you're used to."

Both men remained scrupulously silent, each struggling with his own stung pride.

"Sometimes what we do," she continued, "is bring them in, complete with lawyers, and we let them know that we're on to them. On the surface, it's not much, but occasionally, it shakes things up a little. With Gino, we could let it slip on the street that we know he screwed up the Vermont job and is being eyed for murder." She held up a finger. "We are the ones who gave his signature to ATF, after all. We want him, too. Maybe putting the word out gives us somebody who's pissed off enough at him to squeal." She smiled apologetically. "I know you were hoping for more, but at least we're pretty sure who we're after now. And my bet is that you'll get something on Gino before we do, probably by flashing his photo around back home, like to that motel clerk. If you do, let us know, and we'll grab him so fast, it'll spin his head."

The two Vermont cops exchanged glances and stood up simultaneously, reading her cue that the conversation had come to an end.

Farber looked up at them quizzically. "What's your pleasure?"

Willy demurred. "I guess we'll get out of your hair," Joe offered. "I like the idea of passing his mug shot around St. Albans. If you would, maybe you could send a copy north over the computer right now. Then, like you said, if we get lucky, we could come back to be in on the arrest."

He stuck his hand out, and she rose to shake it. "I want to thank you and your crew for all the help, though. We didn't have a name or a face when we got here. Wouldn't have found them without you."

Willy took his turn shaking her hand. "Sorry we didn't get more time to work together," he said, making Joe shake his head in amusement.

Both men said a few more niceties, gave her Jonathon's e-mail address, dropped by Benjamin Silva's office to say good-bye, thanked Rog personally on the way out, and finally found themselves back out in the hallway.

"You're soft on her," Joe said as soon as the door closed behind them.

Willy stared at him, wide-eyed. "What?"

"Lieutenant Farber. I thought I was going to have to call Sammie and tell her she had competition."

"Oh, right — spare me," Willy complained, taking a few steps backward. But his face had turned red.

Joe laughed and shoved his colleague toward the elevator bank. "Don't worry. Your secret's safe with me."

"Fuck you, Joe. You are so full of it."

Gunther hit the down button, pleased at having put Willy on the spot. Joe was inordinately fond of Sammie Martens — a colleague of theirs back home and currently Willy's love interest. But he knew of her self-admitted track record with men, and he was no more optimistic than anyone else that she and Willy would make a lasting couple. As a result, anything he could do to delay what looked like the inevitable, he would.

They stepped into the elevator. Willy, still smarting, channeled his embarrassment by glaring at his boss accusingly. "So that's it, then? We beat feet with a picture of some guy who may not even be our torch, and hope we get lucky? Glad I could be a part of this. Good use of my time."

Joe let him finish before saying with a conspiratorial smile, "I only told her we'd get out of her hair."

Strictly speaking, the Silver Lake area where Gino Famolare lived had no official designation. It was no more than a neighborhood straddling Newark and Belleville, a few blocks northeast of Bloomfield Avenue. That last detail, however, was significant for two reasons. Not only did Bloomfield, commonly referred to as simply the Avenue, run diagonally, southeast to northwest, across almost the entire county, neatly splitting it in half, but what remnants there were of the Mafia still dominated most of this corridor. When the racial explosion hit Newark in 1967, it was said that the rioters did not cross the Avenue because, according to Willy, "they knew they wouldn't get out alive."

Certainly, it was true enough that Silver Lake did feel and look different from the East Orange area that Joe and Willy left when they departed the task force offices. Unlike the crowded urban sprawl encircling it, Silver Lake felt more suburban, even small-town. Buildings were serried and low, sidewalks crowded with leisurely strollers, and several of the signs were almost quaint in what they advertised: a butcher, a baker, a neighborhood social club — mostly written in Italian, cementing the locale's predominant ethnicity.

Willy, however, saw something else. Looking around as Joe navigated the car through the narrow streets, he commented, "Not what it used to be."

"Which was?"

"Little Italy, all the way down to street vendors and overhead banners. You could walk three blocks and not hear a word of English." He pointed at a Starbucks as it slipped by. "You wouldn't have seen any of that."

Joe once more tried to get him to open up. "Almost sounds like you lived over here."

Willy laughed uncomfortably. "Felt that way sometimes. A lot of New York cops lived here back then. Cheaper." He paused before conceding just a little. "And a lot of bad shit went down that nobody talked about. The NYPD brass didn't mind, either, since it took the heat off them — out of state, out of mind."

Joe knew of Willy's checkered past — a year on the New York force before shipping out to Vietnam and a traumatic tour of duty ending in emotional chaos and alcoholism. He didn't doubt that his colleague had tasted more than one forbidden fruit while on the job — he'd been in the right time and place to do so.

Which was exactly why Joe now didn't want to know any of the details.

"We getting close to Famolare's address?" he asked instead.

Willy gestured up ahead. "Two more blocks, take a right, second left."

Joe followed directions and quickly found himself in a quiet, leafy neighborhood of substantial houses and well-kept lawns.

"This guy drives a truck?" he asked, looking around.

"Don't be too impressed," Willy cautioned. "The whole town is full of hoaxes and scams like this — things looking like what they aren't. These houses would run you three hundred grand and up out in the burbs. Here they go for half that, sometimes less. This is old-time Mob territory — like a rent-controlled neighborhood for Italians only, so it's a little different. But sections right next door don't have that kind of protection. They look the same on the surface — fancy digs and big lawns — but you better think twice before going out at night. Doors are barred, windows wired, Dobes and rotts run around the backyards, hoping you'll jump over the fence. The riots did a number on all these areas, and none of them have really come back. In the seventies, you could buy mansions for the tax bill alone. It's getting better, but it's slow." He pointed suddenly. "There it is. On the left."

Joe slowed the car and pulled over opposite a large, low gray house with a porch running along its front. There was nothing particularly distinguished about it. It shared the stolid bearing of its neighbors. But there were clear signs of better times gone by, when it and its brethren had been symbols of the upward mobility so cherished in the 1950s.

Willy was scanning the block, twisting around in his seat. "We gonna do a sit-and-wait?"

It wasn't a complaint. Despite his hard-earned reputation for cutting corners, Willy could be a patient man, especially when he was on a scent.

"Unless you have something better," Joe answered him. "Farber's chances of success notwithstanding, I figured we can't lose by at least seeing a couple of the players in motion."

"Works for me," Willy said, "but I think we better get off this street. Even lying low, we'll probably get burned before the day's out. Too many people around here learned to spot a surveillance while they were sucking mother's milk."

Joe pulled away from the curb.

In the huge, crowded maze that was the Port of Newark, Gino Famolare maneuvered his eighteen-wheeler with practiced grace past towering stacks of shipping containers. A constant flow of workers and loading machinery crisscrossed before him like minnows avoiding a large fish. He was heading for the company's main depot, coming off a week of driving, looking forward to some time off, and a whole lot more besides.

He backed into a slot alongside a fleet of similar trucks, collected his paperwork and travel kit, and swung out of the cab. He walked toward the dispatch center, exchanging greetings with other drivers along the way, and filed his trip with the woman behind the counter, also handing over the keys.

In exchange, she gave him a wad of phone messages and a check.

The check, he was expecting; one of the phone slips, he was not.

He crossed over to a pay phone mounted on the wall, knowing from the name on the slip that the use of his cell would be breaking one of this man's cardinal rules. "Too many people sniffing the airwaves," was how he put it. "They can still tap a line, but they have to find it to tap it." Given the man's reputation, Gino wasn't going to challenge his logic. He dialed the number.

"Tito," he said after the third ring was answered. "It's Gino. You called?"

"Thought you should know," Tito's voice came back. "That trip up north? Not too clean."

Instinctively, Gino glanced around. He was the only one on this side of the counter, and the dispatcher was back at her console, well out of earshot.

"What do you mean?"

"A kid died."

"Bullshit."

"Fine," Tito said, and hung up.

Gino stared at the phone. The abruptness was just Tito. It was his message that cut deep. Gino had his pride, after all, and it had just taken a direct hit.

CHAPTER 14

"That must be the missus," Willy said, slouched in the passenger seat, his eyes at half-mast. They'd been watching the house for five hours already, moving the car from place to place to keep suspicion to a minimum, sometimes parking over half a block away. At the moment, they were situated on a side road that T-boned into Famolare's street, not quite across from his home. An attractive woman in her mid-forties, solidly built and well tailored, had opened the front door, purse in hand, and was impatiently standing there, apparently waiting for someone who was taking their time.

The explanation appeared moments later. A young woman stepped into view in a short skirt, skintight tank top, and what looked like motorcycle boots. The green of her hair radiated in the sunshine. Despite the cold nip in the air, the girl's midriff was bare and her light jacket open to better display her wares.

"Man," Willy added. "I bet things get a little strained in that household."

The body language between the two

women bore him out, as the girl flounced by her mother, uttering some unheard comment, causing the latter to glare at her in speechless irritation before slamming the door.

They crossed the yard to the car in the driveway.

"Follow them or sit tight?" Willy asked.

"Sit," Joe responded.

The car — a Lexus — backed roughly into the street, its movements reflecting the anger of its driver, and sped away to the west.

Not two minutes later, a second car pulled into the same driveway from the opposite direction.

Willy grunted, surprised. "You know that was going to happen?"

"No clue," Joe answered, watching carefully.

A man swung out of the car, locking the doors and pocketing the keys. He was dressed in jeans and a work shirt and was carrying an overnight bag.

"That our boy?" Joe asked.

Willy glanced at the rap sheet before him. "Gino Famolare, in the flesh. Guess he just missed them."

"I don't think so," Joe said quietly. "Look."

They watched as Famolare studied the street down which his wife and daughter had just vanished, apparently checking to make sure they weren't coming back.

"My bet," Joe said, "is that he likes a little quiet time after coming off the road. By the bag, he may have been gone a few days."

"Why not just head for a bar?" Willy asked. "That's what I used to do."

Joe laughed softly. "Yeah — that clearly worked for you."

"Up yours."

They settled back to wait, expecting nothing much to happen, when — twenty minutes later — the door opened again and Famolare reappeared, wearing slacks, a sports shirt and jacket, and looking freshly showered.

"Oh-oh," Willy said, straightening up. "The boy is restless and on the prowl."

"Could be," Joe agreed, starting the engine.

They followed Famolare's car onto Bloomfield Avenue heading back toward Newark's downtown.

"Business meeting?" Joe wondered out loud.

Willy wasn't wavering. "I could smell the cologne a block away. He's going to see his squeeze. Maybe she's downtown 'cause he's a cheap bastard, or maybe they're meeting in a hotel because she's married to Tony Break-Your-Legs or somebody, but it's a broad. That much I guarantee."

They went from Bloomfield to Martin Luther King and traveled into the city's middle, up to the scaffold-clad courthouse with its statue of Lincoln sitting on a bench out front. There they turned left onto Market, driving east.

Willy smiled. "He's headed for the Neck. I should've known. Perfect."

"Why's that?"

"Most discreet area in the county. It's called Down Neck 'cause of how it fits between the Passaic and the harbor, or the Ironbound 'cause it's surrounded by railroads. Huge Portuguese population."

"Sounds charming," Joe commented skeptically.

"Oh, no," Willy protested. "It's really great. Good food, good people. They police their own in the Neck. The cops never have to worry. Damned near the safest place I know."

"Sounds like Chinatown in New York," Joe said.

Willy shook his head. "Way different. Chinatown, you get the tongs and the gangs — everybody scared to death. The cops don't go in 'cause they're afraid they'll get killed. In the Neck, it's just peaceful — or else. You kill your wife here, nobody calls the cops until your body's found in the gutter. No muss, no fuss. Everybody's happy."

In fact, having now entered the Neck, Joe noticed the whole mood of the street change. From downtown's feeling of a clock stopped in an era of black-and-white, Market Street in the Ironbound was almost festive. Banners were hung over the road announcing an upcoming festival, stores and shops were decorated with colorful signs, many written in a language Joe couldn't read. And the sidewalks were full of people laughing, relaxed, and looking utterly at home.

"There he goes," Willy said as Famolare took a right down a side street.

Joe followed him, falling farther back in the dramatically thinned traffic. He eventually pulled into a parking spot a few streets down as their quarry stopped opposite a very pleasant two-story wood-sided house.

"Ah." Willy smirked, enjoying himself. "The advantages of separate bank accounts and a little income on the side."

Joe was half hoping a fat man in a business suit would appear on the house's doorstep, but unfortunately, Willy had hit it right on. As Famolare emerged from his car, a beautiful young woman with long dark hair threw open the door and came running down the steps into his arms. They kissed warmly before he draped his arm across her shoulders and escorted her back into the house.

Willy laughed. "What're we goin' for, boss? A quickie or some quality time? I say we grab something to eat — like you said, the man's been on the road for days."

Inside the house, Peggy DeAngelis threw her arms around Gino's neck, pushing him off balance against the closed door, and kissed him passionately, her hips grinding into his.

"God, I missed you," she murmured between kisses.

He stayed silent, his hands coasting along the thin fabric of her dress, feeling the heat of her skin radiating beneath it. She wasn't wearing much — just a pair of thong underwear — and as his fingertips discovered this, his own excitement began building. After receiving the news of the fatal fire in Vermont — an irritating and bothersome complication, not to mention a black mark on his reputation — he had thought of Peggy right off as the perfect antidote. Staking out his own house afterward, he'd thought his wife and kid would never leave for the latter's weekly session with the shrink.

He pulled away long enough to savor the young woman before him, her eyes shining, her lips moist. He unbuttoned the top of her dress and buried his face between her breasts, breathing in her warmth.

Definitely the cure for a bad day.

Jonathon Michael left the farmhouse and got into his car, rolling down the window now that the sun's effects were taking hold. The nights were still cold, and snow was still piled against the north walls of most buildings, but there was no mistaking the feeling of spring in the air.

Michael's car, like those of most cops, was as much office as vehicle, so he drove a mile up the road, pulled off under a tree with a view of Lake Champlain in the distance, and started reviewing his notes.

He'd been driving back and forth ever since Joe Gunther's departure south, chasing an angle he'd thought of only out of despair.

He opened the map that he, Tim Shafer, and Gunther had consulted days ago at the state police barracks. Then, they'd unsuccessfully tried extracting an explanation from Joe's pattern of arsons and farm sales. Now Michael felt he was seeing one slowly coming into focus.

Methodically, he filled in a Post-it note and stuck it to the map, right over the property he'd just left, recently purchased from one of the farmers that Gunther had identified among his land sales. Michael's motivation had sprung from the primary list of buyers Joe had compiled from town clerk records. What if he hadn't probed deeply enough? Might not individual interviews with each buyer be more revealing?

In fact, they had been.

Wolff Properties — a loaded name for a realty firm, Michael had thought the first time he visited — was located in downtown St. Albans, on the first floor of one of the short, squat, red brick buildings facing the town's historic Taylor Park, where a small, captured British cannon stood comically on guard, pointing — some thought tellingly — directly at the health food store.

Michael walked by the picture window

filled with photographs of listed properties and entered a long, narrow room that ran straight to the back of the building, lined along one wall with a row of four desks, reminiscent of a string of abbreviated docks at a marina, each desk having a dinghy-like chair hanging off its far end for visiting customers.

"May I help you?" asked a woman sitting at the first dock. There was a young man on the phone two stations behind her who barely glanced up at his entrance — not the curiously named and smooth-talking John Samuel Gregory he'd met last time.

"I'd like to see Mr. Wolff, if he's in."

"And who should I say is calling?" she asked, getting up.

Michael showed her the badge he had clipped to his belt under his jacket. "My name is Jonathon Michael. He knows me."

"Oh, my goodness" — she paused — "I hope everything's all right."

He gave her a reassuring smile and joked, "You haven't robbed a bank today, have you?"

She looked startled, as if the question were serious. He quickly eased her concern. "Sorry — old joke."

She laughed uneasily. "Right. I'll see about Mr. Wolff."

She was back in under a minute, gesturing to Michael to follow her into a side office, beyond which was a conference room with a large white-haired man standing over a pile of papers fanned out across a table.

"Mr. Michael, Mr. Wolff," the woman said, retreating and closing the door behind her.

Clark Wolff crossed over to Michael with his hand extended and his best salesman's smile. "Good to see you again. Still digging around the real estate business?"

As before, Michael noticed that Wolff spoke in an almost theatrical tone, unexpectedly soothing. "Something like that."

Wolff offered him a seat before settling himself opposite. "How may I help this time?"

Jonathon chose his words carefully, not wanting to reveal too much too soon. "We're looking into a situation that involves several properties south of town. In the process, I discovered your office brokered not just the Loomis farm but a few others as well, and that some of those deals were kept very much under wraps."

Wolff's smile didn't fade, but his eyes narrowed just a fraction. "And you think there may be some irregularity with that?"

Jonathon also maintained his poise. "If there is, now would be a good time to mention it."

"There is not, Detective," Wolff said firmly. "Discretion is just that, for the most part, especially so in real estate. As you can appreciate, emotions run high when properties change hands. Sometimes it's helpful to keep a low profile."

"Like getting someone to buy his neighbor's land so no one will know you're actually behind the purchase?"

Wolff agreed. "For example."

"Why would emotions be that hot?" Jonathon asked innocently. "Surely, buying and selling property is what you do."

Wolff crossed his legs carefully. "The realty business is a little like the stock market sometimes," he explained slowly. "What may seem like no big deal to us can be misinterpreted by others."

"As in the purchase of eight farms covering a relatively small area?"

Wolff froze for a moment. "Eight?"

"That's how many have changed hands recently. When you look at the map, seems like a lot of activity with no logical explanation."

Wolff pursed his lips. "What's the nature

of your investigation, Detective? Can I ask that?"

Jonathon smiled indulgently. "You can ask. Are you denying that you've been involved in eight land deals down there?"

In fact, Jonathon was bluffing here, since of the eight transactions that Joe had identified, only five had been traced back to Wolff's office, meaning the remainder were either coincidental or just better disguised.

The Realtor stood up and crossed over to the papers that were spread across the far end of the conference table.

Jonathon expected him to retrieve a document to aid in his explanation. Instead, the older man merely placed both hands flat on the table, looking like an ancient and worn-out prizefighter.

"Detective," he said, not looking up, "I have been in this business for almost fifty years. Chances are, I've set foot on almost every piece of real estate in the county, in one capacity or another. That has sometimes put me in awkward situations. I've been accused of fleecing widows and robbing destitute farmers and raping the environment and being a multimillionaire at everyone else's expense." He finally swiveled his large head to look at Jonathon directly. "But I have done none of those things, including making a million bucks. I *have* tried to conduct myself with honesty and integrity, and I have bent over backwards to get to know people and to prove that it has never been my intention to do anyone harm or to cause anyone distress."

He straightened to his full height. "If you have something to tell me or to ask me, spit it out, because while I may conduct some of my business discreetly, I have nothing to hide from the authorities. That having been said, I am also not going to divulge private aspects of a business deal that may cost me everything if word gets out."

He stopped speaking and waited, putting Jonathon squarely on the spot.

The latter cleared his throat quietly, wishing Gunther were there to keep him company. "Sorry, Mr. Wolff. I didn't mean to imply you were up to anything. It was just that the pattern of sales I noticed might play into our investigation. You can understand why that got my interest."

Wolff smiled tiredly. "What I understand is that you have things you can't tell me, and I have things I don't want to tell you. Since you're the one who came to me, maybe you can convince me why I should be more forthcoming."

Jonathon pondered that for a moment.

He had no proof that Wolff was any less honorable than he claimed. During his research, the people he'd interviewed had all said Clark Wolff was a straight shooter. But there were rules of engagement all cops tended to follow, and revealing inner aspects of an ongoing case to an outsider, no matter how trustworthy, was a definite violation.

"Mr. Wolff," he said, "the Vermont Bureau of Investigation is the state's primary major crimes unit. We do not investigate misdemeanors. We handle murders, rapes, drugs, arson, and all the other headline grabbers. You can take it from me that the reason I'm here is not trivial. If I sense your holding back is with the intention of impeding my work, a few leaked details about a business deal will be the least of your worries. Is that convincing enough?"

It was a credit to Wolff's maturity and experience that he didn't simply blow up and throw Michael out. Instead, he chuckled after a pause and said, "All right. Let's tiptoe into this and see how far we get. A little mutual back-scratching, okay?"

Jonathon didn't answer, nonplussed by the man's apparent imperturbability.

"For example," Wolff continued, "you

said I'd done eight deals in that area. I only know of three. Whose math is off?"

Jonathon extracted his notepad and consulted its contents. He recited the eight names of the farmers who'd sold out.

Wolff absorbed the list and answered, "I arranged the Loomis sale, as you know from before, as well as Cooper's and Chauvin's. I'd heard unrelated news — or so I thought — about a couple of the other farmers. That Beatty had been killed by his tractor and Martin put in the hospital for something with his lungs. Of course I knew about how Loomis's barn burned down; and I won't deny that I knew Noon was in trouble because of a couple of milk spoilage episodes. But he came to me. Before then, I'd never even met the man. As for the others, I honestly didn't know their properties had been sold. Which is troubling, because I should have. It means a competitor worked fast and quietly and set in before anything was listed."

Jonathon's brow furrowed. "But you bought them out, through proxies. Are you denying that?"

"I absolutely am. I'll even admit that I would have dearly loved to have gotten those three farms. They said they sold to me? Personally?"

"To your office."

"What's that mean?"

Jonathon was confused. "One of the people out there, I guess." He gestured toward the other room.

"Except for Karla," Wolff explained, "they don't work for me. I give them a phone, a desk, and an association — meaning the credibility of my good name. In exchange, I get paid a small percentage of every deal they make. Who signed the paperwork?"

"I couldn't read it," Jonathon admitted. "I assumed it was you, since the signature was written over Wolff Properties." He pulled a copy of one of the sales agreements out of his pocket and handed it to Wolff. "That's not your signature?"

The old man stared at the document for a long time, plainly working out what was going on. He finally shook his head.

"No. It belongs to John Samuel Gregory. One of my associates."

From the tone of the man's voice, Jonathon could tell that all this suddenly made sense to him. But he wasn't happy.

CHAPTER 15

"Mr. Wolff," Jonathon Michael asked, "what the hell is going on?"

Clark Wolff kept staring at John Gregory's illegible scrawl at the bottom of the sales agreement. "In a word," he finally answered, "ambition."

Jonathon pointed to the document. "That's not legitimate?"

Wolff returned it to him. "Oh, it's good, all right. In more ways than one. Good in fact and good for the firm. I just didn't know anything about it."

Jonathon remained silent, expecting his exasperated expression to be eloquent enough.

Wolff understood, explaining with a sigh, "All right. What I will tell you is that we are trying to put together a very ambitious project — a development which will both benefit the community and make us very wealthy, but which will be tricky and time-consuming to pull off. A years-long commitment. In my case, I'm motivated for the sake of my children. This will take long enough that I expect they'll benefit more

than I. But for John, who is young and single, time is of the essence. As with most people his age, he thinks time is against him."

"What's the project?"

"I'd prefer not to say."

Jonathon didn't argue the point — yet. "Then what is Gregory up to that caught you by surprise?"

"We are supposed to be working as a team," the Realtor said shortly.

"You don't agree with these purchases?"

Wolff slowly pulled out a chair and sat heavily. He rubbed the bridge of his nose before answering. "In all honesty, I can't say that. They fit the overall scheme we've laid out. From what you showed me, the prices paid and the financial terms are in line. And," he added with a sad smile, "aside from your being here, they haven't attracted undue attention. So I suppose I shouldn't complain. I just wish he hadn't acted behind my back. It was a risk."

"How so?"

"You create bad blood; you can make a mistake. A deal like this only works when you keep your whole team informed. John's an outsider. He doesn't know the folks around here like I do. Going solo just to make a point is a little like navigating a

ship without a pilot, just to see if you can do it."

It was time for Jonathon to put one of his cards down on the table, in the hope that the other man might do the same.

"Mr. Wolff, it looks like mistakes *were* made, by who we're not sure yet. Farley Noon's barn was an arson, it looks like Loomis's might've been, too, and we're suspicious about what might have led to a couple of the other sales on that list."

"What are you saying?" Wolff asked darkly.

"Right now, that unless you open up a bit more, that timeline of yours is likely to get a whole lot longer. You know how things get when cops start talking about arson and murder."

"Murder."

"Talk to me, Mr. Wolff."

Wolff stared at the opposite wall for a few moments, clearly weighing his options. "You don't have anything concrete linking my firm to any of this yet. Is that correct?"

"I'm sitting here already," Jonathon answered him ambiguously. "And we've barely started connecting the dots."

Still, the older man wrestled. "Why does the exact nature of the project make any difference?" he asked plaintively.

"People have died," Jonathon said patiently, knowing he'd already won. "Surely, that's not a serious question."

Wolff ran both hands through his hair and pushed himself up off his chair. "Come on," he said, leading the way to a door at the back of the conference room.

He unpocketed a batch of keys and turned the lock on the door with one of them. They stepped into a darkened room with its curtains drawn. Wolff hit the light switch to reveal what looked like a military command post — a document-laden table, the walls covered with maps and charts and oversize photographs. At a glance, Jonathon recognized that the area of interest was the same swatch of land between the lake and the interstate, just south of town.

"Looks like an invasion plan," he commented, glancing around.

Wolff was thoughtful before he answered. "In a way, it is." He crossed to the most generalized map, which included Plattsburgh in New York, the whole of Lake Champlain, northwestern Vermont, and even a slice of Canada. "You ever drive over to New York State from this part of Vermont, Detective?"

"Sure."

"Takes a while, doesn't it? Either taking the ferry from Burlington, leapfrogging across the islands, or almost entering Canada to get across the water."

"Yeah."

"For years, people have talked about solving that problem by building a bridge from Plattsburgh to Burlington," Wolff explained. "Hooking I-89 to the New York Thruway."

Jonathon laughed uneasily. Up to now, he'd thought of Wolff as a reasonable man. "I heard they once talked about putting a landing strip on Mount Mansfield, too," he said. "Still didn't make it likely. I mean, convenience aside, there aren't enough people in the whole state of Vermont to justify that kind of expense."

"The incentive doesn't come from this state. It's federal."

Jonathon's brow furrowed. "Are you serious? All this is about a bridge?"

Wolff switched to another, more detailed map. "Look at how the Champlain islands line up — like stepping-stones. With the proper funding and momentum, a little connect-the-dots would result in making this backwater an overnight hub, with pre-existing interstates — now all linked — heading off in four different directions."

Jonathon was baffled. "What for?"

"Homeland Security," was the simple response. "I have it on good authority that the federal government wants to turn St. Albans into a major northern Homeland Security traffic circle — a jumping-off interdiction point extending along the border from the Atlantic to the Great Lakes. There's a string of about five such centers being discussed. The only hitch with this one is Lake Champlain." He tapped the map with his finger. "Ergo, the bridge."

Jonathon was tempted to challenge Wolff's logic, but he'd already seen so much foolish money expended in the name of national security that a mere billion-dollar bridge paled by comparison. What might seem nonsensical to him — considering that the entire border was unguarded — didn't mean there might not be government funding to make it happen.

He indicated the map. "This is why the properties you and John Gregory are buying could be worth a fortune? Because they're directly in the path?"

Wolff merely waggled his eyebrows in agreement.

Jonathon ran this through his brain. Now that he'd discovered the rationale behind the purchases, the larger scheme had little meaning. Clark Wolff could have detailed plans of a landing base for alien spaceships. The crucial point remained not the credibility of the project, but that the people behind it believed it was feasible. And that it involved more than enough money to kill for.

He couldn't resist one question, however, since he knew Joe would ask it of him in turn: "You said 'on good authority.' We're pretty tied into Homeland Security, given who we are. I hadn't heard anything about this."

Wolff's answer surprised him. "It doesn't matter. I trust my sources — very highly placed and reliable. But in the end, even if this project doesn't go through, these land deals are still sound, in and of themselves. I'll still make money, even if not what I was hoping. The only real difference is that I've expended more capital than I would have normally. I'm very extended right now."

"Is that where John Samuel Gregory comes in?" Jonathon asked. "Guys with three names are usually loaded. Doesn't he drive a Porsche?"

Wolff's voice flattened somewhat. "Yes, he does."

"So you're more business partners than you let on."

"It's my project," Wolff said stubbornly.

Jonathon let his silence speak for him.

"Yes," Wolff conceded. "We are partners because of his personal assets."

"Tell me about Mr. Gregory."

"He's from down south. His father's a highflyer. There's always been money in the family. He came into the office half a year ago, papers in order, looking for a place to work out of. For a while, he functioned as they all do out there, but he's smart and ambitious, and, of course, there was the money."

"Of course."

"Anyhow, when I found out about this" — Wolff waved an arm at the surrounding maps — "I needed someone to go in with me. I actually thought I'd have to create a consortium, which made me very nervous. Turned out, John was enough."

"Had enough," Jonathon corrected him.

Wolff scowled slightly. "Whatever. The point was that we stood a better chance of keeping this to ourselves as a result, at least until it didn't matter anymore. At some point, you have to announce what you've got going — all the hearings and meetings and permits and whatnot. But by that time, we were hoping to have a major chunk of what we needed, so it wouldn't matter as much."

"How far along are you?"

"About fifty percent of that goal — where news breaking out wouldn't have hurt." He surveyed the room ruefully. "Although a wild guess tells me none of that's going to matter much now."

He returned to the door and held it open for his guest. "Might as well go back to where it's more comfortable," he said.

Jonathon walked by him, allowing Wolff to reverse his security routine — switching off the lights and dead-bolting the door.

The Realtor sighed slightly as he sat back down at the conference table. "Probably for the better."

"What is?"

Wolff was suddenly looking older. "All my life, I've seen this as a good business — matching people to their dreams, building businesses where people don't have to drive an hour to get what they need, adding vitality to communities that are fraying around the edges. It was a good feeling. Even when the tree huggers or the antidevelopment types called me names, I could always see the value in what I did." He shook his head. "But not if people are going to get hurt. You'll have to prove to me that what you're saying is true, but I'll do what I can to help clear the slate one way or the other."

"I'll be damned," Gunther said, folding his cell phone and slipping it back into his jacket pocket.

"Gee," Willy snorted. "And I had you pegged for sainthood."

"That was Michael. He's been doing a little homework. Turns out most of those land deals I was telling you about, below St. Albans, tie into a single realty business — an ambitious old-timer and a rich flatlander hoping to make a killing."

Willy perked up. "For real?"

"A *financial* killing," Joe said wearily, and then he corrected himself. "Well, maybe more, as it turns out. But here's the kicker: When Michael asked the old guy where the younger one came from, he was told 'down south.' Turns out that was true Vermonter talk. He meant Newark."

CHAPTER 16

Lil Farber was wearing a pair of half-glasses, in jarring contrast to the .40-caliber handgun strapped to her waist. She looked up from the document she'd just extracted from the copier outside her office and gave the new arrivals a pensive gaze.

Her greeting was guarded. "Thought you boys had gone home."

"Got bored. Came back," Willy answered.

"We received some new information," Joe explained.

"About Gino?"

Joe chose not to mention how their off-the-books surveillance had netted them Gino's girlfriend. "No. Somebody else. From North Caldwell."

"Ritzy neighborhood," Farber commented. "You still talking arson? That's not our usual turf."

Joe waggled his hand from side to side. "It's getting complicated. This may be the money behind the arson."

She laughed shortly, her interest piqued. "You can take the hoods out of Newark, but when they need something done, it's hard to fight old instincts."

"All roads lead back to the Brick City," Willy agreed.

Farber collected her paperwork and led the way into her office, speaking over her shoulder. "What's the name of this new target?"

"John Samuel Gregory."

"Ooh-la-la," she chanted, circling her desk. "Sounds veddy posh. That real?"

Joe answered her, sitting down, "We have no reason to think otherwise."

Farber squared up to her computer and began typing. "Okay, let's see what we got . . ."

It didn't take her long. In a couple of minutes, she murmured, "Seems you're right about his interest in money. No convictions, but he just ducked indictments for money laundering and tax evasion and is listed as a fellow traveler in a couple of other scams."

"Any Mob connections?"

She hitched one shoulder, still typing. "Call them Mob contacts. Hard to say how connected he really is. Things have gotten looser than in the old days, when only southern Italian Catholics could join, but it still doesn't look like he was Family —

not even in the vague way Famolare is. That having been said, he has certainly played with players." She looked up at them. "Wild guess has it you want a copy of this?"

"If you would," Joe answered, adding, "You told us digging into Famolare's business, friends, and neighbors would be like hitting concrete. The same true for Gregory?"

She sat back and smiled at them. "Nope — knock yourselves out. I like going into the Caldwells myself. Reminds me of the life I turned aside to become a caped crusader."

"Oh?" Willy asked.

She shoved herself out of her chair and poked him in the stomach. "Gotcha."

There are three Caldwells, all located in Essex County's northwest corner, North Caldwell being the fanciest. If Caldwell and West Caldwell can be described as upscale suburbia — with the attending shopping malls and restaurants to keep them functioning — North Caldwell represents the Olympian Heights, where the biggest commercial enterprise deemed appropriate is a country club. Its rolling streets are secluded and treelined, its houses palatial and generously surrounded by manicured lawns. There may have been more rarefied acreage available — nearby Upper Montclair comes to mind — but the home turf of the Gregory family hardly played second fiddle. As Lil Farber drove her car along the area's peaceful, pampered, hilly avenues, she estimated some of the larger property taxes at $60,000 per year.

She slowed near the bottom of a large apron of greening grass, the weather down here being warm enough to have stimulated some early spring growth, and pulled over to the curb in full view of a Mount Vernon aspirant, albeit with an excess of red brick and white trim.

"Chez Gregory," she announced, "or shall I say, Grégoire?"

"Any idea where all the money came from?" Joe asked their escort.

"Some," she said, pulling a pad from her purse. "I dug around while I was online at the office. There's nothing criminal about the family that we know — I guess that's John Samuel's specialty — but I wouldn't swear they're all squeaky-clean, either. In any case, the old man is Edward Cummins Gregory III, if you please. He's listed as a venture capitalist and philanthropist. Also a major patron of the arts and a collector of Hispano-Americana, whatever that is. He makes all the shows, sits on all the boards, backs all the right causes, and is calculated to be worth about a hundred million bucks. He's married to Jennifer Whitcomb Gregory, of Chicago, and together they're the parents of three children, of whom John is the youngest and clearly a mistake, since at twenty-six, he's twelve years younger than the next one in line."

"What do the other two kids do?" Joe asked.

"Sister Susan is a thoracic surgeon, working in San Francisco; brother Frederick — five years older than Susan — heads up the family foundation and works with Dad in the venture capital business."

Joe liked that — the eldest, the closest to the father, knowledgeable of the business, and, he hoped, less than impressed with his little brother. "Where's he hang out?"

Farber referred back to her notes. "Lives a few streets away; works ten minutes from here, in West Caldwell."

"You have anything else?"

She shuffled through a few more pages. "Not much. The society pages approve of the senior Gregorys — Jennifer's kept in shape and wears a size four, Edward floats around in a yacht — they dance, they party, they pose well for photographs, but I got the impression that that's where it stops. Phrases like 'the very private couple' and 'the charming but tight-lipped Gregorys' made me think they draw the line."

Willy snorted from the back seat of the car. "Makes me think little Johnny was banished to Siberia with a bankroll and a Porsche and told to keep his nose clean."

"That's what I'm thinking," Joe agreed, and asked Lil, "Did you see anything about Frederick's social life?"

Farber pushed her lips out thoughtfully. "I didn't check specifically, but when I ran the name Gregory, all I got was the parents."

"Sounds like he lets Mom and Dad have the limelight," commented Willy.

Lil glanced over at Joe. "Off to meet Prince Fred, the heir apparent?"

"Yeah."

The office building Frederick Gregory worked in was a low-key, elegant, modern structure bordered by enough trees, reflecting pools, and stylish brick retaining walls to shield it entirely from the bustle of nearby Central Avenue. Once past the self-effacing entrance gate, all three of them felt like they'd been transported to some Connecticut estate. Perhaps typical of such places, there was only a number on the street announcing its existence, no corporate or business logo. Presumably, if you needed the services of the Gregory Foundation, you called ahead and were given directions.

They parked in a well-appointed lot peppered with a few elegant and expensive cars and walked into a lobby under the supervision of an attractive young woman with very cool eyes sitting at an imposing curving desk.

"May I help you?" she asked.

Joe took the lead, Farber having made it clear that she was there solely as a local presence.

"Yes. We were wondering if we could see Frederick Gregory. I'm afraid we don't have an appointment."

She gazed at him as if he'd just asked her to leap from the building's roof. With polite incredulity, she asked, "You're asking to make an appointment, is that correct?"

Instinctively, without Willy having made a sound or a gesture, Joe reached back a couple of inches and grabbed his colleague's wrist, keeping his smile on the girl. "Actually, I'm hoping he might be able to see us now. It's a matter of some importance to him — something fairly delicate, I'm afraid."

He heard Willy sigh.

"And you are?" she asked.

"Nobody he'd recognize," Joe answered. He'd encountered this situation before and hoped a time-honored approach might do the trick. He reached into his pocket and extracted his wallet, adding, "I don't wish you any disrespect, but maybe this will help us all out. Can I borrow a pen?"

Clearly mystified, she complied. He scribbled a note on the back of one of his business cards, which he shielded from her, and then asked for an envelope. He slipped the card into the envelope, addressed it, and handed it to her.

"I think if you give Mr. Gregory this, he'll make time to see us. He is in the building?"

Still holding the envelope, she studied him for a few seconds, as if running through a mental inventory of scams she'd been warned against. Finally, she picked up the phone, spoke a few quiet words, and, with a very thin smile, motioned to a couch by the window. "Have a seat, sir. This should only take a few minutes."

They retired to their designated perch and watched as a second elegant, well-dressed woman appeared from a side door and picked up Joe's note.

Farber leaned in close to him. "What did you write?"

" 'John may be misbehaving again,' " he told her quietly. " 'We need to talk now, if you can.' "

Farber chuckled. " 'If you can.' Very accommodating."

Joe smiled in response. "Don't want to seem pushy."

"You're really counting on John being the black sheep, aren't you?"

"That I am."

Three minutes later, Joe nodded toward the side door. The same young woman as before was gesturing to them to follow her.

"Showtime," he murmured, and nodded, smiling, at the receptionist, who merely stared at them as they crossed the lobby.

Without comment, they walked single file down a muted hallway appointed with oversize Ansel Adams prints glowing under museum lighting, until they reached an unmarked pair of double doors. These their escort opened and stood back to let them pass.

It was a boardroom, very rich, very

quiet, with a very expensive mahogany table in its center and a man sitting at its far end. The doors closed behind them.

"Mr. Gregory?" Joe asked.

"Not to be rude," the man answered, "but I'd like to see your credentials — all of you."

They filed down the length of the table, and Lil and Joe laid their IDs before him. Willy dropped his in the man's lap, where it pointedly lay ignored.

"Special Agent Joseph Gunther of the Vermont Bureau of Investigation and Lieutenant Lillian Farber of our own Essex County prosecutor's office," the man read aloud. "Sounds high-profile." He looked at Farber. "I take it you're the official liaison, or is there some local interest here?"

"We have an interest. Could I see your identification, too, please?" Farber said. "Can't be too careful."

"I hope not," he agreed, removing a slim wallet and displaying his driver's license. He then retrieved Willy's battered leather badge case and slid it across the table to him, unopened. "Have a seat."

Clearly considering some sort of response, Willy hesitated as the other two pulled out leather chairs. To Joe's relief, he ended up simply sitting. Not that Joe took too much comfort from that. No matter how short this meeting might be, he was betting it wouldn't conclude without Willy expressing himself somehow.

"You're here about John Samuel?" Gregory inquired of Joe.

"We are," Joe admitted, pursuing the thin line that had gotten them this far. "It's kind of a courtesy call, really, not that we aren't interested in what you can tell us about him. But he has gotten himself into some trouble, which we thought you'd like to know about before it hits the papers."

Frederick's expression hardened slightly — the disapproving older sibling. "What kind of trouble?"

Joe pretended to look uncomfortable, skirting the fact that he had no hard evidence yet. "Ah. That's a little awkward. My prosecutor would have my head if I said too much. We are talking felony crimes, though. Several of them."

Frederick's voice was flat. "Is he under arrest?"

"Not yet." This was actually a real concern. By speaking to John's brother now, there was a risk that Frederick would call the little troublemaker and tell him to vanish. But Joe was working on instinct. Based on Lil's research, he guessed that

243

Frederick Gregory would more likely protect the family name than John himself. John's presumed one-way ticket to the Vermont backwaters struck Joe as having been Frederick's one show of generosity. Also, the threat of brother tipping off brother was most likely moot in any case, since Jonathon Michael's questioning of Clark Wolff had undoubtedly reached John Samuel's ears by now.

"Mr. Gregory," Joe continued, "in order to keep this as unmessy as possible, I'd like to know a few things about John. Without going into detail, we do have a strong case against him, but the faster we can wrap it up, the less the media will have to chew on. You'd be perfectly within your rights to call a lawyer or just throw us out, but I'm hoping you won't do either."

Frederick pursed his lips, his irritation visibly growing. "What do you want to know? Perhaps we can start there."

"I'm guessing John was the black sheep of the family, given how you and your sister turned out. An unexpected late birth, your parents caught by surprise, John was probably overindulged on the one hand, and left to his own devices on the other."

"You could say that," was the terse reply.

"Too much money, too little supervision?"

"Basically," Frederick agreed.

"What happened?"

Gregory sat farther back in his chair and crossed his legs. "Now it's my turn to be discreet, Mr. Gunther. While I have no love for my brother, I also don't want to give you any more than you have or need."

"I'm not asking for incriminating details. I'm not even a cop in this state."

Gregory pointed at Lil. "She is."

Farber laughed. "With what they're building against him, we don't have to worry. He'll be an old man before we get a shot at him. I doubt my boss will even care."

Frederick shook his head slightly. "What a fool," he murmured, almost to himself.

"What happened?" Joe repeated gently, grateful to Farber for playing up what they had against John.

"You're right, of course. Spoiled, amoral, and rich to boot. John was a nightmare from the day he learned to walk. Susan and I became the firewall between him and our parents early on, until she got so sick of it, she went as far away as she could get. My mother and father, Mr. Gunther, are not incredibly equipped to deal with someone like John, so I got stuck with him."

He rose and crossed to a window overlooking a terraced concrete fountain surrounded by low trees. "He became involved with some people down here — a shady financial deal, let's call it — that necessitated his leaving the area." He was speaking to the view.

"Why Vermont?" Joe asked.

Gregory turned to face them. "He went to college there a few years ago — University of Vermont. Never graduated, of course. He was thrown out before the end of sophomore year. But when I asked him where he wanted to go he chose Vermont."

"He let you dictate terms like that?" Joe asked, surprised at the acquiescent implication.

Gregory smiled thinly. "Money played a large role. Quite a bit of it, in fact — a big enough allowance to make it worth his while. John is nothing if not self-serving."

"Did he tell you what he was doing up there?"

"We are not pen pals."

"That was your mistake," Willy commented.

Gregory gave him a hard look before responding, "I don't think so. It wouldn't have made any difference."

"What about what got him into hot

water down here?" Joe asked. "How aware of that were you?"

"Only of the end results," he said bitterly. "And that because he came to me once they were on to him."

"Who was?"

Gregory stared at him in silence for a slow count before finally saying, "A man named Dante Lagasso."

Gunther glanced quickly at Farber, who just barely shook her head. The name meant nothing to her.

"I take it Lagasso was Mob-connected?" Joe asked.

"I think that's fair to say."

"You should've let them have him," Willy said.

"Whatever his faults," Gregory reacted icily, "he is family."

Willy laughed harshly. "Don't run your coat of arms up that flagpole, asshole. His faults caused the death of an innocent kid."

Joe glared at Willy as Gregory bowed his head in shock. But while he didn't approve of Willy's outburst, Joe couldn't fault his passion. As usual, in his insensitive, impolitic, trenchant way, Kunkle had spoken only the truth as he saw it. The problem being, of course, that what he saw was based solely on prejudice and speculation.

But he'd also flattened the last of Gregory's reserve. The man looked up from Willy's verbal blow and asked wonderingly of Gunther, "Is that true?"

It was no time to equivocate. "We believe so, yes."

Gregory reached for the back of the chair he'd just vacated, as if to keep from falling over. "My God," he said.

"What did you expect?" Willy asked.

Joe leaned forward slightly and fixed his colleague with a look. "Enough," he said in a quiet, firm voice, wondering if Willy's insistence was based on belief, or merely on having been put in his place by Gregory upon entering.

Whatever his motives, Willy recognized that he'd reached his limit. He settled back in his chair without further comment.

"Don't be too hard on him," Gregory said tiredly, regaining his seat like an ancient arthritic. "He's perfectly correct. We should have held John accountable long ago. Now we have only ourselves to blame. Can you tell me the details of this death? I might be able to do something to atone for what we've done."

Joe was already shaking his head. "Mr. Gregory, there will be time for that later on. If and when we get there, I'll tell you all you need to know. You and the boy's family can work out whatever you want then. Right now I need you to be straight about John's criminal connections here in Newark."

Frederick Gregory gave him a hapless look. "I knew about Lagasso because I had to pay him off. I didn't know the details and John never told me. He basically took the attitude that I owed him the favor of saving his bacon."

"How 'bout before? This couldn't have been the first time."

"God, no. John was getting into trouble from before he reached high school."

"Who did he tend to run with?"

Frederick placed his hand against his forehead, half thinking, half wishing he could forget. "Let's see . . . There was one kid named Santo. I remember that because I couldn't think of a less likely name for him. A real little monster — black leather, motorcycle boots. He was one of the worst John got involved with who caused problems."

"What sort of problems?"

"They were teenagers. What do you think?" he asked peevishly. "Vandalisms, petty theft, drinking, getting girls pregnant

. . . generally carrying on like the juvenile delinquents they were. I was constantly paying off the police or parents or business owners to keep it out of the papers. Santo took full advantage of that, let me tell you. If it hadn't been for John and our running interference, little Santo would have been in Rahway a long time ago."

"Is that where he is now?"

The reaction was a bored "I haven't the slightest idea."

"And you don't know his last name, either?"

Gregory sighed impatiently. Joe knew that the interview was running on fumes.

"Massi. That was it. Santo Massi. If you could dress a cockroach in black leather, that would be him."

"Who else?"

The rich man made a face, his earlier guilt having yielded to the bother of reliving unpleasant memories. "I don't know, Mr. Gunther. The point of all this was to make it go away. Not keep notes."

"Both names sound Italian," Joe persisted. "Did John hang out where there was a strong Mob influence?"

"I think he liked the allure, but then he was truly broad-minded when it came to lowlifes, because he'd go down to Irvington, too, and the docks. Blacks, Jews, Italians — it didn't matter to John. Just as long as they were unsavory and he could rub them in our faces."

Now it was Joe who wanted to end the interview. He stood up. "All right, Mr. Gregory. We'll let you get back to your business. Appreciate the time."

Gregory was startled, far more used to being the one who shut down a conversation. "Wait. What about John Samuel?"

Joe didn't answer at first, letting the others file toward the door. His emotions had traveled quickly and variously in the short time he'd known this man, from sympathy for a philanthropist saddled with an unsolvable problem, to a growing conviction that Frederick viewed the world as a collection of troubles that could be bought off or, if not, disposed of, preferably by others.

In this case, Joe was happy to oblige. "We'll deal with him and let you know."

CHAPTER 17

Lil Farber was sitting at her computer again, this time waiting for a document to appear on the screen. There was a glitch in the system, and things were running slow.

"You boys lay it on thick, don't you? Connecting Gregory's brother to a murder you have no clue he's involved with."

Willy was dismissive. "We have a clue. We just don't have the evidence yet, which is why it would be handy if you got that thing working."

Farber looked at Joe in wonder. "What do you see in this guy? He is such a jerk."

Joe smiled. "I wouldn't leave home without him."

A flicker on the screen drew Farber's attention. "Here we go. Dante Lagasso. A lieutenant in the Facci family — same outfit as Tony Hands, so there's a tie-in — usual assortment of activities. Spent half his life behind bars. Loan-sharking, assault, grand larceny . . . ouch — vehicular manslaughter; wonder what that was about? Bunch of other stuff, including fraud and blackmail. Let's see . . . 'Associates.' What've we got here? Apparently, he once ordered a warehouse burned down after the owner couldn't pay him back."

Farber stopped to laugh. "Unbelievable. A note here says that the arson had all the hallmarks of Vinnie Stazio, except that Stazio was already dead. God — what's not in one file, of course, shows up in the next. All the arson information we were looking for yesterday is in the Organized Crime records. Tell me that makes sense. Damn, we have got to get this crap into one database. Drives me crazy."

"What else did you find?" Willy asked, ignoring her woes.

"Suspicion was the job was done by a student of Stazio's," she continued reading. "Possibly Gino Famolare. Jesus — right there in black and white. God knows where else in this pile of crap his name might be lurking." She slapped the computer with the flat of her hand and sat back to look at them. "Do you know, nine times out of ten, I get more from Google than I do out of our own files?"

Willy gave vent to some frustrations of his own. "Bet neither one of them can tell you Gino has a girlfriend he keeps Down Neck." Joe winced. Even for Willy, this was clumsy.

Farber frowned. "How do you know that?"

"We hayseeds followed him right to her."

She leaned forward and switched the computer off, a telling gesture, to Joe's mind. The spirit of cooperation was now officially in disrepair.

"Meaning you staked him out?" she asked icily.

Willy was unrepentant. "You had zilch. Patted us on the ass and said we didn't know how things were done in the big city, so bye-bye and we'll let ya know when somethin' comes up. Well, so much for that. You can't even get your computer to work, and we got a fresh angle on your guy in one afternoon. You want to know where the candy lives?"

Farber ignored him, standing up to face Gunther. "I guess you wouldn't mind if I did the same thing in *your* backyard, right?"

Joe was surprised, embarrassed, and genuinely apologetic. "That's not the point. It was a breach of protocol, and I'm sorry we didn't tell you. There was no malice intended, believe me. You've been great with us. It was kind of spontaneous," he concluded lamely. "I guess we got our dander up."

Farber stared him straight in the face for several long seconds, letting him absorb her irritation.

Willy, watching them both, finally burst out, "Fine. We'll get the fuck out of Dodge, then." He moved toward the door.

"Don't go on my account," she said quietly, still looking at Joe.

Willy froze, trying to interpret what had just happened. He stayed silent, however, letting his boss find out. Willy was used to having insults hurled at his back. This was something new.

"We're okay?" Joe asked dubiously, only half believing he had figured her correctly.

She finally broke eye contact and strolled to the window, where she sat on the ledge. "Yeah, you and I are okay. You messed up, you said you're sorry. We're both cops. I know how it feels. You, though," she spoke directly to Willy, "you're a whole different game. I'm not so sure I'm crazy about having you underfoot anymore."

It was a Willy moment in the making — a golden opportunity for him to choose from among a variety of sarcastic replies. In fact, his hesitation seemed to Joe only an inability to select one over another. The shock, therefore, was that he chose none.

"Yeah. Sorry," he said quietly. "You didn't deserve my shit."

Farber smiled thinly, but was apparently satisfied, probably knowing by now that even so slight an apology was a miracle. Joe, on the other hand, was less surprised this time, having seen Willy's flip side before, especially with those he respected. As in his relationship with Sammie, Willy could be protective and obnoxious in side-by-side sentences.

Farber merely headed back to her desk. "All right, then," she said, sitting down. "Tell me about the girlfriend."

Gino Famolare was sitting in his den at home when the phone rang.

"Gino. Frank. How you doin'?"

"Good, Frankie. You been behavin'?"

His long-retired older neighbor from three doors down laughed. "God. I hope not. You?"

"No way."

Frank laughed again. Gino waited. This was not a social call. It wasn't that kind of friendship. The two men were less pals than they were members of the same fraternity, in this case the nebulous labyrinth of Organized Crime of which Frank, unlike Gino, had actually once been a soldier.

The entire neighborhood was populated with people of a vaguely similar background.

"So," Frankie resumed, "you been on the road?"

"Yeah. Way up north."

"Lotta snow still up there?"

Gino played along. The sound was off on the TV set, muted since the phone had interrupted, but it was just a string of commercials right now. Nothing he cared about missing.

"Mostly melted — a little bit here and there. You know how it is."

"Yeah, yeah . . . You were gone about a week, right?"

Gino well knew that his older neighbor kept an eye on the street. It was one reason he'd never had Peggy over when the wife was out of town. "Yeah. A week."

"Right." There was a telling pause as Frank finally decided to stop circling the reason for his call. "You have anyone over today?"

Gino stopped watching the screen before him, suddenly alert. "What's up, Frankie?"

"It's not like it's any of my business, but I just wondered. A couple of guys were waiting for you."

"How, 'waiting'?"

Frank chuckled. "Oh, you know the routine. One of 'em naps; the other one keeps his eyes open. Then they switch."

"What'd they look like?"

"One older, one younger. Couldn't see all that good, since they stayed in the car, but they kept moving so as not to be too obvious. The younger one looked like he had somethin' funny goin' on with his left arm. Can't be sure about that, though."

"Cops?"

"That was the weird part," Frank admitted. "If they were, they were using the dumbest cover I ever saw. I mean, they did look like cops, but the plates were from outta state."

"You see where from?" Gino was by now sitting forward in his chair, his feet off the ottoman, the TV program abandoned.

"Oh, yeah." Frank laughed. "That was the other thing. Vermont. They even have cops up there?"

Gino hadn't given that question much thought until now. "I guess they do. Thanks, Frankie. I owe you one."

"Nothin' to it. Happy to help."

Gino wasn't quite so sanguine that there was nothing to it. Staring sightlessly at the den's far wall, he was thinking that if the news of that kid dying in the barn fire was the first shoe dropping, then this little tidbit had to be the second.

And it was a lot closer to home.

"Is that him?" Willy asked, craning to see through the car's back window.

Lil Farber was sitting in the passenger seat, with access to the outside rearview mirror. She quickly checked the mug shot in her hand. "Santo Massi, John Samuel Gregory's old playmate, looking a little the worse for wear — as advertised."

Joe was watching in his own mirror as the man they were discussing, once the swaggering, leather-clad teenage hood of Frederick Gregory's memories, lurched out of a bar in North Newark and stumbled over to a parking meter where he caught his balance. His pallor was luminescent under the streetlamps, and he was skeleton-thin, but the resemblance between man and photo was unmistakable.

They'd been waiting for him for just under five hours, sitting in the car sharing nary a word, each so inured by years of past stakeouts as to barely notice the dullness any longer, their inbred impatience replaced by something like tranquility.

Most of the day just past had been spent in research and debate at Lil's office, as they'd struggled to map and make reasonable the relational tangles of this case. In the end, connections had been made, however tenuous in places, between Gino Famolare, his mentor the late Vinnie Stazio, and the now incarcerated Antonio "Tony Hands" Lamano; between Lamano and Dante Lagasso — once the bane of Frederick Gregory's checkbook — who both worked for the Facci family, and John Samuel Gregory; and finally between Lagasso and Santo Massi, who had been used in the old days by Lagasso for odd jobs, until Massi's recreational habits with drugs and alcohol made him too unreliable.

But unreliable to the bad guys was hoped to be good news to the investigators, since, among this cast of potential interviewees, there were precious few available to try cracking. Stazio was dead, and Gino, his wife, daughter, and girlfriend couldn't yet be approached, Lamano was ancient and in a far-off prison, and Lagasso was still active enough to not even acknowledge their existence without legal counsel, much less engage in conversation.

And conversation was what they were after — which made Massi the only possibly rusty link in the criminal chain opposing them. He was broke, he was strung out, he'd been all but cashiered by his pals, but he was still marginally on the inside. Most of all, he was John Gregory's former co–juvenile delinquent, and — they were hoping — the man John had called for the name of a good arsonist.

To Lil, the best approach was to avoid the very routine she'd outlined in her office: calling the man's lawyer for a meaningless chat with both of them "downtown." Instead, she'd urged merely grabbing him off the street and putting the fear of God into him. They had nothing on him, after all, and it was clear from his recent history that they probably never would — several times, already, he'd been taken to area ERs as an overdose and just barely brought back. Santo Massi was drifting into human transparency, on the edge of vanishing altogether. A conversation with the likes of such a creature, she'd reasoned, didn't need to follow protocol.

Besides, she'd said to counter Joe's protests, assuming Massi did give them something, no prosecutor in his right mind would ever want him later as a witness. Better to just treat him as an anonymous source and not clog up the process with the living dead.

Joe had argued Massi was so shaky that they could sweat him in Lil's office and easily get what they wanted. But Willy, unsurprisingly, had sided with Lil. Massi was their only shot, and given how ancient loyalties were often the last to die, they'd doubtless need every advantage they could get to make this one chance succeed. Finally, he'd added, all they were talking about was a conversation. Santo Massi himself was of no interest to them. They just needed to be set on the right track.

Warily, with few other options, Joe had conceded, feeling in the pit of his stomach that this was fundamentally wrong.

His head seemingly cleared enough for him to proceed, Massi tentatively released the parking meter and stood independently for a few moments on the sidewalk, looking dazed and indecisive. Finally, he took a step in their direction, then two, established a vague momentum, and set off on some goal he only possibly recalled.

It wasn't to be. As he drew abreast of their car, Willy and Lil stepped out, boxing him in.

"Santo?" Willy asked him.

Massi blinked carefully several times, studying the unfamiliar face, his eyes inevitably wandering to the emaciated arm.

He raised his eyebrows. "Whoa — bummer."

"You Santo?"

Massi scowled theatrically. "Yeah . . . I mean, what's it to ya?"

"I want to make sure I give money to the right guy."

"Money?" The man's tired, beaten face creased into a smile. "Sure. I'm Santo."

"Good. Get in the car." Willy moved aside, as if ushering a woman through a restaurant entrance.

The smile vanished. Both the gesture and the invitation had too many poor connotations.

"You got money for me, I'm ready for it."

But Willy shook his head good-naturedly. "Do I look like I got money? I gotta take you to him. A buddy from the old days."

Santo still demurred. "Who?"

"John Gregory. You remember him?"

The man's pleasure was clear. "Johnny — again? Wow. Good timing. Sure, I remember." He stooped down to peer into the darkened car. "He in there?"

Before Willy could answer, Massi straightened abruptly, his face watchful. "That's not Johnny."

Lil saw her opportunity. From being there merely to impede his retreat, she now stepped forward and placed her hand gently on Massi's shoulder, making him jump.

"That's Joe," she said softly as he spun in her direction, falling against the car.

She looped her arm around his waist to steady him, her face close to his. "Wow. Easy, there."

"You're pretty," he said simply.

"Thank you." She smiled. "Would you like me to ride in the back with you?"

Willy played along, backing away so that the rear door yawned open invitingly. Lil slid her hand up Massi's back, lightly massaging his neck.

"Come on, Santo. I'm starting to get cold in this night air."

Whatever reserves he was clutching slipped away. "Sorry."

She steered him into the car, sliding in after him, as Willy slammed the door and got in the front. Unbeknownst to Massi, the door beside him had been disabled, just in case he should want to leave.

"Hey," Joe said brightly from behind the wheel. "How're you doin'?"

"Good," Massi answered cautiously, the claustrophobic reality of being among so many strangers growing again. "Joe, right?"

"You got it." Joe reached across the seat back and awkwardly extended a hand in greeting. "Glad to meet you."

The movie in his head now totally off track, Massi shook hands distractedly. "Sure."

Joe put the car into gear and pulled away from the curb, turning left at the first intersection to head west, as instructed earlier.

"You sure you know Johnny?"

"Yeah," Lil said comfortingly. "He said to tell you that Vermont was ripe for the picking. That you're nuts to stick it out here."

That familiar reference seemed to lessen his anxiety a notch. He smiled broadly. "Nah. He can have it. I'm a city guy. I need the action."

The three of them were quietly pleased by what they were hearing. John Gregory hadn't been in Vermont very long, and yet not only had Massi not been surprised to hear of him in that context, but they'd all heard how he said "again" when Johnny's name had first been mentioned. They seemed to be on the right track.

"Yeah," Lil followed up. "I know what you mean. I'm kinda that way, too."

Santo attempted a seductive leer. "I bet. What'd you say your name was?"

"Lil."

He nodded. "Pretty. Did I say you were pretty, too?"

"You did that, yeah."

"Is that where we're going?"

Lil was momentarily nonplussed. "Where?"

"Vermont."

She and Joe laughed. "That's a long trip, Santo," she said. "No — Johnny's back in town for a visit. To check on you, among other things."

"Oh — right." Massi sighed, not unhappily, and rested his head against the seat cushion, sliding down a bit to get comfortable.

"Tired?" Lil asked him.

"A little. How much money are we talking about?"

"I don't know, but Johnny said he owed you a lot for all the good times you had together."

Massi smiled and closed his eyes. "Good times."

"With more to come," Lil intoned soothingly. She touched Joe on the shoulder and indicated in the mirror for him to take a right onto Bloomfield.

Santo Massi lapsed into sleep, mercifully for Lil, who could only go so far with such small talk. Also, they had a way to go yet, and she'd been slightly nervous about how to keep him adequately entertained during the trip.

They were headed to what her task force squad, and in fact most of the prosecutor's office, had once called home: the abandoned campus of the Essex County psychiatric hospital, a huge and sprawling ghost town of old brick buildings scattered across hundreds of acres of currently prime, rolling, and ready-to-be-developed real estate.

Fifteen minutes along, she tapped Joe's shoulder again and murmured, "Take the next driveway to the right."

It was enough to stir Massi from his slumber. He sat up and blinked groggily out the windows, just as Joe drove them through the campus entrance, immediately losing the commotion of a crowded and bustling Bloomfield Avenue to the contrasting darkness and isolation of the empty hospital grounds.

"Where are we?"

Lil patted his arm. "You never been here? It's a little bit of country we got right in the city. It's cool."

On that level, she was correct. At its peak, the century-old complex was a completely self-contained community, shut off from its environs, with a separate power plant, golf course, swimming pool, fire department, and a layout suggesting a sylvan retreat far from the troubles of the surrounding world. Closed for over a decade, the center hovered between decay and a faintly chilling sense that all its ghosts might still be lingering. This impression was only enhanced by the surrounding blackness, offset but feebly by the moonlight shifting through the trees and the sweep of Joe's headlights across the peeling, gap-windowed faces of a parade of gloomy buildings.

Understandably, it was enough to fully revive Massi's earlier suspicions.

"I don't like this. What is this?"

Willy gave up his earlier soft touch. He turned in his seat, purposefully placed his left arm on the edge of the seat so its ghoulish, sticklike profile was in full relief, and said, "A place for a quiet conversation, far from anyone and anywhere."

His eyes now wide, Massi looked from one of them to the other. "What do you want? I haven't done anything. Where's Johnny?"

"Up ahead," Lil instructed Joe. "Next one on the left."

Joe had already driven by some of the larger institutional buildings and was now amid a semicircle of ochre-colored brick homes, set even farther back among the trees. According to Lil, these were the former staff residences where the county had housed the various task force squads in the years immediately following the hospital's closure. Like some cast-aside movie set, these houses were still endowed with lawns and shrubs and even visiting deer who would emerge from the woods by the dim light of dusk.

But it was also ghostly quiet and empty and looking the worse for wear, and offered to someone with Massi's darkening imagination only the promise of grim tidings and pain.

He began to twist in his seat. "Who are you guys? What do you want from me?"

"Would you believe we're cops?" Lil asked, displaying her badge.

If her hopes had been that this would increase his paranoia, it worked.

"No, I would not," Massi exclaimed, now convinced he'd been kidnapped for the proverbial ride of gangster lore. As the car slid to a stop, he grabbed the door handle and yanked on it several times, his entire body heaving with the effort.

"Let me out. I don't *know* anything."

"We think you do, little man," Willy argued.

Massi's eyes welled up. Despite what he'd just been told, his panic was now in control.

"Don't kill me. Please. I mean, maybe I do know something. I just don't know what you want. But I wanna help. I really do."

Lil reached out suddenly and grabbed his flailing wrist, bending it over painfully and freezing him in place. He arched his back and began stuttering, "Ow, ow, ow."

"Calm down," she said quietly. "We're going into that house."

She worked him backward out of the car and handed him over to Willy, who switched to an armlock as Lil dug the building's keys out of her pants pocket. Joe killed the engine unhappily and joined the three of them on the front stoop. Even given the success of Lil's plan so far, he hated being a part of this.

Massi was simply repeating in a small, plaintive voice, "Oh, please, oh, please."

Lil opened the door and ushered them into a small, dusty hallway, lit only by what moonlight managed to seep through the dirty windows alongside the front entrance. She led the way into a side room and backed off, her job done. This was Joe and Willy's interrogation. It was time to become merely the escort.

In the filtered half-gloom, Willy steered Massi into the room's middle and hooked an upright chair with his foot and dragged it over. He sat Massi down hard in it and stepped back so their quarry could see all three of them standing before him, their faces shrouded in darkness but their body language clear.

Massi was weeping by now, his alcohol-and-drug-racked mind succumbing to the terror of finally being on the receiving end of the kind of interview he'd only nervously witnessed before. His brain filled with the pleas and screams and crying of those memories, he fell from the chair onto his knees and held his clasped hands out to Willy in supplication. "Just tell me what you want. I'll tell you everything. I swear I will."

Joe watched him with his throat dry. He'd seen such scenes before, in combat long ago, when military officers applied whatever they deemed necessary to get what they were after. Of course, none of that would happen tonight. Even having lost the argument, he was in fact running this interrogation and was thus guaranteed that all of Massi's terror would be entirely self-induced. Nevertheless, it was unsettling not only to see this pathetic man's disintegration but to realize how it stimulated in Joe an unwelcome, unpleasant, but undeniable adrenaline rush. As a far younger man, he'd been more like Willy Kunkle than he liked to admit, and had put people through the wringer simply because he didn't have the patience to pursue the truth less violently.

For a moment, wrestling with all this, it was all he could do not to leave the room. Instead, he chose to get the whole thing over with as quickly as possible, hoping some rationalization would help later on.

Feeling like a hypocrite, he stepped forward, crouched down, and took Massi's hands between his own, in a grotesque parody of a priest receiving confession.

"Look at me, Santo," he said in a quiet voice.

Massi was still switching his attention from Willy to Lil, both of them now standing back to either side of Joe, looking as if they were but one command away from unleashing holy mayhem.

"Look at me," Joe repeated.

Massi's eyes briefly settled on Joe's face.

"You had contact with John Gregory recently. Tell me about that."

A small crease appeared between Massi's eyebrows. "Johnny? I haven't talked to him in years."

Joe hesitated. Not only had they assumed Santo Massi to have been the most reasonable conduit between John Gregory and Gino Famolare, but he'd all but admitted to seeing Gregory earlier.

Joe tried a more oblique approach, gently releasing Massi's hands and using his voice to cut through the man's terror. "But you know what Johnny's been up to."

Massi's expression opened up hopefully. "I know he called Dante for advice."

Joe relaxed a bit. "Dante Lagasso?"

"Yeah, yeah. Lagasso. I was in the room when Dante told Tito about how Johnny called him up a few weeks ago."

"What was Johnny after?"

"A torch. Dante finally gave him Gino Famolare, after everybody'd agreed to terms." Massi was speaking fast, his eyes eager to please.

"And what were those?" Joe asked, feeling the relief that accompanied a long-sought-after reward.

"Forty grand total, with twenty percent going to Dante for making the connection."

"Isn't that high?"

"Yeah, but it was an out-of-town job, in unfamiliar territory. It was like an eight-grand surcharge."

Joe leaned forward on the balls of his feet, getting his face as close as possible to Massi's and cutting off the latter's view of the two others. Massi stared into Joe's eyes, as riveted as if he'd been hypnotized by a snake charmer.

"Was there any explanation," Joe asked, almost whispering, "why Johnny wanted a torch?"

But here Santo Massi proved a disappointment. "Money?" he asked hopefully.

Joe persisted. "Good guess. How many fires was this contract supposed to cover?"

Massi was clearly confused. "One . . . I guess. I mean, forty Gs is fat for one, like I said, but it's cheap if you got more, and Gino isn't cheap."

"Do you recall the date of this conversation?"

"Are you kidding?"

Joe let that pass. "Did you meet with, or do you even know, Famolare?"

"No, but he's kind of famous, if you're into that kind of thing."

"Do you know if he was paid for the job?"

"Yeah. But later, I heard Tito say somebody died in it. Tito said Gino would probably be pissed when he heard that, 'cause he's such a perfectionist."

"Tito is connected to Gino in some way?"

"He knows him, is all. Tito's kind of like Dante's secretary, not that I'd say that to his face."

"Do you know Tito's full name?"

Massi looked at him blankly. "No. It's Tito."

Joe stood back up and glanced over at Lil and Willy. "I think we're done here."

Without comment, they both left the room to return to the car.

Massi stared up at Joe with his eyes wide and pleading again. "What're you going to do?"

"What we said we were," Joe answered him, reaching into his pocket and extracting his wallet. "Pay you off and thank you for your time."

He handed Massi a hundred-dollar bill, more by far than he normally would have paid — a surcharge to assuage his own guilt.

Massi held the money as if he might be asked to read aloud from it. "That's it?"

Joe had already moved to the door, and now turned back. "What do you mean?"

"You're not gonna kill me?"

Joe scowled at him, irritated at what the man's life choices had forced Joe to do to him. "That what you want?"

Massi held up both hands, still holding the bill. "No, no. I'm sorry."

You are that, Joe thought, wondering if he should even react. Finally, he couldn't resist. "The way I see it, you'll kill yourself fast enough anyway."

Massi nodded. "Yes, sir. Sure will." After a pause, during which Joe just stared at him, Massi added, "How'm I gonna get home?"

Joe nodded toward the hundred-dollar bill, as disappointed in himself as disgusted at Massi. "Take a cab."

CHAPTER 18

With the intervening desk hiding most of his body, Ben Silva's head floated just above the wooden sign labeled "Director" perched on the table's edge, at least from Joe's slouched and bleary perspective. It made him think of the Wizard of Oz, which in turn reminded him of how little sleep he'd just had. He tried to concentrate on the conversation.

"From Lil's report," Silva was saying, "it looks like we have enough probable cause to rub Gino's hair the wrong way. At least, we can access his trucking company's logs and find out if and where he was driving on the days those fires broke out. It's a limited search — I doubt a judge would give us more leeway than that, based on what we've got — but it's a start. Plus," he added with a tired smile, "it'll let him know we're looking at him."

"He's gotta know that by now," Lil told her boss. "The Vermonters staked out his house and followed him to his girlfriend's love nest Down Neck. If everybody on his block hasn't already called him by now, I'd be very disappointed in the Brotherhood."

Silva raised his eyebrows questioningly at Joe and Willy.

"You didn't know about her before we did your job for you," Willy said in his usual diplomatic mode.

"Peggy DeAngelis," Lil intoned, reading from a sheet of paper and covering any potential awkward silences. "Aged twenty-two, a couple of years of community college, does temp work typing and some modeling. Father is Augustin DeAngelis. He works on the docks, is definitely connected, did some time years ago for extortion and assault, but has been clean ever since. Peggy's digs are worth about four hundred grand, and they're owned by a holding company I didn't have the time or energy to try tracing. Suffice it to say that she is showing no financial distress."

Lil folded the paper and looked over at Willy, adding, "And no, it doesn't look like her name appears in any of our or anyone else's files."

"Well, there you have it," Silva said brightly. "We owe you one, Agent Kunkle."

Willy didn't do well with this sort of reverse psychology. "Whatever," he growled.

"I should warn you both, though," Silva went on, "that the truck logs probably won't do us much good. That particular company is Mobbed up enough that whatever we find will be whatever they want us to."

"Then what's the point?" Willy asked.

"Mostly to apply heat," was the answer. "It's cat-and-mouse. We get 'em when we can, but otherwise, we mostly pressure them in the hopes they'll either quit or make a mistake. Also, just as you did in finding Santo Massi, every once in a while, you fall over someone who'll actually tell you a few things."

"Like the girl," Joe said softly.

There was a momentary stillness in the room. Silva smiled. "You want to talk to the girl?"

"Why not?" Joe asked. "Seems like she would be the ultimate pressure point for Gino, at least. She may also tell us something. But talking to her would show him we know what's up. That screws him up professionally and personally. Especially," he added with a slight smile, "when we interview his wife and kid afterward."

Silva laughed. "Ouch — hardball." He nodded toward Lil. "Okay. Set it up."

Tito Malossini came up behind Santo Massi with a stealth belying his enormous bulk. Santo was at the bar, as usual, at one of the city's dozens of so-called social clubs, where only certain people were welcome.

Tito slipped a large hand onto Santo's shoulder and held it there purposefully.

"Hey," he said in greeting.

Santo looked up nervously, spilling some of the drink he had halfway to his mouth. "Hey, Tito. How's things?"

"Good." Tito's voice was flat and uncompromising. "Come on back." He tugged at Santo slightly in encouragement.

"Now? I haven't finished my drink."

Tito merely looked at him.

"Right," Santo conceded, replacing the glass on the bar. He slid off his stool and accompanied the big man through the large, plain, undecorated room to a narrow door in the middle of the back wall. There were only about four men in the place, and none of them so much as glanced in their direction.

Tito opened the door and stood aside.

Feeling much as he had the night before, when that car door had opened up and its dark interior exerted its force on him, Santo followed the invitation with dread. He hadn't really figured out who those three were last night.

This man, on the other hand, he knew.

"Does Dante want to see me?" he asked hopefully, crossing the threshold.

The answer was flat and curt. "No." Tito gave him a little shove before following him into the dark room.

Joe Gunther was old enough by now that his concept of female beauty had shifted away from the universal norm. To him, the youthful denizens of catalogs, magazines, mall displays, and TV shows had all become a little surreal, as if the majority of them — at least from a distance — ran the gamut from animated mannequins to overendowed, asexual children. Beautiful young women weren't something he encountered very often, in any case, and the women he did see regularly, like Gail and Sammie Martens, were too practical, business-minded, and lacking in vanity to qualify as models. Also, he'd come to cherish the lines he saw in those faces and the experience he could see in their eyes.

All of which made meeting Peggy DeAngelis with Willy and Lil in tow a shock, in spite of his having once seen her from a distance. When she opened the front door to his knock and stood three feet away from them, he felt rooted in place, his mouth half open in greeting but speechless.

"Yes?" she asked them.

"We're the police," Willy said, his voice tense. "We need to talk to you."

Joe cut him a glance, having seen this kind of reaction before. Whether it was his deformity, bad luck as a teenager, or simply his usual orneriness, Willy had his own way of responding to aesthetic wonders.

Real concern furrowed DeAngelis's forehead. "What happened? Is everything all right? Is it Gino?"

"Oh, it's Gino, all right," Willy said bluntly, "but not the way you think."

He stepped up onto the threshold, forcing her to either yield or get pushed back. Still smiling politely but looking worried, she yielded. Willy led the way into the front hall.

"Gino's fine, Miss DeAngelis," Joe said quickly. "We just need to ask you a few questions."

Peggy was by now looking thoroughly confused. "I don't understand."

Now acting eccentrically even for him, Willy was almost bristling. "We'll use simple language," he said caustically.

Joe shook his head wearily. He touched Peggy's shoulder lightly to reassure her. "Don't mind him. Bad day. It is true, though, that Gino's gotten himself into some legal trouble. We do need to talk."

Her fingers hovered at her mouth. The gesture somehow made her look almost coltish. "I don't know," she said doubtfully.

"Could go harder for him if you don't talk to us," Willy said.

"But I don't *know* anything," she protested. "What do you think he's done?"

Willy's response was rich with an overstated puritanical resentment. "He's screwing around with you, for starters."

Her mouth dropped open as Joe finally swung around to face him from inches away, his expression grim. Willy muttered, "Okay, okay, fine," before Joe could say a word, and went to stand behind Lil.

Joe returned to Peggy. "I'm sorry. Maybe we should start over again. My name's Joe Gunther. I'm from Vermont. The cranky guy's Willy Kunkle, and that's Lieutenant Lil Farber, from the Essex County prosecutor's office. You are Peggy DeAngelis, right?"

"Yes. Why are you from Vermont?"

Joe was grateful for Willy's lack of a response. He gestured to the living room behind her as he spoke. "Mind if we sit down? It's a bit of a long story."

"No, no," she said immediately, which automatic courtesy he'd counted on.

They all settled on a sofa and a couple of armchairs.

"What exactly do you know about Gino?" Joe asked in his best fatherly tone.

She concentrated as if she'd been asked a test question. "He works at the docks as a trucker, drives an eighteen-wheeler, and" — here she shot Willy an angry look — "I know he's married, which is something he's trying to end."

"Does he tell you about the trips he takes?" Joe continued.

She smiled, which suffused an already perfect face with a sunny radiance. "He sends me postcards sometimes."

"Could I see them?"

She half rose from her chair before shaking her head. "I'm not sure I should do this. I don't think he'd like it."

Joe looked up at her, his elbows on his knees, trying to appear relaxed and casual. "Why's that? You want to help him, don't you?"

She frowned. "Of course. That's what I'm saying."

"We're here already," Joe explained point-edly. "You do realize that not cooperating will just turn a small investigation into a big deal — attract a lot of attention and involve lots of people."

"Aren't you supposed to have some piece of paper you have to show me?"

Joe and Lil both laughed. He explained, "That's only when we're about to search a place or arrest someone. We're just here trying to make sense of a few things."

"What things?" she asked, still standing.

"It's a bit complicated, Peggy, and we're figuring it out, but my colleague's tough-guy imitation notwithstanding, we may end up finding Gino's got nothing to do with any of it. You could help us with that and make this go away twice as fast."

"Clearing him of suspicion?"

"We just want to know the truth," Joe equivocated.

She hesitated one last time and then nodded slightly. "All right. I'll be right back."

She left the room, and they heard her climbing the stairs two at a time with rapid, light footsteps — still a kid inside that fully adult body.

Lil waited until she was sure Peggy was out of earshot. "So," she asked, "you two always work this well together? You ought to write a how-to book."

"Cute," Willy growled.

Joe rose suddenly, holding his hand up for silence, and moved to the hallway door, listening to something upstairs.

"Stay put," he said over his shoulder, before following the girl's example and heading for the second floor.

On the top landing, he could more clearly hear Peggy's voice speaking in an urgent whisper, down a short hallway and behind a partially closed door. He approached it quietly and pushed it open.

Before him, sitting on the edge of her bed, Peggy was talking into a phone. She raised her eyes to his as he filled the doorway, her expression so much like a child's in trouble that he had to smile.

"Calling Gino?" he asked.

She paled visibly. For a moment, he thought she might even try to hide the phone behind her back. Instead, she ducked her head slightly, as if for privacy, said, "Never mind. No message," into the receiver, and reluctantly hung up.

"I couldn't get him," she admitted.

Joe leaned against the doorjamb. "You didn't have to come up here to do that. We wouldn't have stopped you making a call.

For that matter, we can leave, if you want."

She seemed on the verge of tears. "How much trouble is he in?"

Joe decided to play it straight, within limits. "It's looking pretty bad."

"Did he kill someone or something?"

"Why do you ask that? Has he ever been violent around you?"

She shook her head. "No, not ever. He's always very sweet."

"But . . . ," Joe suggested.

"No, no. No buts. It's just that I could see him getting angry at someone if he was pushed."

"He has," he reassured her. "I think you already know that in your heart."

He crossed the room and sat beside her, leaving a couple of feet between them. She was dressed in a skirt and a white button-down blouse, but as utterly sensual as that had made her appear downstairs, it now enhanced her seeming innocence.

Joe reached out and squeezed her hand briefly. "We're not here to hurt you, Peggy, but I also don't want to lie to you."

She wiped a tear from her eye. "I've never loved anybody so much."

"It happens a lot," he said philosophically. "People are rarely all bad or all good, and they rarely reveal themselves entirely to the ones who love them. I guess maybe sometimes they're being self-protective, but it can be the other way around, too — they just don't want to hurt who they care about the most. But whichever way it is with Gino," he added, looking directly into her eyes, "the fact remains that he's broken the law and brought some real heartbreak to others. I'm not here to judge him, Peggy, and I'm sure not here to wag my finger at the two of you. But make no mistake about it — I will do everything I can to hold him accountable."

She was crying openly by now, making him feel at once guilty and hopeful.

"Do you have those postcards?" he asked gently.

Without a word, she reached into her night table drawer and withdrew a small bundle of glossy cards. She was still holding them when the phone rang.

As she leaned over to answer it, he relieved her of the cards.

"Hello?" she asked in a tremulous voice.

Joe could hear a man's voice on the other end, although not what he was saying. He began nonchalantly leafing through the cards, a collection of unremarkable nature shots, for the most part — mountains, animals, a few with historic buildings. They were from all over the eastern seacoast.

"The police are here," she said. "They say you've done something bad . . . I don't know. They haven't told me . . . Yes, they're still here . . . No, no . . . Gino, I haven't told them anything. I don't have anything *to* tell them. I don't even know what they're talking about . . . I'm sorry, I'm sorry . . . I'll do it right now . . . Can you come over? Please. I'm really upset . . . Okay, okay."

She covered the phone with her hand and looked apologetically at Joe. "I'm really sorry, but you all have to leave."

Joe put the postcards down on the bed and stood up. "Can I ask you one favor?"

She was clearly unhappy with that, but he spoke anyway. "It's only to be careful. People in love do things they sometimes regret. Please, next time you two are together, ask him what's going on."

The voice on the phone squawked again, and now looking confused, she turned toward it and answered, "I did, Gino. They're leaving now. I told them."

She looked up at Joe. "He wants me to see you out — make sure you're gone."

Joe nodded. "Fine with me."

She put the phone down on the bed and escorted him back downstairs to the entranceway, where he stuck his head into the living room and announced, "Gino's on the phone upstairs. We've been officially thrown out."

The other two silently got up and filed out the front door. Joe hesitated on the threshold and looked back at Peggy. "Think about what I said, okay? You've got a full life ahead of you."

She smiled sadly, as if she was already beyond believing such things. "Thank you. You're a nice man," she said, and closed the door on them.

Willy leered at him. "Ooh. Got lucky?"

Joe ignored his most obvious meaning. "Yeah. One of Gino's postcards was mailed from Vermont."

The cell phone clipped to Lil's belt went off. She answered it, exchanged a few sentences, and hung up.

"That was Silva. He thought we'd like to know: Santo Massi was just picked up in a Dumpster with a bullet in his head."

"Gee," Willy reacted. "That didn't take 'em long."

"Gino?" Lil asked Joe.

Joe pushed his lower lip out thoughtfully. "Could be. Santo broke the cardinal rule, talking to us. Could be it was just an example."

"Still," she suggested, "we could roust him and play Twenty Questions, just to keep him off balance."

Joe gazed up the street for a moment. "If you're talking about getting under his skin, we might as well stick with the plan: Let's have a chat with his wife next."

CHAPTER 19

Gino was angrier than either Dante Lagasso or Tito had ever seen him. He was pacing back and forth in the now closed social club from where Tito had taken Santo for the last ride of his life.

"Who the fuck is this Joe Gunther? You told me Vermont was hayseed country — bunch of Deputy Dawgs — in and out with no problem. Now the son of a bitch is fucking up my life."

Lagasso was stirring a small cup of coffee. "I'm not the one who killed someone."

Gino stared at him. "How the hell was I supposed to know the kid would get horny for some goddamn cow in the middle of the night?"

Lagasso shrugged. "Shit happens."

Gino returned to pacing. "Shit happens. That's the best you can do? Quote a bumper sticker? You're supposed to check these deals out, Dante."

"They looked solid," Lagasso said placidly.

"Solid?" Gino exploded. "Is that why you

had Santo whacked? You steered me into swampland, Dante."

"Santo's different. He was overdue for a correction. I'll give you that. The Vermont cop figuring him out so fast just means he's good at his job. Look, you're not the only one with problems. Santo screwed me up, too, connecting Johnny to me. We're all just gonna have to weather this out. Shouldn't be a big deal, now he's dead. Once they finish buzzing around, they'll figure out they got nothin'."

"Right," Gino said bitterly. "And in the meantime, my life is a fuckin' nightmare." He pointed at Lagasso. "And you're carrying some of the freight for that."

Lagasso ran out of patience. He glanced at Tito, who slowly rose from the seat he'd been occupying in the room's far corner.

Gino instantly read the body language. He held up his hand apologetically. "Okay, okay. I'm sorry. I know I fucked up. I didn't mean it, all right? I'm just a little upset."

Lagasso moved his finger ever so slightly, and Tito sat back down, his expression unchanged.

"It's not the first time the cops have come sniffing around," Lagasso said.

"It's the first time they've visited my girl-friend and then gone yapping to my wife, for Chrissake. I've been shut out of my own house. She changed the fucking lock."

"The girlfriend didn't take you in?"

"That's not the point. It's my house."

"You got caught fooling around. Bad luck."

Gino ran his hands through his hair, staring at the ceiling. "I could kill that cop."

"Not a great idea. Why not just settle down with the girl? You never liked the wife anyhow. Times are different. People won't care."

Gino stabbed himself in the chest several times. "I care. It's a matter of pride. I do good work — clean work. I'm known for it. I worked hard for that reputation. It means something to me that people know I been thrown out of my house and forced to live someplace else, all because of some screwup."

"You're making too much of it," Lagasso said, sounding bored. "You're crazy about the girlfriend, the wife is crazy about your money. Everything'll work out. Enjoy playing house while you can."

Gino stared at the wall for a while, breathing hard, trying to control his anger.

"Goddamn John Fucking Samuel Gregory," he finally said. "He started all this. It's always the rich guys that'll cause you a world of shit. Be nice to repay the favor for once."

Lagasso was done for the night. He admired Gino for his abilities and didn't mind the finder's fees he generated. But the guy could be a pain — thin-skinned and quick to blame everyone else for his problems.

"Go home and get laid, Gino. Things'll look better in the morning."

"Hey."

"Hey, yourself," Gail responded, her voice tinny and distant over the telephone line. "How're things in Sin City?"

"Close — they actually call this the Brick City."

She laughed. "Ow. That doesn't sound like much fun. I thought every city was brick — sounds like it should be a metaphor for something."

"According to Willy, the whole place is a metaphor for Murphy's Law."

"Is that true for what you're doing down there, too?"

Joe was in his motel room, as he was so often when he called her from the road, with the curtains open and the lamps off, watching an urban kaleidoscope of lights flitting across the walls.

"No, not really," he answered, not bothering with details. "We're making headway. It's hard when you're dealing with crooks of the Italian persuasion. Pretty close-mouthed bunch. How're things with you?"

"Actually," she conceded, "they may be livelier here than they are down there. This battle between the pro-GMOs and the antis is really heating up. We've had a few arrests on the capitol building steps."

"You're kidding. I thought you were locking horns with a bunch of big-business lobbyists."

"Oh, no. I even got handed a threatening note, and that was before things got exciting."

His attention sharpened suddenly. "What kind of note?"

"Ah, damn," she exclaimed. "I knew I shouldn't have mentioned it. I wasn't going to, either. It just slipped out. It's nothing, Joe. A slip of paper. I don't even know how it ended up in my hand. People give me stuff all the time."

"What did it say?"

"Something about how I'd better not

play with fire. That's not it, exactly, but close enough."

Joe felt a chill go through him at the phrasing. " 'Fire' was the word used?"

"Yes, why?"

"Just a coincidence — the case I'm working on. When did this happen?"

"Joe, before you get all Sherlock Holmes on me, it was no big deal. You should see the chaos around here. The building's packed every day. All the committee meetings have been moved to the big room, which isn't big enough. The phone rings all the time, the mail is almost arriving in boxes, and emotions are running very hot. One little message is nothing in comparison. I wish I hadn't brought it up."

"It's okay," he soothed her. "Did you at least mention it to anyone?"

"Like one of your boys in blue? No. It didn't deserve that much attention. And before you ask, no, I haven't gotten anything else like it."

He decided to change the subject, sensing in her voice less an assuaging of concern than a tone of impatience. "How's the battle going?"

"Frustrating. You'd think in this state, at least, there'd be more support for the organics and traditionalists, especially since a lot of the organics are going that way purely for the money. Some of them are about as crunchy-granola as Adolf Hitler."

"He was a vegetarian."

It was the wrong quip at the wrong time.

"Not funny. You get my point," Gail said tersely. "The bottom line is, the dumb bastards calling the shots at the state level don't seem to have any idea that Vermont isn't Kansas or Ohio. And when people like me point out what should be as obvious as shit on their shoes, all we get is corporate-speak and lame one-liners."

Joe opened his mouth to apologize, when he suddenly reconsidered. His joke hadn't deserved such anger. She knew he was agreeable to most of her positions, especially this one, since they'd already discussed it. He'd merely been made the whipping boy for her pent-up frustration. Reasonably, the apology, if she cared to make it, was hers.

She didn't.

After a long and awkward silence, she said, "Well, it's getting late and I still have work to do. Good night, Joe. Stay safe."

The line went dead.

He held the phone for a few seconds

more, his eyes on the ceiling. "You, too," he said softly.

At the far end of that dead phone line, Gail sat on the sofa in her condominium living room, paying no attention to the nighttime view of Montpelier's distant lights, fanned out like luminescent spray from the dominant beacon of the gold-topped capitol building.

She'd been rude and preachy and self-centered with him. She'd felt interrupted in midwork when he called, irritated when he predictably focused on the threatening note, and angry when he joked about an issue that was consuming her every waking hour.

She pressed the tips of her fingers against her temples briefly, closing her eyes. What was happening? It wasn't him. He was as stolid as ever — reliable, supportive, loyal, and kind. Nothing if not predictable. He'd given her no reason to act the way she had.

And why had she lied about not getting any more threats? She opened her eyes and looked over at the second slip of paper she'd received, just two days ago, lying like a curled-up leaf in the center of her coffee table. "Back off or pay the price," it read.

The way she was feeling now, those words had more meaning than their writer could have ever imagined.

Farther north still, in the tiny, somewhat hardscrabble village of St. Albans Bay, just a mile or so west of St. Albans proper, John Samuel Gregory unlocked the door to his upscale condo and tossed his keys onto the table by the lamp. He paused to admire once more what the lighting revealed — dark-painted walls, expensive carpeting, modern furniture, and recessed spots. He liked this place. The whole area was a dead-end, hayseed, hole-in-the-wall dump. The people were total woodchucks, as dumb as they were gullible. And the women were as easy to impress as kids craving ice cream — and most of them about that experienced in the sack. But this apartment was just right — big, new, well laid out, and with a great view of the bay and the lake beyond — a miracle, given the other buildings in town. Within its distinctly urbanized confines, he could reach back to what he'd enjoyed before his banishment here, and imagine what comforts lay ahead once his plans became reality.

He walked down the hallway and entered the cavernous living room/dining room/kitchen combination, slipping off his designer jacket and draping it over the back of a chair in passing, heading for a side table laden with liquor bottles and crystal glassware. He mixed himself a Scotch on the rocks — the Glenlivet, only, thank you — and wandered over to one of the leather armchairs facing the view. It was dark, of course, past midnight, but there were pinpricks of light always visible, from down both arms of the bay's embrace — twinklings from other houses and from the occasional passing boat.

He was feeling pretty good, even with the reaming he'd gotten from Clark Wolff earlier that day. He'd told the old man where to get off, of course. He wasn't going to take any crap from a sorry loser like that. But, in fact, he hadn't been as pissed as he'd let on. He had the old man dead to rights, after all — he'd bought the damn properties, even if he had done it on the sly. And as for any "improprieties," as Clark had put it, both he and the cops could shove them where the sun didn't shine. Suspicions were just that without proof. And as far as Johnny could tell, nobody had anything close to proof.

He took a meditative sip and stared out

into the darkness. The lights in this part of the room were dimmed almost to extinction, allowing him a view out the window with minimal reflection.

Not that he could afford to be careless, of course. The cops were working up a lather, talking to everyone they could find. Johnny was confident but not foolish. He didn't have any direct way to contact the torch — that son of a bitch hadn't even given him his name — but he would call Dante in the morning, just to make sure that end of things was covered.

Johnny frowned. He really could have done without these complications. It had all started out so well. Like injecting those cows with penicillin — not bad for a city boy — or even better, the old coot and the tractor. That had really been fun, skulking around in the dark, rigging the brake lines like he'd practiced in that garage near the interstate. He'd sort of felt like James Bond. And when the old guy had killed himself good and proper in the crash, nobody had been the wiser.

But the fun was definitely fading.

Johnny took another swallow. Maybe things weren't so goddamned rosy, after all. Since the cops had talked to Wolff, they sure as hell wouldn't take long to get to him — or to turn his life inside out. That wouldn't hold up to too much scrutiny. Then word would leak out, the papers would grab hold, and, all of a sudden, it might not be quite so easy to pull off the scheme they were shooting for.

He squinted slightly, concentrating on the dark void ahead of him, visualizing a string of lights from the fantasy bridge spanning the black water. Christ, what a plan. And, my God, what a pile of money.

There was a movement outside, a ghostly shifting of sorts, floating in the air before him. Gregory sat forward slightly, trying to distinguish between the darkness, the slight reflection in the glass, and his own imagination.

He saw it again and suddenly realized it had nothing to do with the view or the lake or anything outside. It was a shape, a human being, coming up behind him fast and sure, and as he watched, frozen in the split second in which all this occurred, he recognized as in a flash photograph what the figure was carrying in its upraised hand. It was a hook on a handle, used on boxes or hay bales or animal carcasses.

And he watched in helpless disbelief as it came down upon his head.

CHAPTER 20

Lil hung up the phone and stared moodily out her window. "Damn."

"What?" asked Willy, sitting in her office with Joe by his side.

"Still no Gino," she said. "We've got people on his house, at the docks, at all the social clubs we know about, and at Peggy's, but nothing so far. He might've left town. God knows, he probably has a dozen places to call home, after all the time he's spent on the road."

"What did you get on Santo's murder?" Joe asked. "Maybe there's something there that could help us."

Ben Silva was leaning against the doorjamb, listening in. "The Murder Squad's got it," he said. "But they're already smelling a cold case in the making. The guy was dumped in the trash, he owed money to everybody, he was a risk to all his old buddies, and he had filthy enough habits that he still might've been killed by a pissed-off stranger who wanted a hit off his needle. I doubt we're going to get much from that direction."

"Sounds like we're wasting time here," Willy said, confirming Joe's suspicion that his colleague was ready to head home.

"Maybe not," Joe said quietly.

"What're you thinking of?" Lil asked.

"I don't want to step out of line," he said. "Willy and I are on foreign ground, after all. Gino's become a live case for you, and our interest in him has got to play second fiddle. I understand that. Still, when I was talking to Peggy, I felt like we connected."

"You want to knock on her door?" Silva asked. "Pick up where you left off?"

"In a way," Joe admitted. "I don't see where it can hurt, except, of course, for the change of status I just mentioned."

Silva made a face and looked at Lil. "You have a problem sending him in, assuming she'll open the door?"

He suddenly asked Joe, "Can she go in with you?"

But Lil answered that. "No. Probably better he fly solo. I don't have any objections."

"He's good at the touchy-feely stuff," Willy said out of the blue.

Silva shrugged. "A little unorthodox, but it works for me. It's not like we won't be right outside. For that matter, we could wire you. You run into trouble, all you have to do is shout."

"I'm okay with that," Joe agreed.

Lil stood up. "Let's do it, then."

An hour later, Lil, Joe, and Willy pulled up opposite Peggy's house in the Iron-bound. Another suspiciously nondescript car was already parked nearby.

"Cool," Willy commented. "Undercover. Almost like it's a secret."

Lil laughed as she killed the engine. "Yeah. Well, we tried painting 'Normal Ci-vilian Vehicle' on the doors, but the bad guys figured it out."

She turned toward Joe and patted the wireless receiver on the seat between them. "You all set?" She hooked a small headset over her ear.

He fumbled under his shirt and turned on the mike taped to his chest. "Test, test, test."

"Loud and clear," she said. "You're good to go."

"Have fun," Willy said from the back.

Joe got out, checked for traffic, and crossed the street. He climbed the now fa-miliar stoop and rang the doorbell. After a minute, the door opened and revealed Peggy DeAngelis, this time dressed in jeans and a sweatshirt, and sporting a bruise above her left cheekbone.

Joe's face fell. "Peggy, I'm so sorry. I know I'm to blame for that."

"It was an accident," she said defensively.

"It was, in a way," he agreed. "You didn't plan on my coming into your life and causing trouble."

"Well, you did and you still are," she answered, her eyes welling up. "What are you *doing* here?"

"Trying to right a wrong. I'd like to find Gino and start sorting this out."

"You want to arrest him."

"Only if I have to, Peggy. I'd like to talk to him first. Right now all we have is a bunch of questions, suppositions, whatever you want to call them. But they need confirmation, and only Gino can help us there. For all we know, he might be able to set us on a whole new track, but we won't know till we can talk."

She shook her head, her arms crossed over her chest. "I don't know."

He faked a shiver, although it wasn't that cold. "Let me in, Peggy. We can discuss this. You can ask me anything you want."

"I'm not supposed to do that."

"And you're going to let that stop you from doing what's right?"

She stamped her foot in frustration. "I don't *know* what's right. I only know what everybody else wants."

He tried soothing her. "That's true. I understand that you're feeling pushed around. I would be, too, in your shoes. That's why I think it would help if we sat down and talked about it a little, just to see if we can clear things up."

But apparently, through some inner process of her own, she'd reached a different conclusion. She stepped back from the open door and prepared to close it. "I'm sorry. I don't believe you. You just want me to tell you where he is, and then you want to arrest him. You'll have to leave. I'm sorry."

She shut the door, although his last glance of her told him she was as unsure of herself as ever.

He returned to the car and settled into the passenger seat, switching off the mike. "No go," he said simply.

"Yeah," Willy said. "We heard you, Romeo. Any other bright ideas, or can we throw in the towel and go home?"

Lil cast a glance over her shoulder at him. "Running out of gas?"

"Something like that."

She looked at Gunther. "What *would* you like to do?"

He pointed out the window. "I'd like to follow her."

The other two looked in the direction he indicated. A small red Mini Cooper had appeared in the alley beside the house. At the wheel, wearing dark glasses, was a still-unmistakable Peggy DeAngelis.

"Oh, shit," Lil murmured, switching on the ignition and then fumbling for her radio. "Eight-A-two to eight-A-six. She's in motion, guys. Heads up."

The undercover car down the street stayed still and silent.

Lil checked for traffic as the little car zipped out of the alley and sped away toward Market Street.

"What the hell are they doing?" she asked, finally cutting a car off with a screech of tires in order to make a U-turn.

"Eight-A-two to eight-A-six. Get your asses moving. You're on an empty house," she yelled into the radio before chucking it aside.

Willy checked out the rear window as they pulled away at high speed, trying to catch up. "They're waking up," he reported. "Coming after us."

But Lil didn't care any longer. Both hands on the wheel, she was just trying to keep Peggy's car in sight.

Whatever else could be said about Peggy DeAngelis, she was a fast and sure driver, weaving in and out of traffic as if it were standing still. Surely, inexorably, Lil began losing ground.

"How 'bout calling in extra units?" Joe suggested. "You know she's going to meet him."

"Movie stuff," she said shortly. "Besides, we don't know any such thing. For all we can tell, she's pulling us off so he can leave the house and go someplace else." Lil made an abrupt evasive move, almost hitting a car that was easing out of a parking space. "Damn, she's fast. Push comes to shove, I'll get her for speeding."

"You think he was hiding in the house?" Joe asked.

"Don't be dumb, boss," Willy suggested, trying not to fall over in the back. "It was a hypothetical."

"Like what he said," Lil confirmed, gunning through a gap between two cars ahead of her and then stamping on the brakes to avoid hitting a pedestrian.

They were near Newark's center, where

the courthouse on its slight rise lorded over a commingling of major streets. As the light ahead turned red and traffic bunched up before them, they lost all sight of the Mini.

"She at the light?" Lil asked.

"I don't know," Joe answered, craning to see.

"Hang on," Willy ordered, and before either one of them could speak, he was out of the car and trotting up ahead on foot.

He didn't bother cutting over to the sidewalk, but stayed among the cars, hoping to use them for cover. The effort was in vain. Her vehicle was so small that by the time he discovered it at the very front of the pack, he was close enough that he had to stop dead in his tracks. But his movement drew her attention. Through her back window, he could see her eyes lock onto his via her rearview mirror, and he knew he'd been burned.

Without hesitation, as if responding to an electrical jolt, Peggy's car sprang from its place in line and shot straight into the busy intersection, the epitome of its driver's pure adrenaline.

But that's where her luck ran out. Her skill perhaps hampered by seeing the one cop who'd really scared her earlier, she collided first with one car, then with another, like a pinball running free, and finally, spinning and spraying bits of glass and debris, she was catapulted into the space between the front and rear tires of a tanker truck carrying gasoline, which was immediately hit by a bus.

Willy watched, stunned and stationary, surrounded by an audience of cars filled with transfixed onlookers as caught by this sudden chaos as if a volcano had suddenly erupted right before them.

The sounds of metal and glass and rubber subsided briefly, enough that for an instant, Willy distinctly heard the cheerful chirping of a distant bird, before the first shouts began rising from all around.

But Willy stayed rooted in place, still watching what was left of Peggy's tiny red car. He could see her moving slightly through a twisted side window, her long hair shifting in a shaft of sunlight. But by the same light, he could see a sparkle of liquid freely flowing from above her — from the body of the punctured gas tanker.

"Stand back," he yelled at the people approaching the crash site. "It's going to blow."

But, of course, nobody listened. He probably looked like a deranged cripple, standing in the middle of the street, surrounded by cars, waving his one arm.

The explosion, ignited by Peggy's overheated engine, began as an air-sucking whoosh, but then blew out with full force, picking up people and tossing them through the air, and sending Willy staggering back, covering his face against the heat blast, until he collided with Joe, who'd come running up behind him.

"Jesus Christ," Joe said, catching his colleague by the shoulders. "What the hell happened?"

The initial fireball quickly faded back to a roaring column of white-hot intensity, looking as if the earth's molten core had burst through the crust in a single shaft, heading right for the sky.

"She saw me," Willy said simply, sounding as small and abashed as he'd been irascible back at her town house.

Joe was startled by his subdued tone of voice. "What? Are you okay?"

"She saw me," he repeated in a stunned monotone. "Tried to run."

Joe stared at him as Willy continued looking at the fiery tangle of cars and trucks and people. Around them, sirens began closing in from afar, offset by a few horn blasts from motorists who didn't know what had happened. In that sudden, vulnerable moment, Joe realized that Willy had been as struck by Peggy DeAngelis as Joe had been — by her beauty, her youth, her clear, almost breathtaking innocence. But where Joe had engaged her by talking, Willy had done just the opposite, as if she represented a threat to him personally.

Joe squeezed Willy's shoulders, at one with his friend's sense of loss, the memory of this vibrant young woman so clear in his mind.

He wanted to say something useful, far beyond soothing, but he was hard put to speak at all. Transfixed by the white-hot flames, knowing who lay in their embrace, having spoken with her and yearned for her safety mere minutes ago, he was trapped by a paralyzing stupor of futility, waste, and guilt.

For he and the man beside him, as they'd done before to uncountable others over the years, had brought confusion and fear to Peggy DeAngelis. Who knew why she'd run just now and placed herself finally in the middle of this inferno? Where there was no doubt whatsoever was that Joe's appearance in her life had marked the beginning of the end.

He glanced at Willy's pale, suddenly vulnerable profile. If but a few of those same thoughts were presently going through his head — especially commingling with his earlier harsh words to her — it was no surprise why this should hit him so hard.

"Come on," he urged. "We better get back to the car. Find a way out of here."

Tito's voice came through the closed door. "Gino. You up?"

Gino was using one of the Outfit's houses they were sure the cops knew nothing about, in an upstairs apartment he borrowed whenever he needed to lie low.

He was stretched out on his bed, reading a magazine, wishing to hell he could be someplace else, preferably with Peggy.

"What d'you want?"

"Got a phone call."

Gino sat up slowly. Only a couple of people knew where he was — trusted people he'd assigned to watch both his home and Peggy's place.

"Who from?"

"Fredo."

That meant Peggy's. He slid his feet off the bed, got up, and crossed over to the door. When he opened it, Tito towered over him, a cordless phone clutched in one meaty hand.

Gino took the phone. "Thanks."

Tito faded from view like a ghost, always amazingly quiet.

"What?" Gino asked the phone.

"I got bad news," said a disembodied voice.

Gino scowled. "And I'm supposed to guess what it is?"

"It's Peggy," Fredo conceded, abandoning his plan to be subtle. "She's dead."

Gino felt his heart lurch. His body tingling and numb, he reached out for the nearest wall.

"What do you mean?"

"She was killed in a car crash. I'm real sorry."

"A car crash? What the fuck are you saying?" Gino slapped the wall with his hand. "What the fuck was she doing in a car? I told her to stay put, where I could find her. You stupid son of a bitch, talk to me."

"That cop came to visit her — the one you told me about — and right after, she drove off, real fast. I don't know why. Maybe to lead them off, maybe 'cause she was scared. But that's how it happened. She peeled outta there, they took off after her, and *bam.* She got hit by a gas truck."

"A gas truck? What kind of gas truck?"

There was a confused pause at the other end. "Like what brand?"

What should have infuriated Gino merely sent him slowly sliding down the wall until he was sitting on the floor. There was a loud humming inside his head.

"What type of gas, Fredo?" He spoke quietly.

"Gasoline," Fredo said with relief, happy to have the answer. "She burned to death."

There was dead silence as both men were brought up short — Fredo by the realization of what he'd just said almost cheerily, and Gino by the excruciating irony of the nature of Peggy's death.

"That cop," Gino finally said, hearing his own voice as if it were coming from far off. "Was it the older one?"

"Yeah, Gino," Fredo said nervously. "The one you said was from Vermont — who talked to her before."

Gino didn't respond.

"You there?" Fredo asked.

"Joe Gunther."

Fredo hesitated before asking, "What? Oh . . . yeah. Are you okay?"

No answer.

Fredo tried again. "Sorry. Dumb. I mean, is there anything I can do to help?"

"Did you kill him after he killed Peggy?"

Fredo was clearly stumped this time. Having been there, he knew Gunther hadn't even seen the accident and that Peggy had caused it herself. Finally, for want of a more self-protective answer, he risked admitting, "No."

"Then forget about it," Gino said flatly, his voice dull. "I'll do it myself."

Gino wasn't the only one receiving bad news by phone. At last back in flowing traffic, two hours following the crash, and heading toward the arson task force office, Joe answered his cell phone.

"Gunther."

"Joe, it's Jonathon Michael."

"What've you got?" Already, Joe's apprehension rose. There was something about the younger man's voice that told him to prepare for the worst.

"Kind of a weird development, to be honest. John Samuel Gregory was found dead in his condo a couple of hours ago."

"Dead how?" Joe asked, his wording catching Willy's attention.

"Dead murdered," Jonathon answered. "So far, we can't figure out who did it or what was used, but he has a good-size hole in the top of his head, like somebody hammered him with a railroad spike."

"Wild guess," Joe suggested, "you have no clue."

"Nothing," Jonathon admitted.

"Who do you have on it?"

"Right now it's Tim and me. The forensic team is still here, collecting stuff."

Joe was already shaking his head. "Jonathon, you need more help. You've got three arsons, two homicides, maybe a third if the tractor accident was intentional. Not to mention possible flimflamming by the Realtors, with all the legal mumbo jumbo that implies."

"I hear you, Joe. I've been calling around. More people'll be coming in, but they got to clear their decks first. We're talking maybe a couple of days before I can rally a team."

"Get hold of Sammie Martens, then," Joe urged. "She may be in the far corner of the state, but I happen to know she's got a light load, and she'd be perfect for this. Until the others show up, at least, it should help. You don't have time to wait."

"You got it. Will do."

Joe hesitated a moment, thinking back to what had happened so far in Newark — the deaths of Santo and Peggy, Gino's vanishing act, the fact that neither Tito nor Dante Lagasso would ever open up, at least not before bevies of lawyers had earned their keep. Aside from a few useful facts, this little field trip had garnered nothing but disaster.

And considering the present mess, it was unlikely that Joe and Willy would be allowed much more room to move. Farber and Ben Silva were deep into it now, and their tolerance for these previously laughed-at Vermonters would be wearing thin.

Finally, there was the most nagging consideration of all: If John Gregory — the presumed instigator of this whole string of events — had been murdered, then who killed him? And why? The evidence linking a Newark arsonist to Gregory was circumstantial at best. Had chasing it also made Joe miss a far more complicated scenario than a lucrative, if bloody-minded, land deal? It was certainly looking that way.

Had Joe dropped the ball big-time?

"I'm coming home, too," he suddenly added. "With reinforcements."

"You done down there?" Jonathon asked, surprised.

"That's one way to put it."

CHAPTER 21

A beautiful view, Joe thought. Soothing, tranquil, encouraging of meditation. The setting sun cast the distant Adirondacks into bold relief and made the calm waters of St. Albans Bay look like a mirror framed by the flat, forested land of its cradling U-shaped shore.

A far cry from Newark's tangled, crowded, sharp-angled bristle.

"You all right, boss?" a soft female voice asked from near his shoulder.

He turned away from the picture window to gaze upon the scene behind him. A large, modern, urban-style condo, something out of a men's magazine for the upwardly mobile, swinging single male living in an anonymous metropolitan center.

Except, of course, for the blood.

"Yeah, Sam," Joe said to her. "Just wondering what the hell's going on, is all."

"We'll figure it out," she said supportively, and quickly moved over to one of the lab technicians, who was putting away his equipment after a full day of trace evidence collection. Joe watched her at work — earnest, high-strung, responsible to a fault, constantly worried she might let something slip, Sammie Martens was as dedicated to her job as a bloodhound in pursuit.

And for all of that, she was also as vulnerable, insecure, and in need of praise as a child being judged by her elders. He'd often thought that her romantic connection to Willy Kunkle was either the most counterintuitive of lifesaving medicines or a recipe for disaster. Two more volatile personalities he was hard put to imagine, and yet, by now, they'd already been together for several years.

Joe continued surveying the scene — the designer chair facing the window, the blood down its back and covering the floor behind it. The body had long since been removed for autopsy in nearby Burlington, but it was clear what had happened. Joe could almost see, as if they were visible, the killer's footsteps as he'd entered the large room from the hallway, approached the chair across a rug-covered, silent floor, and killed John Gregory where he sat.

Whoever he was, he'd been in here before, Joe ventured. And he'd had a key.

Sam reapproached, her conversation

with the technician concluded. "What do you think?"

"Not a stranger killing," Joe said. "You up to snuff on what's been going on?"

She nodded once, sharply, a tiny reflection of her military past. "Jonathon filled me in on the local background, and I managed to squeeze just enough out of Willy to hear that things didn't turn out too well in Newark."

"You could say that," Joe admitted ruefully.

She digested that before asking, "Did anyone besides Clark Wolff and Gregory know they were working a land deal together?"

"Not that Wolff will admit to or knows about. That was the whole point of the secrecy."

"And as far as we can tell," she continued, "Gregory hasn't pissed anyone off a whole lot since he's been here."

Joe half smiled. "Well, I've clearly got some reservations now. But no, you're right. So far, we don't know of any run-ins."

Sam was nodding to herself, her brain in overdrive. "On the other hand, you lost track of Famolare what? A day or two ago? Plenty of time for him to drive up here and do the dirty."

Joe couldn't disagree. He'd considered it himself. "For what reason, though?"

"He might've thought Gregory squealed on him." She pointed at the chair. "That he pointed you in Gino's direction. That would've explained why you were in Newark checking him out."

"Could be," Joe conceded. "Seems a little extreme. Wasn't the first time the police had sniffed up his pant leg."

"Except that we don't know what kind of relationship the two of them had."

Joe pushed his lips out contemplatively and lowered his chin to his chest. "I'm not sure what we know anymore." He let out a sigh and straightened his back suddenly, eyeing the hallway to the front door. "Guess it's time to see what forensics has to offer."

The office of Vermont's chief medical examiner was buried on the edge of Burlington in the middle of a concrete maze, otherwise named the Fletcher Allen Health Center. A new facility, hard-won and much appreciated by its occupants, the so-called OCME was a far cry from its prior self, tucked away in the basement, just off from the loading docks. It did have, however, a couple of eccentricities: a row of pleasantly appointed windows, each with a myopic view of a concrete wall, and a set of directions that made finding it at the end of a perplexing tangle of hallways and elevators a challenge of orienteering.

The health center was undergoing change, as it had been for years. In a seemingly random process, suggestive of the workings of an unsupervised, dinosaur-size, ADD child, the controlling powers of a massive reconstruction project had pulled down walls of the old hospital, erected others that had left heads shaking in wonder, started building garages that no one had budgeted, and otherwise worked to sow chaos where on paper — a long time ago — there'd once been an organized, well-designed, and reasonably priced renewal plan. By the time Joe pulled into the parking lot and began the standard odyssey of finding his destination, the cost overruns were legendary, the accusations of at least incompetence too numerous to count, and the changes of management evocative of the proverbial revolving door.

Whenever he successfully reached the ME's, Joe always felt like a small boat that had finally found harbor in bad weather.

The feeling was enhanced by the personality of the woman in charge, Dr. Beverly Hillstrom, who had been the chief medical examiner for over twenty years. A no-nonsense tall blonde with a frightening intolerance for laziness, incompetence, or any show of disrespect, she was also very responsive to all forms of perseverance, dedication, and courtesy.

She and Joe were a matched set.

After changing into some pale green scrubs, Joe was allowed by the administrative assistant to find his way down the gleaming hallway to the autopsy room at the end, he being a regular enough presence here to be considered part of the family.

There, standing opposite one of her ubiquitous assistants on loan from the medical school, Dr. Hillstrom was gazing down at the prostrate body of the late John Gregory, a scalpel poised in her right hand.

She looked up at Joe's appearance.

"Special Agent Gunther," she said, smiling in welcome. The two of them, despite a fifteen-year friendship, always referred to each other by title, which struck him as eccentric, although it clearly pleased her.

He gave her a slightly mocking bow. "Dr. Hillstrom."

She in turn inclined her head toward the student. "Maria Carlita from Argentina. This is Special Agent Joseph Gunther from the Vermont Bureau of Investigation."

Joe and the young woman exchanged nods, handshakes at autopsies being occasionally awkward.

"I would ask to what I owe the pleasure," Hillstrom continued, "but I have a sneaking suspicion he's lying right here."

"You've got that right," Joe agreed, stepping up to the table and looking down at the cadaver. It had been opened up like an unzipped canvas bag, its contents largely removed, and the top of its head had just been removed like an oversize yarmulke, revealing a bloodstained brain. This process was done by first cutting the scalp from ear to ear over the top of the head — so that later the mortician would have no visible incisions to deal with — and then peeling the remarkably rubber-like face down and under the chin to reveal the cranium.

"Well," she said brightly, "your timing couldn't be better."

As well he recognized. The next step in this procedure was to extract the brain and move it to a side table for closer scrutiny, which is why Hillstrom currently had the scalpel in her gloved hand.

"So far," she continued, "all we've found is a normal, healthy, otherwise untraumatized young male. Of course, we won't know anything about his blood chemistry for some time, but I saw no indications of any chronic abuse."

After a few quick and expert swipes with her knife, which use she made sure Maria Carlita noted, Hillstrom cradled the brain in her cupped hands.

"What you saw at the scene is all there is, as far as I know," she said, placing the brain on a scale reminiscent of old-time grocery stores, reminding Joe of how many items in this room might come from local hardware and restaurant supply outlets. "A single blow to the head with a long, pointed object."

Hillstrom recorded the brain's weight before transferring it to a work surface beside the sink, where she proceeded to slice it in sections with a large knife, from the outside in, parallel to the axis of injury. Joe watched, intrigued, his imagination conjuring up the picture of a cake being cut away until the track of a single candle could be revealed from the side.

Sure enough, after a series of cuts, Hillstrom reached the traumatized area, where they both could appreciate how something long and pointed had penetrated the brain to about three inches.

"Any guesses on what was used?" Joe asked.

She cast him a sideward glance. "You know better than that, Agent Gunther. I will tell you it was rounded, tapered, and slightly curved. If that helps."

"Curved?"

She used the tip of the carving knife as a pointer. "Follow the arc of the blow. This is the brain's front. Impact came from behind and above. Taking note of the distribution of small bone fragments and the bruising, and factoring in the natural swing of an arm coming down as it might while splitting a log, you can see how the lethal object had a distinct hook to it."

"He used a hook?" Joe asked.

This time she straightened. "Someone did, yes. I have no idea of the assailant's gender. I might be willing to add, under the heading of probabilities only, however, that the assault was from a person using their right hand."

"Nifty," Joe said with a small laugh. "So we're looking for someone with a hook for a right hand. That should narrow things down."

The tiniest of furrows appeared between Hillstrom's eyebrows.

"It was a joke," he explained.

She shook her head. "No. That was clear. I was considering the possibility. That *could* be the case — a hooked prosthesis."

"I think I'll stick with a baling hook for the moment," Joe told her. "I'm keeping pirates for last."

Hillstrom didn't laugh, which came as no surprise. Instead, she crossed over to another work surface, where she'd placed the top of the skull, now hairless, clean, and brutally punctured with a single, slightly splintered hole.

"The two things that steer me away from a prosthetic," she persisted, "are the depth of the injury, which is deeper than the standard hook-as-hand replacement, and this." She picked up a small square of something pale, bristly, and vaguely suggestive of a thin slice of hairy cheddar cheese, if slightly more flexible. It, too, had a hole in it.

"This is the decedent's scalp at the point of impact," she explained. "I cut it free and snipped away the surrounding hair to better reveal the entry site."

Again, she used a knife as a pointer. "I'll

be sending it along to the lab for analysis, largely because of this tiny crown of debris surrounding the wound. Can you see that?"

Joe squinted from close up and studied what she was referring to. "You think that was left behind by the shaft of the hook as it slid in?"

She put the skin flap back on the table, clearly pleased. "Exactly. Very good. That's the second reason I don't believe a prosthesis was used. Most people keep their hooks quite sanitized. It's not unlike having clean hands."

Joe laughed. "Right. And, of course, you wouldn't venture a guess on the nature of the debris."

She smiled broadly. "I don't need to. The lab will tell us that." She sobered abruptly, as if embarrassed by her own inappropriate humor. "I don't know how many attacks you've seen of this nature," she said, "but from my experience, you're looking for someone who knew the victim personally and hated him with a passion."

A hint of the smile reappeared in her eyes as she added, "That, of course, is strictly between you and me."

Hillstrom's confidence in the crime lab was well placed. One day later, David

Hawke, its director, called Joe from Waterbury. In the tradition of how things worked differently in Vermont from the way they did most other places, Dave and Joe were old friends, given to working outside — or at least parallel to — official channels. Not content with just sending paperwork to each other in the standard formal fashion, they were equally prone to using the phone or at least an e-mail to add a personal touch.

"Long time, Joe," Dave said after the two of them had exchanged greetings. "How're you enjoying being the other half of a politician?"

It was a pertinent question, of course, and typically asked by a scientist who had to deal with legislators to an inordinate extent, while wishing he could spend all that time behind a microscope.

It was also a question that cut deeper than Hawke could know. Upon returning from Newark, Joe had only spoken to Gail once on the phone, and that only briefly. She'd been on her way to some evening political function and had sounded distracted and under pressure. He'd kept it short and upbeat and hadn't called again. For her part, she hadn't called back at all yet.

"Not too bad," he said vaguely. "I mostly

just stay out of the way. You get lucky with any of that stuff your boys and girls collected from St. Albans Bay?"

"Mostly still plowing through it," Hawke admitted cheerily, knowing that any findings would be unexpectedly early. "But I did get a fix on that little patch of scalp Hillstrom sent me. I thought you'd like to know right off. The residue around the puncture wound is about as Vermont as any I've dealt with — number one on our list of known substances, in fact."

"All right," Joe played along, "I'll bite."

"There are technical terms," Hawke went on, "but I'll try to keep it simple. It's cow shit."

Joe didn't respond. He was too busy trying to fit the information into all the other puzzle pieces he had floating around inside his head.

"Good news or bad?" Hawke wanted to know. "If it helps, there were also traces of hay."

"It definitely helps, Dave," Joe finally said. "I'm not sure how yet, but it definitely helps."

CHAPTER 22

Gino Famolare pulled out of traffic into a convenient parking space directly across the street from his destination. He sat there for a moment, his eyes still fixed forward, his hands on the wheel.

He blinked once, slowly, and let out a sigh as if he'd been in suspended animation for the last several hours. Which he might have been, for all he knew. He was so numb — had been for so long, it seemed — that he had no idea when he'd last eaten, changed clothes, or even used the bathroom.

He focused on releasing the steering wheel, watching his hands drop to his lap as if they belonged to someone else. The radio was on, he noticed, but not tuned to any station. Whatever had been playing back in Newark had long since been left behind. Now there was only static, which, given his mood, was about right.

He switched off the ignition and sat there listening to the engine ticking.

He missed her so badly, it was a physical pain in his chest, like the building of a heart attack. But worse. Had to be worse. He'd heard heart attacks described as crushing or radiating. But this was less a pain and more like a combination of every childhood nightmare, every unrequited longing, every shock of betrayal. He didn't know how to manage it, what to do with it, how to channel it.

But he was working on that last part. If sorrow and loss could be softened by action, he knew the right action to apply. That was one thing he had no doubts about.

He saw a girl walking down the opposite sidewalk, heading his way. She was slim, dressed in jeans and a short jacket. The pants were hip-huggers, and she was wearing a crop-top sweater which revealed her flat stomach. She looked nothing like Peggy except in the broadest possible way, but she was young and athletic and attractive and clearly full of the sort of confidence that beauty bestows upon a woman, even when she herself may not know enough to trust it.

Peggy, of course, had been luminescent. This girl, now drawing near and about to pass his line of vision, was merely eye-catching by comparison. She didn't have Peggy's inviting aura of innocence and experience combined, that made her look both like a child and the picture of every man's sexual fantasy come suddenly and tangibly alive.

Gino remembered when he'd first met her. At a party. His cousin's birthday. There'd been a crush of people. He hadn't been in a mood to go out, but life at home had become something to avoid. So he'd stood in a corner, generally unengaged, nursing a beer.

He'd seen her enter from across the room, a beauty so remarkable she seemed to carry her own light within her. He watched her, as he imagined most men did, as an unobtainable object of desire, suitable only for dreams, and was already relegating her to a mental picture gallery when she veered toward him in order to share his piece of wall. It turned out that she, too, didn't like crowds, didn't want to be here, but wanted to be back home even less.

From then on, whatever Gino imagined about them came true, and almost as quickly. As in a movie come to life, his opening lines drew laughter and pleasure. In what seemed moments, she was touching the back of his hand while she talked, or resting her fingers on his arm.

He opened up, unused to such receptiveness, shared more than usual, finally admitting to things he almost dared her to reject — he was married, had two kids he disliked, drove a truck, worked on the docks. Nothing dampened her warmth, her clear desire to stay in his company. Their leaving the house together felt seamless and natural, their ready agreement to retire to a nearby motel, their natural, easy, incredibly satisfying choreography in bed. Afterward, sheened with sweat, still breathing hard, he looked down into her face, her damp hair stuck to her forehead, and fully expected to see her pleasure fading away. A one-night stand. A good roll in the hay. Ships passing in the night. All the rest.

Instead, he found her eyes bright, happy, hopeful, and pleased, taking him in as if he were the promise of the future incarnate. She reached up and took his face in her hands and kissed him with such passion and relief that he knew then and there that he'd been blessed. They made love three times that night, something he hadn't attempted in years, and parted, finally and reluctantly, as if neither one might survive the separation, however brief.

And Gino made sure their times apart

were only brief. He became a man obsessed, calculating his every move around when they could next get together. He bought her gifts, clothes, exotic underwear, a town house. They made love in its every room, from the basement to the attic; they tried positions they'd never tried with anyone else; they spent countless hours in bed, simply wrapped up in each other, as if letting go would risk drowning in the separate sorrows they never shared, but both knew existed.

On the surface, it was no meeting of equals. He was old enough to have fathered her, for one thing, but it was precisely the age disparity that she hungered for the most. She catered to his whims, his appetites, his need for her, while he supplied the mature shelter and security she'd yearned for all her life. It was arguably lopsided, unhealthy, and grossly manipulative, but in its excess, it was also as numbing as a narcotic and equally addictive.

And now it was over — violated and trampled not just by bad luck, but by the very factors that had already once pushed Gino to the edge of near terminal grief.

For this wasn't the first time a police officer had mindlessly reached into his life and carelessly extinguished someone central to his emotional well-being. Over twenty years ago, Vinnie Stazio had been killed by an off-duty cop for no reason. A moonlighting watchman, twitchy, trigger-fingered, too stupid to yell out at a passing shadow before shooting it, had taken from Gino his mentor, his father figure, and the man who had helped him give birth to his own self-respect.

Vinnie's death had devastated Gino, as much for the friendship it interrupted as for the feeling of impotence it spawned. For mere loss and grief weren't the only legacies of this ancient killing. Humiliation was there, too, since, despite his vow to seek revenge, Gino never acted on it, continually finding ways to avoid seeking out the offending cop and serving him his just deserts.

But that, of course, had been a long time ago. Gino had been young, insecure, grateful for Vinnie's attention, but still largely unformed. While furious and frustrated by the older man's sudden death, he'd still lacked the nerve to set things right.

No longer.

This time the man responsible for Gino's heartbreak would suffer, and he would do so in kind.

Famolare closed his eyes and pressed his fingertips hard against his tear ducts, using the resulting pain to clear his head. He then reached into the back seat of his car and retrieved a woman's photograph and a powerful pair of binoculars. He propped the picture against the dash and focused the field glasses on the front steps of the ornate building across from his parking space — the Vermont state capitol building.

He'd been doing his homework, using the phone, the old-boy network, and the Web to gather information. He knew all he needed to know about Joe Gunther, the man who'd killed Peggy.

He knew Gunther had a woman he cared for.

Most of all, he knew Gunther would soon be feeling the same pain Gino was carrying around in his chest like a stone.

Joe entered the conference room in the St. Albans state police barracks that he and Michael and Shafer had used days ago to decipher the arson pattern just south of the city.

This time, however, although the basic purpose was the same, and those two men were in attendance, the scope had been ex-

340

panded, and with it, the team. Now added to the large table were Willy Kunkle, Sammie Martens, and Ross Braver of the VBI Burlington office, who'd been busy all this time on an unrelated, still-open homicide case. There were also two liaisons each from the Sheriff's Department and the Vermont State Police. Nine officers in all, not counting Joe.

"Sorry I'm late and thank you all for coming," Joe began, placing his paperwork on the table before him. "I know everyone's knee-deep in alligators right now. There's a lot we've been dealing with and still more starting to come together. But it's with that in mind that I thought we better meet so we can all get on the same page."

Still standing, he paused to open a file folder and consulted its cover page. "To bring the newcomers up to speed, let me summarize a bit. In the folders before you, you'll find much more than what I'm about to say, but this is the once-over-lightly."

He stepped away from the table and began pacing as he spoke. "In a nutshell, it seems we're looking at a real estate deal gone haywire. A St. Albans Realtor named Clark Wolff caught wind that the feds were planning to site a major Homeland

Security operations center just south of town but needed to put a bridge across Lake Champlain to better establish an east-west travel corridor paralleling the border. On one hand, it looks ridiculous, but on another — if you look at the map — you can see where someone in Washington might've thought it was a great idea. More to the point, the reality of the thing doesn't matter, 'cause Wolff bit the bait and started buying up farmland where the bridge is supposed to hit the shore.

"The problem was, he needed a lot more money than he's got available, and he didn't want to tip his hand to the local banks and risk spilling the beans prematurely. Enter John Samuel Gregory, a young, rich, ambitious exile from Newark, New Jersey, complete with shady past and connections to the Mob."

"Great," muttered one of the state troopers.

"Exactly," Joe agreed. "It took Mr. Gregory about fifteen seconds after joining Wolff's firm to catch wind of this scheme and up the ante by strong-arming a few deals to speed up the process. From what we've pieced together, it looks as if — without Wolff's knowledge, according to him — Gregory hired an arsonist named

Gino Famolare from back home to come up here and torch three barns that we know of."

Joe paused to hold up a hand. "Keep in mind that some of what I'm saying is speculative. We are pretty confident about two of the fires, since the MOs are almost identical, but the third one — the Loomis fire — was electrical, making it different in origin, and the damage was severe enough that we can't absolutely be sure Famolare was involved."

"You don't even know it was arson," Willy added helpfully.

Joe didn't argue the point. "He's right. We don't. But read the files to see why we're going with that assumption — you'll find mention of some milk tampering we think occurred to weaken the target financially just prior to the fire. And while we're on the subject of things we can't prove, pay attention to the vehicular death of Arvid Beatty, who died when his tractor brakes failed. Similarly, you'll find mention of another farmer named Martin, who was accidentally gassed checking his own silage and sold his farm after waking up from the resulting coma. To be honest, though, he's included only because the sale went to Wolff and Gregory, not because we think the gassing was somehow rigged."

"How solid are you that Wolff knew nothing about Gregory?" Ross Braver asked. "Someone gets killed, it's usually whoever he was sleeping with or in business with."

"True enough," Joe agreed. "And you may be right. My gut tells me he's clean, but he's still on the radar along with everyone else."

"On the land deals," the other state trooper asked, "what kind of acreage are we talking about?"

"That's a little vague right now," Joe admitted, crossing back over to his notes. "Of the eight area transactions we know about in the past few months, Wolff knew of three, including Loomis — the electrical fire I mentioned. He didn't realize his supposed partner, Gregory, had also picked up the tractor death and the gassed guy. But those're only the ones we're sure about. Total, that comes to about sixteen hundred acres. They had more on their wish list."

He looked up at them. "Okay, so far, so good. We know the players, the motive, and the methods. All that seems pretty complete." After a beat, he added, "But there's one small off-key note."

"Gregory got himself killed," Shafer said quietly.

"That's not it," Sammie countered, her eyes bright and glued to Gunther.

Joe smiled, not surprised that she'd done her homework both thoroughly and analytically. "No. Gregory's death was certainly a surprise, but that's not what I meant."

"What, then?" Shafer asked.

"It's the death of Bobby Cutts," Sam answered.

Joe nodded slightly. "There's your oddball from the start. It's the last of the arsons, the only one outside the cluster, the one the Realtors had no interest in, the only one where cows were killed on purpose and the human by mistake."

"You saying we have two separate cases?" one of the sheriff's men asked.

"No," Willy drawled, his voice rich with contempt.

"The arsonist who did Noon also did Cutts," Jonathon explained.

"And Gregory did visit the Cutts farm," Sam added. "He left a business card behind."

"We don't have separate cases," Joe continued helpfully, trying to make the deputy feel less targeted. "But we may have two separate investigations based on separate motives."

Braver, the newcomer, asked, "You say Bobby Cutts died by mistake. Are we absolutely sure about that?"

Joe nodded, happy to field such questions, for all of their sakes. "Absolutely? No. From what we know about his recent activities, and following the logic that most violence stems from sex or greed, we can suspect Barry Newhouse, Marianne Kotch's old boyfriend, and Rick Frantz, the guy she was seeing behind Bobby's back. Jonathon's done some digging on both subjects."

Michael picked up the cue. "While you and Willy were in Newark, I found out they both have alibis for when the Cutts barn went up, but I also ran tests on a variety of sodium chlorate incendiaries and found the timing variances to be pretty wide. Still, for what it's worth, I also don't think either of them did it. Newhouse fits Marianne's description of him — all hot air and laziness. When I squeezed him hard in an interview, the one thing I got for sure was that at heart he didn't really give a damn about who Marianne was sleeping with. Frantz was a little trickier, since now it looks like his coma will be permanent. I had to talk with family and friends and work in from the edges, and I had the extra disadvantage of knowing that he might be capable of arson, being a habitual offender. But there again, I came away empty-handed. There is nothing at all — in his background, his habits, or in anything I could get from the people I interviewed — that would indicate he had anything to do with that fire."

Ross Braver wasn't giving up quite yet. "That all works if there was a grudge against Bobby personally," he said. "What about if he was just a symbol? A way to break his father's spirit and force him to sell?"

"You thinking Billy St. Cyr?" Joe asked.

"Why not?" he answered. "According to the case file, St. Cyr and Calvin Cutts were cat-and-dog for twenty years. Now, all of a sudden, St. Cyr turns into Mr. Nice Guy just before he makes an offer to buy."

"Then why burn the herd?" Sam asked.

Braver was warming to his topic. "That's the beauty. He doesn't want it. He's been telling people he wants to get out of the business altogether. But if you look at a property map, you can see how the Cutts farm makes a big dent into St. Cyr's western boundary. Combined, they form a nice, huge, well-proportioned whole. Pretty as a picture and twice as salable."

"But he could have sold those cows," Sam protested.

Braver shook his head. "Only if he had them to sell, and that wasn't going to happen if Cutts wasn't interested in any deal at all — until his son and whole herd had been killed."

"Jesus," one of the deputies commented. "That's cold."

"Maybe," Braver agreed. "But that's how it's panning out, isn't it?"

They all looked at Joe, who had in fact made the Cutts family his assignment.

"I'd heard an offer had been made," he admitted. "I don't know where it stands right now."

"I do," Tim Shafer announced. "Or at least I know a bit more than that. You'd asked us to look into St. Cyr before you went south."

Joe had completely forgotten. "Too many people involved in all this," he commented. "Good thing I'm not an air traffic controller. What did you find out?"

"We were told that he cut corners whenever he could and took advantage of every government handout. All true. I got an unofficial look at some of his financials. It was like untangling spaghetti, and I didn't go too far into it, but from what I could figure out, he's rolling in dough. He has no incentive to get out of farming, and buying the Cutts place makes all the sense in the world. He's got kids with big plans who want land, too, so that's an additional booster."

"You think he's good for the fire?" Joe asked.

Shafer equivocated. "I'm saying it's possible. Means, motive, and opportunity are all there. He doesn't have a criminal history, but we know what that's worth."

Sam was scratching her head. "I admit I'm the newcomer here, but I thought that fire was set by Famolare, who was hired by Gregory because of their mutual Newark background. If St. Cyr is behind the Cutts burning, how's he connect to either one of them? It seems so totally out of left field."

"That's because this whole deal is out of left field," Willy said, having kept his peace for an unusually long time. "The only hard-core information we got out of Newark was from a juicer who thought we were about to kill him, and even that was about only one of the three fires — which one is anyone's guess. All the rest of it — Vinnie Stazio *maybe* having a student named Gino, Gregory's brother paying off Lagasso, and then Lagasso ordering up a fire that *looked* like a Stazio burn long after Stazio was dead — is just a bunch of conjecture." He pointed to Sam's piled paperwork. "Jonathon's report says that the motel clerk was given Gino's mug shot. Couldn't ID him. Said he had that stupid hat pulled down too far over his face. Same thing for the two farmers who supposedly saw him — too far off to see his face. I mean, Jesus, we've been playing fast and loose from the start."

"Initially," Joe agreed. "But I don't think so lately. Regardless of those failed IDs, Gino's connection to Vermont is solid, and juicer or not, Santo sounded pretty sure of himself to me — and talking to us definitely got him dead."

"Speaking of getting dead," Willy said, "shouldn't we be talking about Gregory?"

Joe held up a finger. "In a minute. I don't want to lose track. Here are some of the issues I think we need to keep in focus: Was Bobby killed accidentally or on purpose, and if the latter, was it personal or symbolic, as Ross suggests? Is the Cutts fire related to the others in some way other than having been set by the same arsonist? What's the real motivator behind Billy St.

Cyr's recent change of attitude? And finally, what was the desired end result of the Cutts fire? If we find someone whose fortunes suddenly improved, we may also have our primary actor."

He now looked at Willy. "Okay. John Samuel Gregory. Who knocked him off and why?"

Braver, not well known to Joe, seemed to like his theories straightforward — and didn't take no for an answer. "My vote's on Wolff. It's a money deal. Gregory did him dirt by going maverick and screwing everything up."

Jonathon tilted back in his chair and rested one foot against the edge of the conference table. "What I'm wondering is, who did he piss off the most?" he asked, before quickly gesturing to his colleague. "Not that Wolff doesn't qualify, Ross. I didn't mean that. But there're others standing in line. Gregory comes from Newark, basically exiled for misbehavior. His brother doesn't like him, the Mob thought he was a welcher when Lagasso squeezed the family firm for what he was owed, and who knows who else may hate his guts around here for all the mischief he's committed? Which reminds me," he added almost as an afterthought, "we shouldn't forget that unless we find out otherwise — which is pretty unlikely — it was also Gregory who hired Gino to torch the Cutts barn. Why did he do that?"

Total silence greeted this question.

"Seems like," he resumed, "we ought to take a closer look at the members of the Cutts clan."

CHAPTER 23

Gino waited patiently in the shadows, indistinguishable from the tree trunk he was leaning against. During the past couple of hours, several pedestrians had strolled by not ten feet away without even imagining his presence.

He was good at this. He could wait forever.

The target had actually arrived ten minutes ago, driving into the condo garage and closing the door behind her electronically before leaving the locked car. A cautious woman, he'd noticed earlier. The kind of caution born of a bad experience. Bordering on paranoia.

But whatever that experience, it had been a long time ago. He could tell that the edge had left her fear. Already, in the few days he'd been doing this, he'd seen a curtain left open a crack, a window left unlatched for an hour to allow some air in. Finally, yesterday, after her half-hour jog with whistle and pepper spray canister, she'd committed the ultimate mistake, punching in her security code on the front door alarm without blocking the keypad from view. He'd been there, of course, binoculars in hand, ready and waiting. Twenty-three forty. The magic number to the kingdom.

Content that she was in for the night, or at least wasn't coming right back out, he eased away from his post, checking all around for possible onlookers, and stealthily crossed over to his parked van.

Quietly, he got into the back, pulled the blanket closed to block off the front seats, and switched on the laptop computer. The van's back windows were tinted, but as an extra precaution, he'd also taped black plastic garbage bags over them. No one passing by would see what he was doing.

The screen's ethereal glow colored his impassive face a pale blue as he waited for the program to boot up. Gino Famolare was on emotional autopilot — all professional, all the time. Despite what he had planned for this woman — a first in his career, given that the farmer kid had been a mistake — and despite the stakes and extra effort he'd put into this job, it remained just that for him. A job.

Or so he was telling himself.

The screen finally resolved into what he was expecting: a mosaic of eight postage-stamp-size images, each of a different aspect of the interior of Gail's apartment. As he watched the tiny pictures, she passed from frame to frame, walking around the privacy of her home, going about the business of settling in for the night.

After learning the alarm's entrance code yesterday, Gino had picked the lock and checked the place out, outfitting it with a series of minute, wireless cameras which he'd hidden behind books, among plants, behind a stack of towels, and elsewhere, until he was sure he had every angle covered, including the bathroom, where he'd made sure to coat the camera lens with antifogging fluid.

He wasn't always this thorough. But then again, his norm was to make sure no people were around.

Not this time. This time the target wasn't a building, but its occupant, and he'd convinced himself that he needed to know her habits, her daily rhythm, as if such knowledge might alter his approach or his overall plan. It wouldn't, of course. He intended to strike in the middle of the night, when she was asleep. There was no point in knowing when she watched TV or brushed her teeth or which side of the bed she used. Simply watching the house for several days and seeing when the lights went off would have been adequate for his purposes.

This all stemmed from some other need.

On the computer, Gail moved into her bedroom and kicked off her shoes. Gino clicked on the image and brought it up to fill the screen. He watched, barely breathing, as she removed her sweater, then her blouse, slipped off her skirt and panty hose, and moved about the room, either putting clothes away or placing them in a laundry hamper. In front of the latter, she also took off her underwear and tossed it into the hamper with the rest, before reaching into a closet, taking hold of a terry-cloth robe, and covering herself once more.

Every movement had been routine to the point of blandness — an attractive woman presuming herself to be without an audience. There had been no shred of sexuality, no enjoyment in doing what might have been seductive in another setting. She had merely been making herself more comfortable.

But it had left Gino sweating in his van, his breath short and his eyes glued to the picture, the complex of emotions gripping him — anger, loss, and lust — all swirling for attention in different and conflicting ways.

He missed Peggy as if a part of him had been amputated. Over the time they'd been together, he'd begun merely blessing his lucky stars that he'd been able to get such a woman into bed. Every time he'd dropped by her tiny apartment to see her, he'd been amazed once again by her beauty, her sensuality, her clear and inviting openness. As he tugged at her buttons and zippers, ran his hands under her clothes, and made love to her in any way he wished, he found himself constantly wondering when she would suddenly bring herself up short, see him as if for the first time, and immediately throw him out.

But it never happened. Time passed, he moved her into the house Down Neck. Her joy in his company never slipped, her expectations that they would forever be a couple never wavered. Her conviction was catching. From simply being unfaithful, which he'd been many times before, he eventually came to feel that sleeping with his wife was cheating on Peggy, and he stopped. He moved downstairs to his den, slept on the couch, and put up with the attending domestic fury. It didn't matter. He didn't care. He had Peggy, and everything was going to work out.

By this time, Gail had stepped into the bathroom. Gino, in a daze, slowly closed the first window and expanded the second, making Gail leap in size just as she removed her robe. He stared at her as she used the toilet and then entered the shower.

It was glass-doored, and the minicamera had been set high, so he maintained a full and unimpeded view of her as she stepped under the water stream, tilted her head back, and let a warm cascade wash over her. He sat transfixed as she reached for the soap, lathered herself up, and went through the clearly memorized, almost soothing routine of a breast exam. She raised each arm in turn and hooked it behind her neck as she caressed and kneaded her breast with the other hand, using the soapy film covering her to ease her motions.

Gino hadn't slept in days. He'd barely eaten and hadn't changed his clothes. He'd stayed at Peggy's house, lying in her bed, surrounded by her things, despite Fredo's constant urging that he beware of the cops. Fredo had kept watch downstairs, his eyes on the street, his panic rising to the point where Gino had finally paid attention.

Still, as he'd formed his plan and put it into motion, Gino had clutched his loss and its metamorphosis into obsessive revenge like a dying man clinging to false hope. Now, his eyes glued to Gail, naked, glistening, self-absorbed, all he could see was Peggy, all he could remember was how she had felt under his hands, and all he could think of was how she had burned alive.

Just as this one was going to. Very soon.

At the same time, an hour's drive away, north by northwest, a light was killed in an upper bedroom of the Cutts farmhouse, and curtains spread apart to better afford a view of the barn's charred remains, now cradled in the snow-free black soil of the surrounding field like the skeleton of an oversize Viking ship locked in an ancient bog, its ribs gleaming slightly in the moonlight, polished by the scorch of fire.

Marie Cutts, barely visible as a black-on-black silhouette, sat by the window, looking out. She was still — to the point of breathlessness — to where all she could feel was the heartbeat she so casually took for granted. Her unseeing eyes were fixed on the center of the cold pyre, her deaf ears filled with the dying screams of her youngest child.

Marie was wishing she was dead, too, as quiet and calm as Bobby in his grave. She'd had enough of the fury that had fueled her for most of her life, that she'd channeled into pushing her family to avoid the shoals her own father had so callously ignored. From the moment she'd met Calvin and seen in him the soundness she lacked at home, she'd laid out plans for a future of prosperity and safety. She'd driven him to be cautiously innovative, to never spend more than they could afford, to avoid work habits born of simple repetition, and to establish others that would stand them all in good stead.

Cal was compliant at first, a willing student, eager to please, hardworking, and patient. He listened carefully to her ideas and put many of them to use. But only at first. Over time, he created his own visions, often willfully at odds with hers, she thought, simply because he could do so. He became easygoing, too friendly and trusting of others. It hadn't resulted in any reversals of fortune — yet — but it reminded her of her socially adept father, and it hung over her head like a sword.

When the kids were born, she shifted her

attention, planning an education for Linda that would make her a farmer's best partner, and a training program for Bobby that would ready him to inherit and thrive.

But there again, she'd been thwarted. Calvin's insidious good nature and independence, so valued by others and so weak at its core, took early genetic hold, making of Linda a rebellious acolyte, more interested in boys than in farming, and downright lazy at home, doing chores only under threat. Bobby, of course, had been perfect, quick and eager and happy to participate in his mother's dream, and for a brief few years, Marie thought she'd caught her golden ring.

But then Linda, of all people, messed things up, marrying Padgett, becoming pregnant, and getting her weak-willed father to betray his own blood for the sake of an interloper.

Marie shifted in her seat, her anger stirring like the lava from deep inside a volcano — just as it always had. *Linda,* she thought derisively. Didn't even like farming, despite all her fakery in pretending to be Padgett's helpmate.

Bobby had once more been the hero, acceding to his father's decision, saying how relieved he was to play second fiddle to a former juvenile delinquent. As furious as Marie had been by the whole turn of events, she'd still been amazed by her son's good grace.

Bobby had been all she'd ever hoped for, her dream incarnate, her comfort in the face of old age. His death had broken her heart and made of life something not worth living.

Back in Newark, Lil Farber and members of her unit, supported by an armor-wearing tactical team, grouped around a scarred, stained, hollow-core door on the second floor of one of the city's tenement buildings. Whispering into her radio to the people watching the fire escape, she called off a brief countdown, nodded to the two tactical men carrying a steel battering ram between them, and stepped back to give them room.

With precision born of frequent practice, the two easily smacked the door's handle on the first swing, sending the door flying back on its hinges with an explosive bang. The men instantly peeled off to both sides, one of them taking the ram with him, while four more with flashlight-equipped shotguns poured through the opening, shouting out who they were and warning everyone not to move.

It was a raid, brought about by a solid tip from a trusted snitch, who said that keeping company with a prostitute at this address and looking forward to a long evening of sex and illegal drugs would be Fredo Loria, Gino Famolare's right-hand man and chief flunky.

The tip proved sound. Sprawled naked on the bed with an equally exposed young woman, Fredo even had the telltale white smears under his nostrils of a recent snort of cocaine. With no small degree of satisfaction, Farber placed him under arrest.

Several hours later, Joe Gunther, staying at a motel on the edge of St. Albans, was dragged from his sleep by the nervous buzzing of his pager as it vibrated across the glossy surface of his night table.

He read the number and the brief message, "Call me now — Lil," and dialed back immediately, propping his pillows against the wall behind him.

"Farber."

"Lil. It's Joe."

She didn't waste time. "Sorry to bounce you out of bed. We busted Fredo Loria tonight, Gino's lieutenant, or best buddy, or whatever you want to call him, and threatened him with the three strikes rule unless he ratted out his boss. He told us something I thought you'd like to know ASAP."

"Shoot," Joe said, the last shreds of fog clearing from his brain.

"I'll give it to you in two parts," she went on. "The easy stuff first. Fredo confirmed that, just as we thought, Gino made three trips to Vermont, the timing corresponding to your three barn fires. But here's the catch, and it ties into what Santo Massi told us the night we grabbed him. You asked him if the forty grand was for one or more jobs, and he said one, meaning the phone conversation he overheard between Gregory and Lagasso was probably about the first one."

"Loomis," Joe said softly.

"Whoever. But what we got out of Fredo just now was that there were only two jobs brokered through Lagasso in any case, each for forty thousand. The third was done off the books."

"Meaning what?"

"Lagasso knew nothing about it. The customer and Gino dealt direct."

"Did Fredo know who the customer was?"

Lil laughed. "You want it that easy? Forget about it. There's one more thing, though: The night we sweated Santo, he told you that later Gino heard about someone dying in — quote, unquote — 'it.' He screwed that up. The death didn't happen in the fire he'd heard discussed, but in the third one he knew nothing about. He just assumed they were one and the same. Fredo remembers otherwise because Lagasso talked about how Gino was on a roll, and that they were all top-dollar deals from out of state."

"Did Gregory do all the hiring?" Joe asked.

"I don't know," Lil answered him, "and nor did Fredo. But, for what it's worth, the price remained the same."

Joe remained silent, thinking.

"There's something else," Lil added. "While Gino never told Fredo who hired him, he was worked up enough about the fatality in number three to vent a little."

"That upset him?" Joe asked, surprised.

He could almost see Lil shaking her head in amusement. "Not hardly. That death ended a perfect record — it was all about vanity. Anyhow, again according to Fredo, Gino ranted how he hadn't wanted any of the jobs to begin with, since he wasn't used to barns and didn't like the way they're laid out. He was also angry about having to kill the cows, so the kid dying, too, really turned his crank."

Joe thought back to when all this started. He, Shafer, and Jonathon had wondered if — given the evidence — the torch might have improvised and that a lack of familiarity with barns might have played a role in making two of the arsons so easy to pair up.

Lil's voice changed to something a little warier. "Joe, Fredo also told us something you're not going to like. That's really why I woke you up instead of waiting till morning."

He didn't like the sound of that. "What is it?"

"Gino's holding you directly responsible for Peggy DeAngelis's death."

"Me?"

"Fredo said he'd never seen him so worked up. 'Out of his mind,' was the phrase he used. Peggy must have given Gino your name, but whatever it was, that's all Fredo heard from him: Gunther this and Gunther that. The punch line is that the last time Fredo saw him, Gino was heading your way to even the score."

"All right," Joe said neutrally, adding this surprise to an already complicated equation.

"That's not really it, though," Lil added,

hesitant for the first time since he'd known her. "He said he was going to settle it 'in kind.' I never asked you. I mean, it never came up. But are you married?"

A cold chill swept through him. "That's what he meant?"

"Fredo quoted him as saying he was going to do to you what you did to him. That's the way I took it."

Joe was already swinging his legs out from under the covers. "Thanks, Lil. I appreciate it. Is there anything else you can tell me — anything at all? What car he's driving, what he's wearing, who he might've called?"

"We went through Peggy's house after the crash. We could tell he'd been living there — or some man had — but to answer your question, no. We've checked everything and everywhere. That's why we busted Fredo. But it looks like Gino's off the face of the earth for the moment. We're still on it, though. Anything we hear that'll help, we'll let you know."

Joe was struggling into his pants with one hand. "Thanks, Lil. I owe you one."

"No, you don't," she said. "You broke open a case we were going nowhere with. Good luck."

Joe hung up, buckled his pants, and hit the phone's speed dial.

"Answering for the Vermont Bureau of Investigation."

"This is Joe Gunther. Oh-two-twenty-four. I need an emergency dispatch of a marked patrol unit to the following address in Montpelier, to pick up a woman named Gail Zigman." He gave the operator the name and number of the street. "This is Code Three. Take her to Waterbury HQ. I'll be there as quick as I can."

"Ten-four," came the crisp reply.

Gunther dialed again.

A very sleepy Gail answered.

"It's Joe. Wake up."

"Joe?"

"Yeah. I hate to do this to you, but you've got to listen, and please do what I tell you. I'm on my way, and I'll explain it in less than an hour."

"Joe, what's going on?" Her voice was now clear, brittle, alarmed by his tone.

"A man may be after you, using you to get at me. You need to get out of the house."

"Who? Why? What's this about?"

"Later, Gail. I promise. I just want you safe right now."

"Okay, okay."

He was pulling on his shirt, almost dropping the phone. "Not yet, though, okay?

Don't use your car, and don't leave the house until a police car shows up. He'll be playing his lights. Right now get dressed and wait by the front door, and then wait till he comes to the door. He's going to take you to Waterbury. That's where I'll find you."

"Is he outside now?" she asked, her voice tight with fear. He knew that all the nightmares she'd learned to control since her rape must be suddenly exploding from her subconscious.

"Not necessarily," he tried soothing her. "He may not even know who you are. I just got a call about this guy from the police in Newark, and I'm only being cautious. He made a generalized threat against whoever might be in my life, and then he vanished."

He heard a hard edge creep into her voice. "Joe, if it was that vague, you wouldn't have called me."

"I'm not lying to you, Gail. What would you prefer? That I overreact, or pretend nothing will happen until it does?"

"I'm scared," she said after a pause.

"I know that. I'm truly sorry. Now please do what I asked so I can start heading your way. Okay?"

"Okay."

★ ★ ★

The trip to Waterbury was the fastest Joe
had ever driven, never dropping under a
hundred miles an hour and often hitting a
hundred and thirty. Only once did he let
go of the wheel with one hand, to confirm
by radio that Gail had been picked up, but
throughout it all, as in a closed-circuit
mantra, he berated himself nonstop.

To put this particular person into this
kind of danger, not only after all they'd
shared, but especially as they had recently
entered some ill-defined and unaddressed
emotional landscape, led to an anxiety he
hadn't felt since he and his late wife had
confronted her terminal cancer over thirty
years ago.

The barn fires, the killing of John
Gregory, the intellectual satisfaction of
trying to solve the puzzle, all melted away
in the face of this suddenly loose cannon
bringing what was normally an exercise at
arm's length to cataclysmic proximity. All-
too-recent memories of how he'd felt
watching Peggy's car burn into the pave-
ment crowded his mind. That death had
made him feel guilty. A similar fate for Gail
— with him directly to blame — would be
devastating.

Joe drove as if his life depended on it.

★ ★ ★

Gino sat in the passenger seat of his van, rendered invisible from the streetlights by the cab's inner gloom. The throbbing blue flashes from the passing cruiser's strobes bounced off the row of apartments opposite him, a paradoxical combination of blinding aggression and colorful harmlessness.

Intrigued after an initial surge of startled apprehension, he watched as the car pulled up to Gail's address and a uniformed officer got out and approached her door.

Something must have happened back in Newark, he thought. His mind immediately went to Fredo — loyal, obedient, but sloppy. Easy for the cops to squeeze, but not someone with a lot to tell.

Gino looked thoughtful as Gail was escorted back to the car and ushered into the front seat.

They hadn't wasted any time, he'd give them that, but, then, he'd also lost a few days collecting himself and doing his homework — target acquisition, as he liked to term it.

But speed was no longer the point. In fact, it wasn't even a factor. In some part of his grief-racked brain — a part he wasn't directly consulting — Gino was actually thinking that he had the entire rest of his life to complete this assignment, regardless of how brief that might be.

He slid down into his seat more comfortably as the cruiser turned around in the driveway and returned whence it had come. He didn't know where she was being taken or how long they'd keep her under wraps. But he knew where she'd resurface. He'd taken the time to study her history, her personality, her habits.

And that's where he'd be waiting.

CHAPTER 24

Joe found Gail in a small meeting room on the third floor of the Department of Public Safety headquarters building in Waterbury. She was sitting at a fake-wood table in front of a cardboard cup of tepid coffee, surrounded by blackboards, motivational posters, and a rickety metal stand supporting a TV and a VCR.

She stood as he entered, but didn't circle the table to greet him. He went to her instead, putting his arms around her shoulders.

"I am so sorry, Gail," he told her again. "When I heard this guy might be in the neighborhood, I couldn't not warn you."

Gently, she placed her hands on his chest and pushed him back enough to see his face. "That was not a warning, Joe. With my history, that was a threat. Telling me not to drive my car or step out of the house? Who is this man?"

Joe pulled two seats around so they could face each other and indicated she should sit. She did so, but cautiously, as if preparing to run at any moment. It was anyone's guess what panic she'd been struggling with — an army of ghosts he could only imagine.

"His name is Gino Famolare," he explained. "He's an arsonist, Newark-born, Mob-connected, and he was hired to burn a few barns around St. Albans."

"And now he's after me?" she asked incredulously.

"Maybe. Like I said, I'm only being careful there. He was overheard saying he'd do to me like I'd done to him, or something like that, before he disappeared a few days ago."

"And you did what to him?"

"It's what he thinks I did. Would you like a refresher on that coffee?"

Gail gave him a flat look. "No."

"Sorry. We — the Newark cops and we — were putting pressure on him indirectly. Talking to his wife, his girlfriend, staking his place out, and in the midst of it, the girlfriend bolted, we don't know why. We chased after her, but she crashed her car and died. Apparently, Famolare made it personal."

Joe didn't mention how easily he understood Gino's motivation, and how thoroughly, in two brief encounters, he, too, had fallen under Peggy's spell. Gino's vow to do unto Joe as Joe had done unto him carried more emotional weight than Joe felt comfortable sharing.

Gail blinked a couple of times, still staring at him. "Do you have a picture of him?"

He reached into his breast pocket. "I thought you might ask."

He laid a mug shot on the table beside them. As with all such photographs, it was debatable whether the subject's own mother would recognize him, but it was all Joe had.

Gail picked it up and studied it. "A wife and girlfriend both."

"Yeah, the girlfriend was young enough to be his daughter. Beautiful, very much in love with him."

"You spoke with her?"

"Yes. Tried to get her to give him up. He had her stashed in a town house in the safest part of town. Quite the love pad."

"And the wife?"

Joe had no idea where these questions were going, or what had stimulated them, but he didn't feel he could quibble. "More like an urban suburb, the way Newark and its surroundings are set up."

She frowned, dropped the mug shot onto the table, and sat back for the first time. "I meant, did you meet her, too?"

"Oh, yeah. Slightly dirty pool. We wanted to know what she knew, and we used the girlfriend as leverage."

"You told her?" It was asked without inflection.

For the first time, a small alarm went off in his head. "He did kill a kid. Burned him alive."

"I read the papers, Joe. Every day."

He pressed his lips together, silenced by the ice in her voice.

"How did the wife take it?" she asked.

"Not well, and it still didn't get us anything. As far as we could tell, he kept her and their daughters in the dark about his activities."

Gail slid forward in her chair and began to stand. Joe reached out to take her hands, but she quickly moved them away and stood on her own. He stayed put, looking up at her.

"Are you okay?" he asked lamely.

She walked to the far end of the small room, putting the table between them again. "That's not a serious question, right?"

About the only time he had ever seen her so on edge was during the days and weeks following the rape.

"No. Of course not. I'm just hoping to put things right."

Her face darkened. "So far, it doesn't sound like you've done too well. Besides helping to get a girl killed, destroying a man's otherwise clueless family, and then siccing the same whack job on me, have you gotten any closer to making the world a safer place?"

He was stunned into silence. Never before had she spoken to him with such contempt.

He rose, too, and moved to the door. "I'm going to put you up at a motel, at least for the rest of the night," he said. "You have any preferences?"

"I want to go home. That's where I feel safest."

Joe hesitated.

"Do you have the slightest shred of evidence this man is even in the state, much less watching my house?" she asked him.

"No. But we don't know he isn't, either. He's very upset, Gail, and —"

"I know the feeling," she interrupted.

He took a breath. "And very determined. The threat he made against you is like a blood oath. We — I — have no reason to think he won't act on it. I can't let that happen. I love you too much."

There was a prolonged stillness between them, punctuated only by the slight humming of the fluorescent lighting overhead.

She scowled suddenly and touched her forehead with her fingertips, as if acknowledging a headache. "I didn't mean to snap at you."

"It's all right."

"I'm tired, is all."

"I know. That's why I suggested a motel."

"Not that way," she explained, her eyes sorrowful. "I'm tired of this kind of stress — I've got enough of my own. I'm running out of reserves."

He took a step toward her, gripped by her implication and the fear it ignited within him — one that had grown over the last couple of years. "We will get him, Gail."

She sighed deeply. "That's not what I mean."

He knew what she meant, but he didn't press her — didn't want the words out in the open.

"I tell you what," he said instead. "Let me put you in a safe place for the rest of tonight and tomorrow, while my guys check your place from top to bottom. After that, you can go home. But it's got to be with twenty-four-hour-a-day protection, both there and at work. Discreet, if you want, but around-the-clock."

He'd expected resistance, but when it came to personal safety, he should have known better. Both her house in Brattleboro and her Montpelier condo were minifortresses, rigged with locks, lights, and alarms.

"Okay," was all she said.

Gino didn't linger for long, but he did take the time to gloat a little, at least. He watched as several unmarked cars drove up the street and parked at various locations along the block. A group of casual-appearing men and women, some carrying oversize briefcases, convened on the sidewalk before Gail's address, hovering like disorganized guests looking for a leader, until one of them worked the front-door combination and let them all in.

With a satisfied backward glance at the small pile of cameras that he'd just removed from the same premises, Gino started his engine and gently pulled away from the curb.

Joe pulled into the Cutts farm dooryard and got out of his car, feeling the soft give of black soil beneath his shoes. It was officially mud season by now, when a half year's worth of subsurface ice finally yields to warmer temperatures and turns all of New England into a soggy sponge for a few weeks. People who think nothing of ice and snow view mud season with loathing for what it does to roads, lawns, and the rugs of front parlors.

"Did you catch who killed my son?"

The voice was loud, sharp, and querulous, as always, but where he'd previously thought of it as an incoming mortar round, Joe was now disposed to consider its complexity. Given what he'd learned since that first snowy day, his presumptions about this family, and certainly about this one member of it, had undergone serious revision.

"How are you, Marie?" he asked, approaching.

"How do you think? You not going to answer the question?"

He put one foot up on the porch and stood looking at her. "We're a lot closer than we were."

"What's that mean?"

"We have a better idea what happened, for one thing."

She pointed at the remnants of the barn,

stark and foreboding. "That doesn't tell you what happened? It sure as hell tells me."

He didn't argue the point. "You see it for what it did. I wonder what brought it about."

She frowned. "What are you doing here?"

"Did you know a man named John Samuel Gregory?"

"No." The answer was immediate.

"You get the paper or listen to the news?"

"Why?"

"Because he was found killed in his condo in St. Albans Bay. Murdered."

Marie's scowl deepened. "Why would I care about that?"

"He was here, at least once."

"The hell you say."

Joe came onto the porch. "Could I come inside for a second? I want to show you something."

"Inside? What?" she asked, startled.

"It's something in the kitchen."

Almost despite herself, Marie stepped back to let him in. He crossed the front room to the kitchen and walked over to the corkboard covered with drawings, post-cards, business cards, and whatnot. He scanned the board's entire surface in vain.

"His business card was stuck here. I saw it last time."

"So what?"

Joe reached into his pocket and pulled out a card of Gregory's that he'd gotten from Jonathon earlier. He handed it to Marie. "It looked like this one. Gregory was a young guy, longish hair, fancy dresser, drove a Porsche."

Marie returned the card. "Stupid car for up here. I remember him. Not the name. I didn't like him — too stuck on himself."

"What did he want?"

She turned on her heel disgustedly and crossed to the sink. "If I didn't dislike you so much, I'd feel some pity for you. You married? I'll send your wife a get-well card. You want coffee?"

Joe played along. "Sure. Thanks."

"He was a Realtor. What do you think he wanted?"

"Did he float a price?"

She was busying herself at the stove, having filled a pot with water. "Not to me, he didn't. I passed him off to Linda."

"How did that go?"

She turned to glare at him. "What the hell does this have to do with anything?

They talked awhile and he left, and that was that. It was a no-sale."

"How much did he say it was worth?"

Her face closed down, and she returned to the sink, removing two mugs from a row of cup hooks above the window. "I don't know."

Joe addressed the back of her head. "Linda didn't report the conversation?"

"Maybe I don't remember."

"Maybe?"

Her shoulders slumped. "It was three times what the place is worth."

"That's quite a figure."

Slowly, not wanting to turn around, she spooned instant coffee into each mug. "Not really. It's what the flatlanders are paying nowadays."

"And you weren't interested?"

"Nope."

He didn't speak for a few moments, watching her ready the coffee, load up a tray, and bring it over to the large, catchall dinner table, which was presently hosting a pile of Lego bricks at its far end.

"No one in the family was interested?" Joe asked as she continued to avoid eye contact.

"You want milk or sugar?"

"No." Gunther didn't move to take the

383

coffee, letting his question float in the air.

"We talked about it," she finally conceded, sitting at the table in front of her mug, which she didn't touch.

He sat opposite her. "What was the gist of that?"

Marie shrugged. "You're the detective. Look around."

"It was never discussed further?"

"Nope."

"About when did all this happen?"

She picked up her mug, but didn't drink from it. "Maybe half a year ago. Before the snow. More'n half a year ago, I suppose. I don't remember exactly."

"And you never saw Gregory again?"

"No."

"Did Linda?"

"Not that I know of."

"Who else was around when he came by?"

Marie rolled her eyes. "Who cares? Why do you always do this? Since the day you showed up, it's been one damn fool question after another. How the hell did you get your job?"

"John Gregory hired the man who killed your son."

She stared at him, her mouth open, her eyes wide, as if he'd punched her in the stomach, which he supposed he had, in a fashion.

"What?" she finally managed in a whisper.

"*That's* why I'm asking these questions."

Her eyes welled up. "You bastard."

He stood and leaned forward, propping his hands on the table, looming over her. "How else does anyone get through to you, Marie? We've got God knows how many people working on this, trying to find out exactly what you want us to find out, and all you dish out is abuse. Answer the question — *please:* Who else was around when Gregory came by?"

She impatiently wiped at one eye with the back of her hand. "We all were." Her voice was flat but under control. She had gotten the message. "It was late in the day. Bobby was back from school, but second milking hadn't started yet. That man drove up in his car, and I went to find out what he wanted. I thought maybe he'd gotten lost. Once I figured what was what, I handed him to Linda. She took him in for some coffee, like you do for folks, and then she showed him out — maybe a half hour later."

"No one else talked to him?"

"We all did, a little. After he came back out, Bobby was waiting. He'd seen the car

385

and spread the word, so all the men ended up standing around and yammering about it like twelve-year-olds. I let them be. Waste of time."

Gunther visualized the scene, having seen its facsimile enough times. "How would you describe Gregory's attitude?"

"Like I said, full of himself. I hate it when men get that way."

Joe sat back down on the edge of his seat, leaning forward to better make his point. "Marie, now you know why I'm asking. Was there anything at all that stood out that afternoon?"

She put her fingertips against her temples, her elbows on the table. "I'm not being difficult, I swear to you. But there was nothing to it." She rubbed her eyes with the heels of her hands. When she spoke next, half her face was still covered. "Why did he do it, Mr. Gunther? Why did he kill my boy?"

It was the first time he'd ever heard her use his name. He reached out and took one of her wrists. She let him lower her hand until he could squeeze its fingers. "We'll find that out, Marie. We're close already. You said Bobby was the one who got everybody interested in the car. Did you pick up on anything going on between Gregory and him, good or bad?"

"Nothing," she repeated.

He sat back, took a sip of his coffee, studied the children's art decorating the wall for a moment. "Okay. Different questions, then. You're going to have to bear with me, though, or I'll leave right now and spare us both."

"What kind of questions?"

"Personal. The ones you hate."

She drew her eyebrows down into a scowl. "Why?"

"Put it together," he told her. "A complete stranger in a fancy car comes by to list your farm with his firm. You turn him down, but there's nothing unpleasant about it. In fact, everyone comes out to admire his car before he disappears into the sunset, never to be seen or heard from again. That's your story, right?"

"That's what happened."

"Half a year later, he hires a professional arsonist to burn your barn down with everything in it, shortly before he gets murdered himself. You see my point? There's got to be a connection to something or someone inside this family."

She nodded without comment.

"All right. Try not to take offense. These are questions only. They don't necessarily

387

mean anything, but they may suggest some ugly ideas."

"Get on with it." A hint of her old edge had returned.

"I asked you a long time ago about how things were in the family. I've got a better idea now that I've done some digging, especially about Bobby, but how're relations between Linda and Jeff?"

He hesitated about telling her that he didn't want another rant against her son-in-law, and so was pleasantly surprised when her response was quiet and measured. "Fine, as far as I know."

"Linda's never come to you complaining about how maybe she doesn't get enough attention from him?"

Marie actually smiled slightly. "If she didn't, she wouldn't be a farmer's wife. That's one reason women have begun getting out in the fields more, to be with their men. It's not just feminism and all that political talk. It's loneliness, too."

"Is she particularly lonely?"

Marie picked up her coffee and held it in her hands, letting the steam drift by her face. "She's always been a dreamer, talking about far-off places, wishing she could go there. She used to spend hours reading *National Geographic* as a child, studying the maps they included sometimes. 'I'm going to travel, Mama,' she used to tell me. It didn't last. She grew out of it, like all kids. And when we did travel, going to Boston or Springfield to shop or see the museums, she didn't like it much. I think that's what ended it for her, seeing the reality. We got lost once in Boston and ended up in a bad neighborhood, and she was amazed at how people lived. That time, she even made a fuss about coming back home — couldn't get here fast enough."

She paused to take a sip. "I don't like Jeff Padgett. You know that. But she does, and she always did, since the day Cal took him in like some alley cat."

"And he's good to her?"

"He's never given me any reason to think otherwise. I'm probably the only person on the face of the earth who doesn't like him."

Joe paused, not sure he wanted to pursue that. She saved him the choice.

"So why's that?" she asked in his stead. "Because I'm a bitter, disappointed old woman who can't stand the idea of people being happy."

He opened his mouth to protest, but stopped. In fact, she might have been right. He didn't know her well enough to challenge her.

"Is Linda," he asked instead, "as enthusiastic about the farm as her husband? When she and I spoke, I thought I picked up on a couple of small things that indicated otherwise."

Marie shook her head. "Farming's a funny life. No money, terrible hours, no security. It's dirty, smelly, and dangerous. Some of the dumbest beasts on earth get to rule your life and kick you out of bed and drive you to ruin. You get stepped on, pushed around, and slapped in the face with shitty tails every day. And that's not even talkin' about the regulations and agencies and inspectors and politics. You've got the organics and the traditionalists and the nonorganics and GMOs and hybrids and antibiotics and more paperwork than they got trees to make paper. And yet every farmer I know — everyone born to it, at least — understands that this life is why we're on earth."

She paused to take a breath before adding, "When you get away from all that crap, and you're just out there, in a field or working the animals, you feel like the people who did this a thousand years ago."

She placed her hand flat on the table's scarred wooden surface. "This is how we all started out — when we left the caves and started working the land. We created the world like it is. Everything else followed from what we started. They try to tear it down and screw it up, and they treat us like dirt in the process — paying a hundred thousand dollars for a stupid car and demanding that bread and milk stay the same price they have been for decades. But we're still here, 'cause in the end, even with their chemicals and fancy seeds, messing with Mother Nature and maybe poisoning the soil, they still need us to make it grow."

Joe gave her a small smile. "A wild guess tells me you argued against letting Gregory list the place for sale."

"You got that right." Her cheeks were slightly reddened with the passion of her speech.

"Who argued for it?"

Her expression saddened. "Linda. Cal wobbled a bit when he saw she was keen on the idea — until he saw the rest of us weren't interested."

Joe nodded slowly. "So the ambivalence I picked up from her wasn't totally off base."

It wasn't phrased as a question.

"No," she admitted. "She's had her troubles. The kids complicated her life. Got in the way of the dreams, maybe. I don't know. I don't like talking about that stuff."

Joe thought about the vitriol he'd seen Marie pour over the heads of this family, visiting her own disappointment on them like a Bible-thumper invoking the devil. No wonder she didn't peer at it too closely.

But he stuck with the topic at hand. "Just how heated did this conversation get?"

Some of her old fire flickered bright. "I told you that. She spoke her piece and it was done."

Joe merely stared at her.

She shifted angrily in her chair. "For God's sake. That's all there was to it. This farm was everything to Bobby, it's been everything to Cal and me, and Christ only knows, Jeff would be nowhere without it, so he sure as hell wasn't for killing the golden goose. Linda said what she had to say and that was that — she gave it up. Why don't you, too?"

She suddenly flared, a second wave building on the first. "Why are you so damned hot on this? We're the victims here. You may be clueless about what happened — I sure don't know why some rich flatlander bastard in a fancy car wanted my son dead — but that doesn't give you the right to harass us just because you have nobody else to poke at."

Joe sighed. Figuring he had little left to lose, he swung for the bleachers. "If I were you, Marie, and I resented this farm for how it reminded me of my father's failure and I hated my husband for giving my son's birthright away, I might do something drastic to force the rest of the family to accept an offer I'd never get again in a lifetime."

Her face drained. Trembling with rage, she stood up, causing the chair to skitter away behind her, and shouted at him, *"My son died in that fire."*

Joe stood also, slowly, deliberately, and spoke in a calm but firm voice. "Your son was killed by accident, Marie. His dying was no one's intention. Maybe that's what hurts the most."

She staggered back as if he'd pushed her, hitting her shoulder against the wall. She gasped a couple of times and finally burst into tears. "You bastard. You total bastard."

He circled the table and approached her. She held both her hands out to prevent him. "Don't you come near me."

He stopped. "Take your time."

Catching her breath, she managed, "I want you out of my house."

He considered arguing with her, or trying to console her — to somehow get across how her outlook and hostility helped make his suggestion appear reasonable.

But he saw it was a lost cause, just as her husband's efforts to explain his giving the farm to Jeff had been futile, and Jeff's persistent kindness and forbearance had been wasted. Marie Cutts was worse than a dog with a bone. She was hell-bent on martyrdom and righteous indignation and was now more committed to her suffering and loss than she could possibly be to the remnants of her family. The death of one of them had laid permanent claim to her spirit, and it would take more leverage than a mere love of the living to dislodge it.

"I'm sorry, Marie," he said at last, and stepped toward the door. "I truly am."

She said nothing and made no motion, so he turned, crossed the front hall, and showed himself out, pausing on the front porch to take in the view that had greeted this clan for generations, now missing its life-sustaining centerpiece.

He sighed and dropped his gaze to his feet, considering the conversation he'd just left, and his suspicions about the tortured train of events that this pain-racked, grieving woman had most likely set in motion.

For it was Joe's growing conviction that Marie had conspired with Gregory to have the barn burned, in an effort to free her family of its tyranny, deprive her son-in-law of her son's rightful inheritance, and yet still receive enough money to put them all comfortably on another track. Except that in a miscalculation of classically Greek proportions, she'd sacrificed that very son in the process — and had created a source of such enormous guilt that only more bloodletting could satisfy it.

Thus the murder of her happenstance accomplice — a hated, swaggering, city-born hustler on the fast road to riches. A man who'd probably accommodated her request for an arsonist to prove to himself that he had the makings of a real operator.

Joe shook his head, forever amazed at how the human species worked to tie itself in knots.

Joe looked back over his shoulder at the door he'd just shut, thinking he might try talking to Marie one last time, when he saw it hanging neatly from a wooden peg set into the wall, as conveniently located as a snow shovel.

It was a wooden-handled baling hook.

CHAPTER 25

Gail blinked and refocused on the man addressing them. As with so many before him, he was wearing a dark suit, immaculately tailored, but this guy had on a shirt with French cuffs, an affectation bordering on the absurd in Vermont. His hair was blow-dried, perfectly coiffed, and had probably cost the price of the small puppy it resembled. He knew nothing about the state in whose capitol building he found himself, and was lecturing them on the fine points of his 100 percent safe, in-house-tested, biologically engineered agricultural product.

Gail hadn't heard a word he'd said.

All morning, she'd been attending such committee briefings, ostensibly conjured up to educate her and her colleagues, and all morning, she'd been struggling to stay focused.

She was sleep-deprived, it was true, having spent the remains of the night in a motel room Joe had rented, staring out of the window. She'd refused his offer of company out of pride and spite, which had further eroded her ability to rest. And the large meeting room her committee was now using for the overflow crowd was hot and cramped and encouraging of napping.

None of which fully explained her distraction.

Gail was scared and paranoid, and angry to be feeling that way yet again.

She sat back slightly and eased her bag open in her lap, glancing surreptitiously for the twentieth time at the face of the man who Joe said might be stalking her. Closing the bag, she made a covert survey of the crowded room, trying to take in all the faces lining the back wall, filling the chairs, and jammed at the door. Nobody set off alarms.

But as soon as she was done, she felt the urge to do it again.

The large man sitting beside her leaned slightly in her direction and whispered, "You all right?"

"Fine," she said shortly, not looking at him. In contrast to their speaker, his suit was cheap, poorly cut, and built to survive a washing machine with impunity. Not that the suit was the issue. Both it and the man wearing it were in fact almost endearing. But he was still her police bodyguard, and his attentive presence only aggravated her emotions. To her mind, he was a neon sign of her own frailty and the danger to which she'd needlessly been exposed — an unintended source of something verging on resentment.

Sammie Martens found Joe back at the state police barracks in St. Albans, leaning on his knuckles and glumly surveying a fanned-out spread of files, photos, and aerial maps littering the conference table before him.

"Stuck?" she asked cheerily.

He looked up with a tired smile. "I feel like I'm on a tractor within sight of the barn, and I've just run out of gas. I need evidence. It's driving me crazy."

She pulled a sheet of paper from her pocket, unfolded it, and laid it between his hands, clearly delighted to be of service so late in a game she'd been wishing to join since the beginning.

"Try this."

He picked it up.

"It's from the crime lab," she explained. "They got some DNA off the sharp end of that longshoreman's hook you found. Perfect match for the late unlamented John Samuel Gregory."

"Huh," Joe acknowledged, reading on.

"That's just what we were hoping for,"

Sam added, by now irrepressible. "The kicker is, there were fingerprints on the handle — fresh ones. Belonging to Linda Padgett."

Gino couldn't believe his luck. The cops up here had either no clue or no manpower — probably both — but it was pretty clear after a two-hour surveillance that they hadn't left a guard on the target's condo while she was at work.

He stretched out his legs. He was hidden among the trees on a hill overlooking Gail's neighborhood, where, aided by his binoculars, he could see most aspects of her home. Cognizant that his good fortune could only be short-lived, Gino retreated from his post, cut back through the trees a quarter mile to a rarely used logging road, and retrieved his van from where he'd parked it behind a half-rotted pile of abandoned evergreen boughs.

Before he got in behind the wheel, he removed two magnetic signs from a pair of oversize cardboard tubes and pressed them onto the sides of the van, instantly transforming it into what he certainly considered the ultimate of ironies: a burglar alarm service vehicle — just the kind of thing Gail might have parked in her driveway.

He then slipped into a pair of similarly marked coveralls, started up the van, and trundled down the road to make the wide loop down and around to Gail's street.

It was a gutsy stunt, appealing to his flair for the dramatic. He'd done similar things in the past, while either casing jobs or actually rigging them for a burning — using various vehicles, wearing an assortment of disguises, including that of a cop. He did it both because he believed in hiding in plain sight and because, in his mind, it infused his naturally secretive and anonymous work with a touch of individuality, even if he ended up being an audience of one. Gino had his pride, after all, and in this instance especially, his pride was deserving of a certain respect.

Parking in the center of Gail's driveway, he swung out of the van, slid open the side door, extracted a couple of metal cases and a clipboard — the ultimate badge of legitimacy — and made a big show of checking the address against some presumed piece of paperwork. Visibly comforted, he marched up to the front door, worked the entry code, and walked inside, fully expecting every step of the way to be challenged and exposed.

With the front door closed behind him,

he placed both cases on the floor, straightened, and let out a sigh of relief. A single half hour, he figured. Then the rest would be history, along with the cop's girlfriend.

Joe checked his watch. He was due to meet Gail at the statehouse after work — not something he wanted to miss, for a variety of reasons. By the same token, he was even more eager to conduct this briefing, since, as with most investigations, his instincts were telling him that they were finally nearing the end. It had not been an easy road — certainly one pitted with emotional potholes, only the latest of which had been his virtual accusation of Marie Cutts for the killing of her own son — something which now was looking doubly offensive, since it appeared far less likely.

Also, in case any shreds of self-congratulation were somehow still threatening, Joe had the missing Gino Famolare to consider, and the specter of the threat that Gino had made against Gail.

He looked up at the group already assembled, sighing at those last couple of thoughts, the pure mechanics of a murder investigation looking tame by comparison. Sam was there, of course, organized with a stack of folders before her, as were both

Shafer and Michael. Willy Kunkle entered as he watched, giving him a single raised eyebrow in greeting. Finally, looking slightly embarrassed, since he was technically their host, one of the troopers from the earlier meeting slipped in and sat without comment. There were no sheriff's deputies in attendance.

"We've had some breaks," Joe started out, quieting them down. "Forensics tied the fatal injury in John Gregory's head to a baling hook, found at the Cutts farm, complete with blood and fingerprint evidence. Sam?"

She opened her topmost folder. "Prints belong to Linda Cutts Padgett. Initially, this was only suggestive of her involvement, and not proof positive — it could have been she grabbed the hook after someone else used it to kill Gregory. But we've taken advantage of this break to get a couple of court orders, and things are now piling up against her."

Jonathon Michael took up the narrative. "Turns out Linda has access to several bank accounts, all aboveboard. One belongs to the family business, another is a shared account she has with her husband, and the third she reserves for herself and her side job as a freelance tax adviser. This is the most interesting one to us, since, about three weeks prior to the fire that killed her brother, she cleaned it out of the almost thirty-three thousand dollars she had in it. There is no record of it being deposited anywhere else, nor is there any indication that she bought a car, vacation tickets around the world, or anything else legit. It just disappeared."

"Gino costs forty grand for an out-of-town torch job," Willy added.

"Right," Sam confirmed, grabbing another folder for consultation. "Which means Linda was still some seven thousand short if Gino was her intention. We have proof of her withdrawing five from the family farm account, no doubt something she hoped the eventual insurance payoff would cover before it was noticed. But that still left the final two thousand."

She waved a sheet of paper in the air. "She also had a safe-deposit box in her name and Jeff's. We don't know for sure what was in it, but we did get a look at the signature card at the bank. With neither one of them having touched that box in over four years, she checked it out at exactly the same time she was scrounging for cash. We have a copy of the bank log, complete with her signature."

Getting into the round-robin, Tim Shafer chimed in, "There was a thought that if she'd gone into that box to get something to sell, maybe she sold it either to a pawnshop or on something like eBay. Sure enough, after checking around here and in Burlington, and looking through her computer files, we found where she auctioned off a diamond ring for twenty-five hundred bucks."

"I ran a check of the Cutts phone records," Willy said in a bored voice. "Little jerk didn't even have the sense to use a pay phone. Close to the same date she was pulling all this other shit, she also placed a couple of calls to a number in Jersey. I had the cops down there run it down — it's one of the Italian social clubs Lagasso's known to frequent."

Joe glanced down the table at the lone state trooper and invited him to join in with a silent nod.

The man smiled and sat forward. "We got hold of St. Albans PD after we came up with nothing on our own computers and found out that Linda Padgett was stopped for speeding and given a warning just outside of St. Albans on the same night we think Gregory was killed. She was heading back into town from the bay."

Joe nodded. "Thanks. On my end, I had the crime lab compare a bunch of John Doe prints they collected at Gregory's house to Linda's. They found several matches. It was their opinion that, given the number of prints and where they were found, she must have spent a fair amount of time there."

"How'd you get her prints to compare to?" Willy asked.

"I collected a bunch of her personal items from home — birth control dispenser, sanitary napkin box, stuff like that — and sent them to the lab."

"She wasn't there?"

"I made sure neither she nor Marie would be," Joe replied, and then addressed them all. "I also had a brief chat with her husband, Jeff, and asked him about the time the whole family discussed Gregory's offer to list the farm. Marie had told me it was no big deal — that Linda had made a pitch to sell and run with the money, but that she'd folded once everyone else went against her. Jeff's story was a little different. He says she really pushed for it, crying, yelling. Told me it was the first time he realized she might not really like the farming life."

"Well, duh," Willy snorted. "You have to

talk to this clown with a two-by-four in your hand?"

"Oh, for crying out loud," Sam muttered to herself.

"Pretty understandable self-denial," Joe explained. "The farm means everything to him. That's partly what made me think for a while that Marie did it."

"And crispy-crittered her own kid?" Willy asked with an incredulous laugh. "I love it. You are hard, boss man."

"Bad enough that the sister did it," Sam said quietly. "So what's the connection between Bobby dying and Linda killing Gregory?"

"I think we better ask her that face-to-face," Joe concluded.

CHAPTER 26

She sat on the ground, using his gravestone as a backrest, her eyes squinting against the setting sun as she took in the view all the way across St. Albans, the bay, the lake with its islands, and to the ragged gray horizon cut like a rough tear by the Adirondack Mountains.

It had been a beautiful day, clear and dry and warm with the scent of spring. She'd longed to sit on the grass like this, using Bobby to rest against as they used to, back-to-back, long ago. But until now it had been too cold or too wet, so typical of this god-forsaken land. She'd been missing his company — his easygoing ways, his willingness to listen, the fact that he never once mocked her dreams, no matter how fanciful.

He was the only one she'd told about John, and he hadn't mentioned it to anyone, as she knew he wouldn't, no matter how uncomfortable he felt. That part made her feel a little guilty at first, before her own enthusiasm overwhelmed her. But she hadn't been able to keep it to herself, and who else was there?

Bobby was great, of course. Understanding and supportive, even if a little confused. He first assumed that she was breaking up with Jeff, naturally enough. It was hard to explain that becoming John's lover had less to do with sex than with the launching of something new and bright and hopeful for all of them. That in this man's arms, surrounded by his things, intoxicated by his presumption of privilege and money, she caught hold of a vision that she could make real for her family — including Jeff.

She pursed her lips slightly. It wasn't Bobby's fault, of course. As good and as sympathetic as he'd been, she knew it hadn't fully made sense to him. He'd been too brainwashed by the whole farming family mystique, and God knows, that was no surprise, given the company he kept. Jeff treated the farm like the Holy Grail, Dad saw it as a sacred trust, even Mom got it twisted up in the Bible, if only from the Book of Job. None of them could be expected to see the wisdom of her insight — the sheer, unromantic practicality of it.

She rubbed her flat stomach with her hand, touching the underside of one breast in the process, and smiled. Okay, truthfully, it hadn't started that way, so altruistically.

She'd been attracted by the man's style — his clothes, his car, the self-confidence in his eyes. He was clean, for one thing, with slim, well-cared-for hands, and smelled great. That first day, the only time he'd been by the farm, to ask if they wanted to list it with his company, she reacted to the whole package like an animal in heat, bumping up against him once at the door, placing her hand against the small of his back, catching a whiff of his aftershave.

It was a small step to finding out where he lived, to dropping by his house after hours one night, to literally stepping into his arms as soon as he opened the door. Not saying a word, she kissed him hard, feeling his hands immediately slipping under her clothes, expertly undressing her all the way to his bed, in total silence, like a tangible, corporeal dream.

That had been all about relief and freedom and unbridled sex. The visionary stuff came later, when she understood that at least some part of this pleasure could be transplanted to her home and husband, who she knew could supply the love that John was incapable of. In the sex was born a greater hunger, and in that hunger, a need that slipped imperceptibly into obsession.

She told Bobby of her affair with John

Gregory, of her attraction to his belongings, his freedom, his money, and his lifestyle. But she didn't tell him of her plans to make a gift of their ilk to her family — how she would end their mother's anger and shame, alleviate their father's crushing responsibility, and allow Bobby and Jeff and her children to taste and flourish in a life beyond cow manure, poverty, and the grinding dictatorship of daily chores.

She didn't tell him how pure serendipity let her appear at John's house one night, when he was distracted by a phone call and hadn't noticed her enter, and overhear him discussing a barn-burning job with a professional arsonist.

So quiet she thought she'd stopped breathing, she listened, transfixed, all horror displaced by the notion that this was like a sign from above — the answer to everyone's problems. The herd and the barn could be destroyed in one fell swoop, the insurance money collected, and the entire farm sold for several times its value.

All because of her sleeping with John.

Her guilt replaced by mission, she made achieving her goal her only purpose. She went at her affair with renewed vigor, satisfying John every way he wished, until she found an opportunity to go through his files and extract the name she'd heard mentioned — Dante Lagasso.

The rest followed naturally. Contacting Lagasso, starting the process, gathering the money. She didn't know when it would happen or who would do it — Lagasso had said that was a rule — and stayed awake for nights on end, waiting for her liberation.

She leaned her head back against the smooth granite of the headstone, closing her eyes to hold off the tears.

Bobby, what the hell were you doing in there? Of all nights? I was giving you a whole new life.

She tried emptying her mind, getting things lined up again. There was a path to follow here — fault to find . . . Right. John. In the end, this was all his fault. If he hadn't come by that day; hadn't flirted with her the way he had, in her own kitchen; hadn't exposed her to . . . everything.

He was the one who killed Bobby in the end, because that's how you had to look at things these days — you had to find the source. The source of evil. And once you traced it, you had to get rid of it. Find the evildoer. John had threatened them all, finally — burning barns of hardworking farmers; seducing married women; driving around in that useless car; killing innocent boys . . .

She'd done well, killing him. She'd set things right.

Joe met Gail and her bodyguard at the door of the overflow hearing room. He'd waited in the hallway until the crowd had dwindled to a handful before crossing the threshold, knowing the cop would hold her back, not wanting her surrounded by a crush of people. And a crush there had been. Joe wondered what the fire marshal's opinion might have been had he been there.

"Worthwhile day?" he asked her as she approached, slinging her bag onto her shoulder and weaving her way through the tangle of chairs. He exchanged friendly nods with the cop, a state trooper he knew only as Mark.

"Not really," she said. "You catch the guy yet?"

"No, but we're making progress." He didn't tell her that the progress concerned only Linda Padgett and that no one had the slightest idea of Gino Famolare's whereabouts.

"Great." She brushed by him, paused as

Mark stepped ahead of her into the hallway to check, and then followed suit, Joe bringing up the rear. He noticed that Mark was keeping a diplomatic poker face.

"You want to switch off a little?" he asked him. "I'll keep her company if you want to follow in my car."

They both looked to Gail, who nodded tiredly. "I'd like to pick up a few groceries on the way."

They stepped out into the setting sun and walked over to the parking lot reserved for members. Joe had parked illegally, half on a sidewalk, and left his badge on the dash, hoping for some mercy from the overworked Montpelier parking enforcement officers. Either they hadn't been by or it had worked.

He opened his passenger door for Gail, asking as she stepped in, "How're you doing?"

She didn't answer, waiting for him to circle around and join her. He started the engine and pulled into the street.

"That's a loaded question," she finally answered.

"He may never show up," he tried comforting her. "It was probably just a lot of hot air."

"Amazing as it sounds," she said, her

voice hard, "that's not very helpful."

He didn't say anything, aiming for State Street instead, and eventually the Shaw's supermarket around the corner, on Main.

"I'm sorry," she said a few minutes later, not looking at him. "I'm tired."

"You may be tired," he agreed. "But you've also had your life turned upside down — again. I'm the one who's sorry."

She suddenly burst into tears, causing him to almost rear-end the car in front of him. As he reached for her with one hand, she caught it in her own and squeezed it, saying, "It's okay, it's okay. I just . . . I don't know."

He pulled into Shaw's and parked haphazardly, noticing in the rearview mirror that Mark was more carefully doing the same, keeping them in sight.

With the engine still running, Joe reached out for her and took her in his arms. It was the first real display of affection they'd shared in quite a white, a realization that filled him with sudden bittersweetness. She hung on tight, her face buried in his shoulder, as he rubbed her back.

"I was so hoping all this was behind me," she said eventually, her voice muffled by his jacket.

"I know. I know. I'm so sorry."

"It's happening all over again," she continued, pulling back slightly to speak. "Getting worse every night. The nightmares, the insomnia. I'm back on sleeping pills that don't work. I check the doors and windows again and again. I can't taste what I eat, and I'm never hungry anyhow."

He kissed her, interrupting, and then said, "I never wanted this to happen."

"You couldn't help it, Joe," she answered. "It's your job. It's the people you deal with. It's your life."

"Still," he soothed her, "it seems so unfair."

Her face scrunched up like a child's. "It *is*. I know that's dumb, and I know a lot of people have had it a lot worse than I have, but I feel like I've paid enough. I've got good things to offer, and I really want to do that. I promise to work hard. But I want to be left alone."

The crying surged once more, and he gathered her more tightly to him. "We'll get you that. I promise. We'll make it work."

They shopped for her few grocery items after that, holding hands, not speaking much, oblivious of Mark trailing behind, his eyes on everything but them. In their separate ways, Joe and she felt bruised and worn, not unlike weary travelers who have just been told they have many more miles to go.

With a couple of plastic bags of bananas, canned soup, and some vegetables, they left the town behind them a half hour later under a sky tinged with the furious last blush of the setting sun, and worked their way in a two-car caravan toward Gail's condo development. Joe was lost in a reverie of futile tactics, all aimed at removing Gino Famolare from circulation. Gail seemed barely awake, slouched down in her seat, staring blankly at the darkening scenery slipping by.

On her street, as they approached the house, a man detached himself from the shadows of her garage door to greet them as they pulled into the driveway — another cop, here already a couple of hours, and assigned to watch the house for the rest of the night.

Joe killed the engine, got out, and circled the car to help Gail with the groceries she had nestled in her lap. As they were sorting out the bundles, Mark pulled past the driveway, sidled up to the curb, and then backed into the driveway beside them, facing out. As he did, Gail stepped out of the way, looking up as his headlights swept

the row of parked cars across the street —
and illuminated the pale, round face of a
man sitting deep inside the shadows of an
unmarked delivery truck.

From her countless examinations of his
otherwise bland mug shot, Gail instantly
recognized Gino Famolare.

She dropped her groceries onto the
ground and grabbed Joe's arm. "My God.
That's him. In the van."

The headlights had moved on and were
now pointing at the car directly behind the
van. But Joe didn't hesitate, trusting in
what she'd seen. He threw her back into
the car, pulled his gun out, and yelled,
crouched in a shooter's stance, "You in the
van. Get out with your hands where I can
see them."

The two other cops instantly yielded to
instinct, the one by the garage imitating
Joe, and Mark, still in his car, turning on
the spotlight by his outside mirror and
shining it on the van.

All three saw Gino's pale blur as he
ducked down behind the wheel, fired up
his engine, and stamped on the acceler-
ator, clipping the car ahead of him as he
spun out of his parking space.

But Mark had anticipated him. As the
van emerged into the street, its rear tires

squealing, the bodyguard drove his car like a battering ram against the other man's rear quarter panel, throwing the van into a skid and causing its own momentum to propel it into a utility pole, where it stopped with a metal-crunching thud.

As Joe and the other cop ran toward the wreck, and Mark piled out of his car, his gun out, Gino stumbled from the van on the far side and began running, limping badly, in the opposite direction.

In his hand was a semiautomatic, clearly visible under the streetlight.

All three officers rounded the crashed cars at the same time and stood for a brief moment, lined up as at the range.

"Gino Famolare. Stop where you are," Joe shouted, some twenty yards away.

His back to them, Gino stopped, still holding the gun.

"Put the gun down, kick it away, get on your knees, and lock your hands behind your head," Joe ordered.

Instead, Gino turned around. The gun was still pointed at the ground. All three cops spread out as Joe repeated, "Put the gun down — *now.*"

But everyone knew what was going to happen, turning what followed into a ritualistic suicide. Gino brought his gun hand up, fired once in Joe's direction, and immediately collapsed in a fusillade of bullets. He lay still and crumpled in the ear-ringing silence, faintly shrouded by a pale gray mist of gun smoke delivered by the cool, barely perceptible evening breeze. A thick rivulet of blood began to leak toward the gutter from under him.

CHAPTER 27

Sammie Martens walked up to Joe outside Gail's condo. There were vehicles everywhere, supplying enough flashing strobes to satisfy a parade marshal, from the initial responders to the post-shoot investigators to the crime scene techs and the arson guys. This last group had been called in to remove all the incendiaries Gino had planted throughout Gail's house.

"You okay, boss?"

"We are now," he answered, nodding toward where the medical examiner was crouched over Gino's body. "Suicide by cop."

"So I heard," she said. "How's Gail?"

Joe hesitated, remembering Gail's oddly shut-down demeanor following the shooting, when he'd hoped she might've been in some way relieved. "She didn't get hurt," he said cautiously.

"Great," Sam answered vaguely, getting to the real reason she was here. "I don't know if this is the time or place, but Linda Padgett's gone missing, and her dad says one of his handguns isn't where he left it.

It's usually locked up, because of the kids, but she knows where the key is."

Joe nodded, his brain cataloging all he knew of this family's complicated dynamics. "How long she been gone?"

"Five hours, give or take."

"Any ideas?"

Sam smiled ruefully. "That's why I'm here."

"Okay," he said. "I got one. Let me check on Gail again and get clearance to leave, and I'll be right with you."

Sunset was long gone from the ridge hosting the cemetery. Now, replacing the swatches of red and orange across the fading blue sky was a canopy of cold, sharp stars mirroring the St. Albans city lights cradled in the trough of land below.

Sam and Joe parked their car well shy of the cemetery gate and made their way slowly and quietly through the short undergrowth of headstones, helped by the night's dim light. Eventually, they made out the dark shape of a figure wrapped in a blanket, bundled up against Bobby's new stone and outlined against the urban glow far below.

Joe gestured to Sam to stand watch from two rows behind as he moved to a spot slightly off to one side of their quarry and cleared his throat, gently so as not to startle her.

She was so motionless, he wondered if she was even alive, a thought that had crossed his mind on the drive over here.

"Nice night," he said hopefully, his eyes on the invisible horizon. "A little cold, still. You warm enough?"

Linda didn't answer.

Joe slowly, almost casually, sidestepped in her direction, causing her to stir at last.

"I have a gun."

"I know," he said lightly, trying to hide his relief. "I just thought I'd pick the next pew, if that's all right. This one right here." He laid his hand atop a headstone two over from her and sat on the ground as she was, using the stone as a backrest.

"Beautiful spot," he commented. "Sad Bobby can't enjoy it."

"What do you want?" she asked.

"I want you to give me the gun and come with me so we can sort this out."

"What's to sort out? I heard you've been asking questions. You know what happened."

"I know there was an accident. That Bobby died when he shouldn't have. That was nobody's intention."

"I killed John Gregory, too."

He wished she hadn't said that. The finality of it worried him. "I'm not so sure that was all your fault, either," he told her.

"I killed him with a baling hook. The one your people took."

He nodded, unsure if she was watching him. "True, but that doesn't have to mean much — there were mitigating circumstances. Life isn't as black and white as you're painting it, Linda. It's not that simple."

"Simple?" she burst out.

He pretended to laugh. "Yeah. I know what you mean. But that's the beauty of the law. It takes things like that into account. Plus, you've got your dreams, your ambitions. Reasons to keep going regardless of what any lawyers might say."

"All gone."

"Your kids . . . Jeff."

"They might as well be gone, too."

He continued staring out at the vastness before him, stretched like a black sheet punctured with hundreds of tiny, light-leaking holes. Personally, her finality struck Joe like an all-too-familiar chord — Gino's decision to die at the hands of strangers, Marie choosing the legacy of a dead father over her own family's happiness, John

Gregory killed because of his own greed, and Peggy dead because of loyalty.

Which thoughts, as they so often did, brought him back to his own life's watershed moment. "I had a wife once, long ago. I loved her like I never loved anyone. I thought losing her would kill me, too."

Linda remained silent.

As did Joe. He was no longer just negotiating with her, he realized. This last admission made that clear. For while it was true that losing Ellen to cancer had knocked his legs out from under him, it had done more permanent damage than he'd ever comfortably acknowledged. It had killed a vital response deep inside him, stunting his ability to love with abandon forever after. It occurred to him now, with sudden conviction, that Gail's increasing estrangement, while fueled by her own ambitions and fears, had also been abetted by his own reluctance — inability, really — to fight for their continuing union.

It was an admission of his own form of cancer — emotional in his case — that he'd been staving off for most of a lifetime.

He pressed his hand against his forehead, overwhelmed by the feelings this released in him, and murmured, "God almighty."

"What?" Linda asked.

He turned to her, embarrassed. "I'm sorry. I'm supposed to be talking you out of doing something foolish, and instead, I'm thinking about myself."

"Your wife?" she asked, surprised to not be the topic of conversation.

"Her — and the woman in my life now. Things aren't going too well with us. They say life never turns out the way you expect, but they make it sound like it's all because of outside forces. That we have nothing to do with it, like it's preordained."

"You said your wife died," she argued. "You didn't make that happen, did you?"

"No. She got sick."

"Then you *didn't* have anything to do with it."

"And you had everything to do with Bobby dying?" he countered, bringing the conversation back around.

"I hired the guy who burned the barn."

"Why?"

"Christ," she let out, her reticence falling away. "Count the reasons: being buried in debt and cow shit, having a crazy mother and a henpecked father and a husband whose head is so deep in the sand, he wouldn't recognize daylight if it hit him in the face. You talk about my kids. What the hell do they have to look forward to?"

"What you set in motion," he tried to explain, "you were doing for everyone's sake. Except that Bobby died by accident and screwed everything up." Joe turned toward her suddenly, as if struck by a revelation. "Don't you see what that tells you? If you'd been coldhearted and selfish, thinking only of yourself, you would have kept going — collected the money, sold the farm, rebuilt a life. But you didn't. You loved Bobby. You love them all. You're a good person, Linda," he stressed, ignoring the patent absurdity of the assertion in the hopes that, this time, at least, he might prevent another death.

"This accident," he continued, "this horrible miscalculation — it meant nothing to John Gregory or to the arsonist. They took it in stride. But to you, who had everything to gain by having the same attitude, it stopped you cold. You couldn't go on. You had to set things right and balance the books. Isn't that true? Isn't that why you're here with that gun?"

She took a while before conceding, "I guess."

"Well, then," he said, working with that small opening, "that's it. You've got one last thing to do, and you're done."

"What?" she asked, startled and clearly confused.

"Get it all out. Tell them what happened — everything."

He could hear the scowl in her voice. "That'll make a good impression."

"What kind of impression do you think you'll leave by blowing your brains out?" he asked, challenging her. "What'll Jeff and the kids be left with then? Gossip and rumors generated by people who'll have no clue what really happened. You think you've messed things up now. Take a wild guess how they'll turn out after you're gone."

"I'll be in jail. How'll that be any good?"

"It'll show you held yourself responsible. Your grandfather drank himself to death. Look what that did to your mother. You want the same thing to happen to the people in your life? Cindy and Mike? Or are you going to own up to your mistakes and show them how it's done?"

She didn't respond. The silence stretched out between them for a long time.

He spoke one more time, very quietly. "You made a mess of things, Linda. I'm not saying otherwise. It's your choice whether that stops now and you own up, or you end your life and cripple your children."

After another half minute of not saying a

word, she finally shook her right hand free of the blanket's folds and laid a large handgun on the ground between them. He could see in the half-light that it was fully cocked.

"Okay," she said, her resignation clear.

That sense of defeat, so at odds with the tone of his sales pitch, left him wondering what favor he might in fact have done them all.

Joe pulled up to Gail's condo around midnight, not surprised to find people still milling about and all the lights on inside. Fatal shootings in Vermont were not the routine they were in large urban areas. Even the experienced cops here took extra time to get it right.

He cut the engine and swung his legs out tiredly onto the driveway, pausing to watch a crime scene tech in the distance set up a photograph that included both the pool of blood and a ruler he clearly didn't want dirtied.

"Anything wrong, sir?"

Joe glanced to his immediate right, where a uniformed Montpelier patrolman was standing in the shadows.

"No — been a long day," he told him. "The senator inside?"

"Yes, sir."

Joe rose to his feet and watched the photographer a moment longer, all the while thinking of both the conversation ahead and the one he'd just left behind. He recalled the first time he'd set eyes on Linda Padgett and how her youthful beauty had so struck him. Now she, in a living parody of Peggy DeAngelis, was done with a life she'd barely begun to taste.

"The choices we make," he murmured.

"Yes, sir," came the voice from the darkness.

He smiled and shook his head, making a mental note to stop thinking out loud.

He didn't use the entry code on the condo's front door lock, but rang the bell instead.

Gail opened up a minute later. She was pale and exhausted. She also looked resolved.

"Hi, Joe." She didn't give him a hug, and he hesitated offering one. "Did you find the girl?"

"Yeah. She's okay. I never told you, what with all that's gone on, but she was the one —"

She interrupted him with a raised hand. "It doesn't matter. I don't want to know."

He nodded, as much in confirmation to himself as in acknowledgment of her request. Never before had she countered him like that.

"Right."

They stood awkwardly in the open doorway for a few moments.

"Well, anyhow. It's safe. I wanted you to know it's all over," he said.

She gave him a sad smile. "Funny turn of phrase."

"Oh, Christ," he said. "No. I didn't mean that. I'm sorry."

But she was already shaking her head. "I think I do — mean that."

He took a shallow breath. "Ah."

She reached out at last and touched his cheek. He quickly turned his head and kissed her fingertips.

She dropped her hand, her expression soft and mournful. "And I'm the one who's sorry, Joe. It's not you. It's me."

"But it is what I do, isn't it? Maybe even who I am."

She didn't argue with him. "You couldn't stop that," she said flatly.

He opened his mouth to answer, but again, she stopped him. "I wouldn't want you to, no matter what you might say now."

"There're other ways I could do the same things," he suggested.

"It would be like being the water boy at a football game," she told him. "And I'd be the one responsible for putting you there."

He saw that was a dead end. "You're sure this is necessary?" he asked more generally.

"This isn't the first time we've been here," she reminded him. "You've been stabbed, beaten, almost blown up — God knows what else. You were shot at just a few hours ago. You're in the middle of all that, taking responsibility, calculating the risks. I'm just the person who loves you, waiting for the bad news."

"Will that change if we break up?"

She pursed her lips, the bearer of bad news. "Over time? Yes. It will diminish. I won't know what you're doing day-to-day. Also, selfishly speaking, chances are greater I won't become a target because of you."

He had to credit her honesty, if not her tact. Still, it was the former he'd been wanting for quite a while now, if dreading its content.

"I realize this is hard for you to understand, Joe, even with your abilities. I've never known a more sensitive man than you. But what just happened brought me back like a slap in the face. It was the rape

431

all over again. I even felt raped. All over again. One of the ploys I used to get me through the rough spots back then was playing the old lightning-can't-strike-twice denial game. They don't recommend it, but it saw me through. Now I see what they meant."

She paused. He didn't say anything, at a loss for words.

"I can't afford to do that again," she concluded.

His heartbeat was rapid, and he knew his face was flushed, but he stayed silent, conditioned both by upbringing and by training to guard his counsel, to listen before speaking, to accept his losses. It took two to avoid the outcome she was suggesting. Whether she was right or not, she was determined to keep to her course.

And he'd never been a man to argue just for the sake of it.

Slowly, so she wouldn't misinterpret, he leaned forward at the waist and kissed her gently on the cheek, enjoying the familiar warmth of her skin on his lips.

"I love you," he said, straightening.

"I love you, too," she responded as he turned to go. "I always will."

CHAPTER 28

Joe hadn't wanted to return to the Cutts farm. As of late, his life was full enough of loss and grief and unanswerable questions to make a gratuitous visit to another emotional black hole impressively unappealing.

Which, of course, didn't preclude his needing to do it anyway.

Not for Marie. Even considering his treatment of her at their last encounter, he still wasn't keen on trying to make amends. Given what she'd always thought of him, that bordered too close to pure masochism.

Calvin, however, was another matter. Belittled by his wife and daughter, diminished by his own mixture of stoicism and self-effacement, Cal remained for Joe a potential touchstone — someone who, even now that his family was reduced to ashes, might have something to say that Joe could use in putting all this to rest.

For that remained an important coda for Joe — something he searched for at the conclusion of most cases, especially the ones extracting their weight in sorrow. In his world — the one that had just cost him

Gail — such bruising needed redress, or at the very least, a moment of observance.

He had no idea how or if Calvin Cutts could supply him with such spiritual liniment, but for some reason, he'd thought of no one else when the need had become clear.

All that having been said, however, he still didn't want to see Marie again, so, like a man obliged to attend a formal ceremony he yearned to avoid, he lingered in his car at the top of the hill above the farm, steeling himself against the inevitable — in this case, his arrival in the dooryard and the usual buzz saw greeting.

Which is when, as if from providence itself, a tractor cleared the horizon to his right and began trundling downfield, aimed directly at the fence beside him. Calvin Cutts was at the wheel.

Joe got out of the car and waited by the edge of the road until the tractor drew abreast and Calvin killed its engine.

The accompanying silence surrounded both men like the palpable warmth of the sun overhead.

Cal nodded at Joe before slowly disentangling himself from behind the steering column and climbing down to the freshly plowed earth.

"Agent Gunther," he said, wiping his hands on his jeans as he approached.

"Mr. Cutts," Joe said, returning the courtesy.

Cutts reached the fence and stopped. Neither man extended a hand in greeting. "What can we do for you?"

"Nothing I can think of," Joe answered. "Just dropped by to see how you were all doing."

It was the kind of statement Marie Cutts would have treated like a grenade pin, but Cal merely shrugged and answered, "Feeling a little caught between a dog and a tree, but I guess we'll sort it out."

"The farm?"

"Always. The insurance turned out to be even less than we thought, and Billy dropped his offer to where it didn't make any sense. Looks like it's back to life as usual."

They were standing side by side with the fence between them, both facing the distant mountain Joe had admired on one of his first visits. Calvin's last comment didn't seem utterly delusional, as it might have from someone else facing his reversal of fortune. Instead, it came across as a simple statement of fact, and, for all of that, Joe was hard-pressed to doubt it. He and Cal were not entirely unalike, after all, from their parentage and age to their general stoicism.

"Could be worse," Cal added. "Some foundation — run by that John Gregory's brother — said they'd help out — pay for Linda's kids' education, replace the herd. Marie didn't want it, of course, but we'll take it — for all our sakes. Still," he continued, "it's not that we couldn't still sell. Jeff could make more money someplace else, and I could even retire, more or less, given my needs." He paused to rub his chin with one rough hand.

"But," he added, "it just wouldn't feel right."

"What about Marie?"

He nodded. "Well, that's part of it, of course. Farming's what she knows. It would be a bad time to uproot her."

When he left it at that, Joe asked, "How's she doing?"

Cal kept his eyes on the horizon. "Not too good. Hasn't said a word since it turned out the way it did — losing both her kids, one way or the other. It's pretty clear Linda won't be getting out anytime soon."

"I am sorry about that," Joe said gently.

Cal finally looked at him with a sad

smile. "So am I. You have kids?"

"No."

"It's interesting," he said philosophically. "They sure can surprise you." After a pause, he added, "But they give you something to love all the way to the end."

That made Joe think of Linda's family. "Is Jeff going to stay put?" he asked.

"Far as I know. I suppose that's the funniest part of this whole deal, when you think about it. He only really stayed because of Linda. Now it's just him and me, basically. A couple of guys doing what they can — like shipwrecked sailors, when you think of it."

He shook his head slowly, as if countering an argument. "No, best to keep things the same. Linda'll know where we are that way, wherever she might be, and Marie can use the familiar routine to get better. Won't hurt those kids, either, knowing we stuck it out."

He bent down and retrieved a clod of earth, which he held in his hand like a talisman. Joe wondered if the gesture would result in some comment combining both insight and hope.

In the end, he wasn't sure it didn't.

"Guess I better get back to work," Cal said.

.